Winter's Captive

Winter's Captive

The Georgia Series, Book 1

June V. Bourgo

Acknowledgements

This book took many years to write. I suppose you could say life got in the way, but realistically, it was probably because I stood in front of myself.

My acknowledgements must start with Meegan Walker, a young, intelligent woman working on her master's degree who took the time to read my first draft and offer an honest critique. Her encouragement set the path for my continued writing of the book.

A big thank you to my readers, Pamela Gregorchuk, Pamela Hartman, Anne Marsh, Carolann Glover McGillivray, Darcy Paterson, Mavis Rogers, and Norma Thompson who all found a part of themselves in Georgia Charles.

Thanks to Diane McIntosh of Bright Ideas Design and author, Susan Juby, for teaching me how to pitch a story.

To my fellow writers, for their creative and emotional support, Carol Ann Higgins Cajigas, Irene Kueh, Patricia Puddle, Chrissy Peebles, and Jayde Scott.

Of note, my husband Dennis, for his shoulder massages when I spent too many hours at the keyboard and for having the courage to tell me when I could improve a scene. I value his creative input and his belief in me.

To all the teachers in my life, living and ethereal, especially Carol Kozevnikov, where my journey to self began.

To all the women in my circle of family and friends,
especially my mother, Mavis Rogers, the matriarch of my family at ninety-five.

Chapter 1

As I hastened deeper into the dense forest, what was left of daylight morphed into dark shadows. On one hand, this scared the hell out of me; on the other, it could be used to my advantage to disappear within the foliage. I willed myself not to look back, instead focusing on the uneven track ahead. I knew it would be Gary who would come. And if he caught me, I wouldn't make it back with him. This place would be my final destination; buried in a grave that might never be found or scavenged by forest creatures that would scatter my bones amongst the debris of the forest floor. This was an even scarier thought and adrenaline spurred me forward pushing my body beyond extremes. Never much of a runner, the speed I was moving surprised even me. The possibility of death can do that.

Pounding feet sounded behind me and I broke my resolve of not looking back. I glanced over my shoulder, almost tripping, but saw no one. My ears picked up the sound of obscenities. *Yes, it's Gary and he's gaining ground.* My lungs gasped for air. *Get off the trail, now.* My eyes searched for a place to hide. The pathway rose up a small incline. I flew over the top and down the other side, where the path veered off to the right. To the left, an old game trail barely visible meandered through the trees.

I slowed and glanced around me. The near darkness provided deep shadows in the trees. A tangle of fallen trees and branches on my left looked like a good spot to hide in. Branches scratched my face and caught in my hair as I pulled myself over the decaying trunks. I tumbled face first into a hollow under a log, filling my mouth with dirt and leaves. The smell of musty, rotting debris churned my stomach. The taste of bile rose into my throat.

Gary charged over the top of the incline and came to a dead stop. *Damn.* I hoped he would miss the game trail and keep going.

"Alright, bitch. Come back now and I'll let you live. If I have to chase you, you're dead! Got it?"

Let me live? Sure you will. Oh God … I feel like a trapped animal. Terrified he would hear my raspy breathing; I tried to control my gasps. There was nothing I could do about the pounding of my heart.

Gary studied the game trail, then the path. "Where are you. That's it. I'm done and you're dead." He took a hesitant step towards the game trail, then turned and disappeared down the path to the right.

The thought of staying put crossed my mind. *No, when he returns he might search for me, guessing that I'm hiding.* I waited a few moments until he was out of earshot and scrambled out of my hiding place, tripping and falling, until I finally reached the old animal trail Gary ignored. *Girl, you made enough noise to wake up the dead.* I bolted down this new track until it merged some time later with a new pathway. Total fear provided the strength I needed to keep going.

Before long, everything turned into dark, distorted shadows. I stumbled forward in the blackness, tripped over a rock and fell. *Okay, I guess*

3

this is where I'm spending the night. I felt my way into the trees. Hopefully Gary had given up and returned to the truck. Tomorrow, they might look for me or hopefully they would leave.

I positioned myself between two fallen trunks and adjusted my gloves and hood, pulling my turtleneck up over my nose to cover my exposed skin. It would be a long, cold night. I chewed on my fist to keep from crying out every time a twig snapped or a night noise sounded. My anxiety increased as my imagination added the four-legged variety to the two-legged ones that already frightened me. With my head resting on my knees, eyes closed, my thoughts wandered over the past few days and all that transpired to lead me into this unexpected and overwhelming circumstance. *Was it only yesterday?*

Chapter 2

Twenty-seven Hours Earlier

Five months pregnant. How could I have missed the signs? The doctor told me that under normal circumstances I'd have known. My thoughts turned to Colin. I played the scene over in my mind. *A definite mindblower.* I imagined his anger and could hear him say, "Georgia, how could you let this happen?" *Hmm ... self-inflicted, like he didn't play a part in it.*

"To hell with him," I muttered, hurrying along the busy street. Ten years of supporting him through law school, waiting for him to feel secure enough to start a family, and, then, five months ago the bastard left me for Julie Newman, his pregnant assistant. *I bet she planned it, the husband-stealing bitch.* He said it was the right thing to do—to leave me for his lover, I mean. I wondered if things might be different if he'd known about *my* pregnancy first.

Well, she could have him. I didn't want a man to stay with me out of obligation because I carried his baby. A marriage needs more than that. I laughed out loud at the thought of the look on Julie's face when she learns about my imminent childbirth. People on the street stared as I snorted with glee. Let her put up with his selfish ways and wash his dirty socks and underwear. She took him away from me, but now, he'd have to support two babies. Nothing could change that. The more people stared, the more I laughed self-consciously, practically crossing my legs to keep from peeing.

This baby could be my greatest revenge. I cringed. *Was I really that bitter? Who am I?* The revelation of my pregnancy still confused me, since I had only found out about it yesterday. However, the baby growing inside of me deserved more than being considered an act of revenge. Tomorrow I was flying home to Vancouver. What a shocker this baby will be for my family and friends. I smiled. As confusing and overwhelming this new revelation was to me, my mother would be happy—her first grandchild.

The past month had been spent in Whitehorse, visiting my childhood friend. Her husband was away on business, leaving us to reconnect and reminisce. We travelled the Yukon Territory with ease. The roads were quiet. Most of the tourist places were closed for the season. But we'd shopped, dined, and hiked all over this vast area. Marion was the perfect host. Her outgoing personality had pulled me out of my shell. My knowledge of the Yukon had been limited a month ago. Travels with Marion, and nights of reading about the history of the area increased my knowledge base. Adding that to the down-to-earth warmth of the northern people, I felt at home here and began to understand the ways of the land.

I entered the restaurant where Marion sat waiting for me. She waved from the back of the restaurant and I gestured towards the washroom, heading straight there. *Relief!* After washing my hands, I held them under the hot water, feeling the heat surge up my arms and through my chilled body. I turned to a full- length mirror and the reflection staring back at me was very serious. My large dark eyes revealed the insecurity I felt about this new direction in my life. I removed my jacket and examined the petite, slim image before me. My hands ran down the sides of my abdomen. A slight bump was the only indication of the new life developing within. My breasts were definitely larger. I stared into my face again and noted for the first time, the glow of a healthy, rosy complexion. My long brunette hair fell past my shoulders in a bounce of curls and waves, framing my cheeks. I ran my fingers through my hair to fluff it up around my face.

A woman appeared behind me waiting to use the sink. I gave her a smile, grabbed my jacket and left the room.

"There you are," Marion chirped. "I ordered the lunch special for both of us. Hope that's okay? We loved it the last time we were here."

I settled in a chair opposite her. "That's fine. We're running a bit late because of me."

"How did it go?"

"No problem, they confirmed my flight home to Vancouver tomorrow. I didn't expect the long line- up."

Marion studied my face intensely. "So … how do feel about going home with the news of your pregnancy."

I let out a long sigh. "It's a little daunting. You know I wanted to have a baby for the longest time, but not alone. Life can really be unfair. My husband impregnated me a mere five weeks after his lover became pregnant. And the whole time he planned to leave me."

"Sounds more like a horny bastard than a husband," Marion said.

As crude as it sounded, it was the right comment I needed at that moment. We burst out in laughter. The waitress delivered our lunch. "Enjoy," she said, with a smirk. We laughed again, knowing she'd overheard Marion's remark. We spent the next twenty minutes Colin bashing.

"Mom will be ecstatic—her first grandchild. It's so hard to fathom I reached five months without suspecting my pregnancy."

"Not really. The doctor covered that. You lost weight grieving over 'numb-nuts' and you're carrying the baby to the back, so you hardly even show at this point. Besides, the baby hasn't moved yet."

"That's all true. I'd attributed the nausea and lack of monthly cycles to emotional stress. There was some spotting in the initial months. I guess I just wasn't paying attention to my body.

"Understandably," Marion said.

"My suspicions were certainly there since I've been in Whitehorse, but I tried to ignore them. Once the tenderness and swelling of my breasts increased, deep down I knew it was time to deal face it. The doctor said the baby should move anytime now."

The waitress cleared away our dishes. "Dessert, ladies?"

Marion spoke for both of us. "No thanks. Just coffee, please. We have a mother-to-be here." She nodded at me with a giggle. "We need to watch what we feed her."

"Congratulations, how far along are you?" the waitress asked me.

"Five months."

Her eyebrows shot up. "Really? You don't look that far along."

Marion threw up her hands. "See? You don't even look pregnant."

"I can't believe a whole month has passed. I hoped the unfamiliarity and anonymity here would help me make some sense of my life and maybe help me find my passion."

Marion looked perplexed. "Your passion?"

"Ya … something to bring the joy and the laughter back." I rubbed my stomach to ease the tension. "Perhaps, it's this baby. One thing I did find out is there's life after Colin."

"Hallelujah! You've done a lot of healing this month and I'm so glad I could be a part of it." Marion reached across the table and squeezed my hand.

"I don't have the answers yet about who I am, or the what, where, and when of it all, but I know who I don't want to be."

"Who's that?"

The waitress came back with the coffee pot. I waited for her to leave before replying.

"A woman who doesn't think for herself, who wears what she's told to wear, and gets coached what not to say at business dinners … can you believe I let Colin run my life that way?"

Marion put her coffee down. "Yes. You know even as a child, you were always the complacent one who never made waves."

"Wasn't I though? I lost myself to Colin because I went along with everything he said. One day, I overheard him joking with a colleague. He told him that the secret to a good marriage was control. He said that everything in my head, everything that I thought, he'd put there. "

"What an arrogant prick."

"Hearing that really hurt me. It was the beginning of my awareness about who I'd become."

My best friend stared at me and then squinted. "You need to become empowered."

"Empowered—what a great sounding word that is," I mused.

We sat in silence, sipping our coffee, lost in our own thoughts. I tried to recall the last time I experienced a sense of power.

"Do you remember the summer we were five and I broke my arm?" I asked.

"Are you kidding? How could I ever forget? I was the kid right behind you, chasing you back to home base. I heard the bone crack when you hit that cement sidewalk. I carried the guilt of it for years."

My eyebrows shot up. "But it wasn't your fault I decided to take a shortcut and jump over that low wire fence."

"Tell that to a five-year-old who could always beat you home," Marion said. "I was about to pass you when you took that jump. I believed I pushed you too hard."

"You should've told me, silly." I reached over and squeezed Marion's hand. "My arm broke in two places." I pointed to a spot above my wrist and another below the elbow. "They gave me anesthesia at the hospital to reset it. Mom took me to bed with her that night and when I woke up the next morning, I felt nauseous. My brother and my two male cousins peered at me through the metal bars of the bed frame at the bottom of the bed."

"Ah yes ... your brother Kris and cousins Jimmy and Kevin. Whenever those three were together, that meant trouble for us," Marion snickered.

I giggled. "They teased us mercilessly, didn't they? Anyway, they stared at me with great anticipation, begging to see my cast. I sat up far too quickly, letting the covers fall to expose my arm. With unprecedented accuracy, I projectile vomited in their direction."

Marion squealed with laughter. "How come I don't remember this? What did they do?"

"They ran out of the bedroom screaming. I felt much better and relished the thought that I, five-year-old Georgia, grossed out three older boys."

We shared another laugh. "Empowerment!" I said.

"Ah…" Marion said, softly.

"Pathetic, isn't it?"

"What is?" she asked.

"That I've been sitting here trying to recall when I felt empowered in my life, and the only thing that comes to mind is an incident at five years of age."

"Hmm—if you can be empowered at five; you can be empowered at thirty."

"Oh Marion, you always find the right words to say. You really are a great friend and I love you dearly."

"And I you. Talking about being empowered, think about this. Perhaps you weren't meant to find out about the baby until you were ready to handle it. These past months would have been a lot harder to bear if you'd known."

I gave her a pensive look. "You have a point there."

We left the restaurant and started towards the costume shop. Today was Halloween. We headed to our appointment to pick up costumes for a party at the community hall tonight. My friend lived outside the city and no one made the long trek up the driveways of their rural neighbors' houses. The small community held a party for parents and kids every year.

Marion turned at the corner, expecting me to follow.

"Hey, I'm going to run to the drugstore down the next block and buy those vitamins the doctor told me to take."

Marion stopped and looked back. "Okay. I'll meet you at the costume store, one block over behind the drug store." She turned away and threw over her shoulder with a giggle, "But don't run, mama."

"Yes, boss. Shouldn't be more than ten minutes."

In the pharmacy section, I found the vitamins that the doctor had recommended for pregnant women, and a pocket book called *What to Expect When You're Expecting.*

"Are these for you, dear?" the salesclerk asked.

I nodded and she added, "Congratulations."

I smiled proudly. "Thank you."

Wow, in one spontaneous moment, I owned my pregnancy. It actually felt good. I pushed my way through the rear door into the back lane—a shortcut to the costume shop.

A cold, brisk wind whipped my long hair across my face. A good indication that winter was on its way to the north. The dirty, narrow laneway served as a wind tunnel, and a sudden gust funneled a swirling cloud of grit and papers against my body. I braced myself against its powerful surge and started down the alley. Stuffing my purchases into my oversized jacket pocket, my wallet slipped to the ground and I stooped down to pick it up.

I heard the sound of running feet and glanced up from where I was crouched. Two men with backpacks wearing ski masks came charging around the street corner at the far end of the alley. I gasped. The taller one held a revolver and I froze. The shorter man pulled off his mask and threw his pack into a parked car. His brown, stringy hair hung to his shoulders and his dark eyes were full of surprise as he noticed me crouched down ahead of them. The two men exchanged looks and nodded.

"You drive." The masked man threw his bag to his partner and headed towards me.

I screamed and pushed myself up to my feet. With little time to run, he caught me by my hood and jerked me to an abrupt stop.

"Oh no you don't … you're coming with us." He grasped my hood tighter, pulling my hair as he dragged me backwards.

"Ow … let me go!" I cried. We struggled and I stomped on his foot. He punched me in the stomach, knocking the air out of me. I fell to my knees clutching my abdomen in pain. *Oh no, my baby. Please don't hurt my baby.* The man pulled me to my feet as the unmasked driver stopped the car beside us.

A group of people entered the lane. I screamed. "Help me, please!"

They began to yell and one of them ran towards us. My abductor pointed his gun at him and the man stopped. They stared as my captor slammed me into the back seat. The masked man jumped in beside me and placed the gun against my head. "And shut the hell up." His snakelike hiss, made my skin crawl. I curled up as far back into the seat as possible and wrapped my arms around me to protect my aching stomach. I bit my lips to keep from crying out.

The engine accelerated and the vehicle sped off down the lane. The car turned one corner and then another, until heading south of town. I bounced sideways across the seat into my abductor. Disgust filled me to the core. I pushed myself back with a shudder and snapped on the seat belt.

Chapter 3

Police sirens sounded in the distance but I never saw the cars

The man beside me smacked the driver on the back of the head. "Idiot."

I cowered in the corner of the seat at the sound of his voice.

The man next to me yelled at the driver. "I can't believe you could be so stupid. We talked about the masks before we hit the bank. We weren't going to remove them until we were out of the lane. Why'd you do that? Huh?"

"I'm sorry. The lane looked empty. I didn't see her stooped down on the ground."

"You messed up, jerk!"

"I know … I know." A silence hung in the air. "Gary, how much d'ya think we got?"

The masked man started to pound the back of the seat.

I began to shake and curled myself into a tight ball.

"You stupid son-of-a-bitch. Damn you, anyway,"

he said, and pulled his mask off.

"Why'd you do that? Now she knows your face too.

Gary sneered. "Because you used my name, asshole. She saw your face and now, knows my name. How long d'ya think it'd take the cops to connect me to you and the bank job? We've done too much shit together, cousin."

"So what're we going to do with her?"

"Keep her 'till we know we're safe," Gary said.

"Then what?"

"Let me worry about that."

I stared out the window, wringing my hands together. My ears echoed with the thumping of my heart as my brain seized with fear. At least the pain in my abdomen stopped and I could breathe again. *This is a bad situation. Think, girl, think. Don't dwell on what might happen.*

The driver turned up a dirt road and travelled along for a while through a forested area to an opening, until we reached a white Dodge cargo van.

"Out of the car." The man called Gary grabbed me by the arm and shoved me through the side door of the van, onto the floor. "Stay put and shut up." He drew the gun out of his pocket and ran the barrel back and forth along my cheekbone. "Got it?" His blue eyes—glassy and lifeless—reminded me of a doll. I cringed, nodded my head and pressed up against the sidewall.

"Bobby, bring the bags."

My body jerked and I sucked in my breath. Now, I knew both their names and faces. Things couldn't get any worse.

They spent the next few minutes counting their money. "Wow ... eighty thou ..." Bobby let out a whistle.

Gary laughed. "I told you, didn't I? Friday payday they always have more money in the upper vault. The biggest pay check we ever had."

The two men zipped up the bags and placed them under a blanket behind me.

"Bobby ... get in the passenger side, I'll drive."

The lack of windows and seats in the back made it difficult to see from my vantage point on the floor. The van retraced the route in and turned right, heading southeast on the Alaska Highway towards Watson Lake and beyond to British Columbia. I hadn't heard or seen any police cars since leaving Whitehorse. Since they didn't know we switched vehicles, I didn't expect any help from them. Hopefully, the police would find my wallet in the lane and with the help of the group, who saw us, identify me.

I studied my two captors. A tall, thin man, Gary wore his hair short to his scalp in the back. His hair hung a bit longer on the top, bleached blond with dark roots. His eyebrows were dark and thick. A gold ring pierced his left ear, with a gold stud beside it. I looked up at the rear-view mirror and caught Gary glaring at me, confident and mean, and very much in control. My stomach rolled over as his eyes pierced mine.

Bobby, shorter and wiry, fidgeted in his seat, drumming his fingers on the armrests. He tossed his head, swinging his long, stringy hair from side to side. His constant, furtive glances at Gary displayed a nervous disposition, causing me to read him as someone who wasn't too sure of himself or of any of this.

If things weren't bad enough in my life, now this. I closed my eyes and tried to organize my thoughts.

"Uh-oh! " Bobby sat upright in his seat. "Flashing lights about two miles ahead. What're we gonna do, man?"

"Stay cool for one thing. Get in the back. Now!"

"What?"

Gary yelled. "Hurry up, man. They don't know what we look like or the vehicle we're driving. But they'll be on the lookout for two men. So get in the back with the bitch, outta sight."

Bobby lowered himself on the floor beside me and pulled me down from my sitting position. My nose crinkled from the smell of stale cigarettes and body odor. I turned my head away from him and covered my face with my hand. Gary slowed down his speed. Bobby jerked his head up. "Wh… what's happening? Why are you slowing down?"

"Stop freaking, man! I'm following the speed limit. Don't wanna attract attention."

The sound of the siren grew louder. "Yes—home free," Gary said. "They whistled right on by, lights flashing and all."

Bobby rolled onto his back and howled like a dog, kicking his feet on the van floor. While my two kidnappers celebrated their getaway, I resumed my sitting position and fought the urge to cry.

Don't let them see you crying. I wrapped my arms around my knees and put my head down, slowly rocking back and forth. *Stay calm.* If there ever was a time to practice the meditation techniques Marion taught me, the time had arrived. Marion ... my best friend, all the way back to primary school. I pushed away the thoughts of how upset she would be at my disappearance.

The sky turned a dull grey as night approached. Gary made a sharp right and headed straight south. The only road in this direction travelled along the Cassiar Highway, an isolated stretch of road heading south through the undeveloped northwestern part of British Columbia, referred to as the "last frontier". Towns were few and hundreds of kilometres apart. There were no amenities here like on the Alaska Highway.

There was no other traffic on this remote highway.

My alarm level rose. *Focus. No one will help you, except you.*

The darkness came and Gary pulled over, giving Bobby a shove. "Hey, wake up. I gotta take a leak."

Gary opened the side door and gestured for me to get out. "I'm sure you need to take a break too."

I stared at him with apprehension. The urge to relieve myself was strong, but the idea of stepping out into the dark with him terrified me.

"Come on," he barked. "We don't have all night!"

Get a grip girl. I climbed out and stretched my cramped legs while they stood next to the van and relieved themselves.

Did they expect me to squat down beside them?

Gary turned and stared at me. Reaching under the front seat, he grabbed two flashlights and shoved one into Bobby's hands. "Here, take her over to those bushes while I check the fluids. And keep your eyes on her."

Bobby led the way and pointed with the light. "You can go there."

"Okay, turn the light away," I said.

"No can do. Gary said to keep an eye on you."

"I'm not going to run away. Where would I go in the pitch dark? You're holding the light."

"Fine. Make it quick." He turned away.

I squatted. My eyes searched the area. The landscape rose sharply uphill on both sides of the road, no pathways. Running away wasn't an option here. *Say something to him; try to personalize your situation.* "You know he's going to kill me, Bobby."

"No ... no ... he'll let you go when we get out of this area." He didn't sound too sure. "And don't use my name."

"I'm pregnant."

"You're what? Bullshit!"

I stood and adjusted my clothes. "Five months. I'm done here."

Bobby shone the light on me, and stepping closer to him, I placed my hand on his arm.

"Please, don't let him kill my baby and me."

He pulled his arm away and gestured for me to walk in front of him. *That went well.* My hopes of getting any help from him were dashed. We were back on the road and travelling further into the wilderness.

Hours later, I opened my eyes and bright sunlight blinded me. A glance at my watch, told me it was six a.m. I must have dozed off. It was cold in the back of the van and I pulled my jacket tighter. *Day 2 of my abduction.*

Bobby was driving. My abductors talked in hushed tones, but I could make out the words. "How do you know she's pregnant?"

"She told me last night," Bobby said. "When I took her out in the bushes."

"What else did she say?"

"She said she thought you're going to kill her. She's afraid for the baby. Are you? Are you going to kill her?"

"Jesus, man. She knows who we are. She can identify us. Do you wanna go to jail? I'm not going back."

"Shit man, what if we get caught?" Bobby was visibly upset. He ran one hand through his hair over and over. His upper body rocked back and forth in the seat. "I mean, jail time for robbery isn't the same as for murder."

"Stop rocking and pay attention to the road. I hate the fact she's pregnant, okay. But she doesn't give two shits about us. She'd turn on us in a minute."

"Yeah, but..."

"You know why she told you she's pregnant? 'Cause she knows you're a pushover. She's trying to get between us. Got it? Besides, if we get caught, it isn't just robbery we face, but kidnapping, and weapons charges. Grow the hell up, man. We gotta do this, so shut up about it, okay?"

"When ..." Bobby whispered, "when you gonna do it?"

A lump rose in my throat, and I swallowed hard to keep from vomiting.

"When we reach the cabin. We'll hole up for a while, bury her out there someplace. No one'll ever find her." Gary turned and caught me looking at them. His eyes hardened. Raising his forefinger to his temple, he pretended to be pulling the trigger of a gun.

My head jerked backward, and my chest constricted. *Oh God, I can't breath.*

Escape. That thought repeated over and over in my mind like the rhythm beat of a perpetual drum. *But where could I go?* Desperation took desperate measures. I would run at the first opportunity. This was a matter of life or death—my baby's and mine.

Gary watched my every move. Mid-afternoon, we pulled into a gas station at the first town since turning onto this roadway. A place called Dease Lake, surrounded by hundreds of miles of wilderness in any given direction.

"Hey, bitch ..." Gary said, "... lie down. Bobby, you fill up the tank and I'll go get some snacks. Lady, if you so much as twitch, I'll shoot the first person I see in this hole." He patted the gun in his jacket pocket. "Then, I'll kill you!"

My heart pounded. There were people here that could help me, but they might as well be on the moon. I crawled up to the front of the van and raised my head behind the driver's seat until I could see out the side mirror. Bobby had his back to the driver's door, watching the gas gauge. I wiggled over between the seats and peeked out the driver's window to the store beyond. A woman stood behind the counter. Gary was nowhere to be seen. A quick glance out of the front windshield told me there were no other cars or people about.

I inched my way across the passenger seat on my stomach and opened the door. Pulling my legs under the dash and in front of the seat, keeping my body down low, I swung my feet out the door and lowered myself to the ground into a crouch position, and closed the door quietly up to the door jam. *Now what?*

I knew if I went around the back of the van, Bobby would see me and if I went around the front, Gary might see me from the store. Instead, I sprinted straight ahead, body bent over, head down low, to the second row of pumps and hid behind them to reassess. One peak back to the van assured me that my abductors weren't aware of my escape. Only one thing stood between me and the bushes beyond—the highway.

I had no choice but to make a run towards them. I charged across the dirt driveway that led into the gas station, aced the highway, and flattened myself in the ditch on the other side. A visual survey told me that there was a short ten-yard dash to freedom. The negative to that was that it represented a thirty-foot run across an open grassy area to infinity beyond. A quick peek back to the gas station made my heart jump. Gary and Bobby were standing in front of the van talking, Bobby had his back to me and Gary was half-turned. With the seconds ticking away before they discovered my disappearance, it was now or never.

Up like a shot, I made a dash across the open meadow. The bushes drew closer. No way would I look back. All my energy was thrust into that run. I was almost there, when my foot went into a hole, throwing me off balance. Down I went, sprawling face first onto the grass. There was no time to check for injury. This time as, pushing myself up, a glance over my shoulder sent shock waves through my body. Gary had seen me. I took off running. Pains shot through my right ankle, but that was the least of my worries.

The bushes were a welcome sight, swallowing me up as I jumped over the smaller ones and pushed my way through the hedge behind them. This wasn't my day. The ground dipped sharply behind the row of bushes and I slid down a muddy embankment, landing thigh deep in a marshy wetland.

It took all my strength to crawl up the side of the wet bank and push myself into a standing position—only to find myself face to face with a gun pointed right at the middle of my forehead.

Chapter 4

Gary's hand shot out and grabbed me by the hair, pulling my face close to his.

"Ow ..." I cried out between gasps to catch my breath.

Spat hit my face as he spoke through clenched teeth. "What did I say would happen if you tried to escape? Huh?"

He shook my head and I dared not say a word He was in control and I waited in despair for what was to come.

"We're going to step through those bushes and walk back to the van as casual and quiet as can be. Now march." Gary spun me around and gave me a push into the bushes. Resigned to my fate, I did as he said. My ankle was aching, but I was able to walk.

Bobby had driven the van up a dirt road that ran parallel to the open meadow. We reached the vehicle quickly and were heading down the highway in a matter of seconds.

"Try that again and I'll pop you right there. You're lucky no one at the gas station clued in to any of this or you'd all be dead, like I warned you."

Gary threw a can of pop and a bag of chips at me. I finished them off in short order, only to keep up my strength. *Great nourishment for a pregnant woman. Not that it mattered. This may well be my last meal.*

"Isn't that the road we go down to reach Uncle Pete's cabin?" Bobby asked.

"Uh-huh. There's the sign to Telegraph Creek."

The van climbed up steep grades and dropped back down to valley bottoms. It was a rough ride on the gravel road, full of twists and turns on a washboard surface. My recent snack sat like a brick in my stomach and once again, I quelled the urge to vomit. *Hang on, girl. Now isn't the time.*

The further we travelled, the more apprehensive I became. Now that I'd tried to escape once, Gary would watch me closer than ever. For sure it would be over for me when my captors reached their uncle's cabin. A check of my ankle showed nothing more than some bruising and there was a scrape on my wrist from the force of my fall on my watch. A plan began to hatch in my head. *No way am I done yet. Soon, escape must be soon.*

Gary mumbled to himself, leaned forward and pounded the dash. "Stop. "

Bobby stopped the van in the middle of the road. "What?"

"We've gone too far. That old bridge up ahead is miles past our turnoff. We'll have to turn around and go back. Keep your eyes open for the turn. These damn logging roads all look the same at dusk."

Bobby swung the van around and sped back in the direction we'd come from. Five minutes later, a popping noise sounded and the van veered to the right.

"Feels like a flat tire," Bobby said, pulling the van over to the side of the road.

"No shit." "You get the jack and tire iron and I'll get the spare." He told me to get out. I dragged my weary body out the side door and a cold wind hit me in the face. My jeans were still wet from my fall into the marsh. The cold air whipped them against my legs, chilling me instantly.

The front passenger side tire was flat all right. This was it. There wouldn't be any more opportunities. As I stretched my legs, I walked in a circle deliberately limping.

Bobby came up beside me. "What's wrong with your leg?"

"I stepped in a hole and fell. I think it's a sprain."

A sadistic laugh came from Gary. "Serves you right for running," he said.

Bingo! They bought it.

"I need a break, please," I said, pulling my jacket collar up around my neck.

Gary glared at me and turned to Bobby. "Take her. I'll remove the tire."

I followed Bobby up a trail, accentuating my injury, until he pointed out a spot for me and turned his back. "Now, don't you run on me, missy."

"Run?" I spat out, with a snort. "With a sprained ankle? Besides it's getting dark." I squatted down, quickly scouting my surroundings. The path continued into the dense forest.

Gary cursed down by the van.

It's now or never.

"Hurry up! I need you," Gary yelled.

"You done yet?" Bobby asked.

"No, not yet."

I could hear metal hitting metal. Gary was having quite a temper tantrum. "Get down here. These lugs are stuck."

"Hurry up, lady. Jesus! Gary's real angry; you don't wanna make him madder." Bobby fidgeted.

"I'm sorry, you go down and help him. I'll be right there."

"What? I can't leave you. Gary'll kill me." Bobby started pacing in front of me.

"What're you doing up there?" Gary yelled.

"I'm not done yet, okay? It's a pregnancy thing. I'm not going anywhere with a sprained ankle. Besides that, it's getting dark."

Gary's yelling and swearing grew louder. Any minute he would come running into the bush after us.

"Okay. I'll go down and help Gary. You come as soon as you're done." Bobby ran off down the path. "I'm coming, don't have a shit fit."

I didn't believe it. *He actually left me alone? Go ... now.*

Up like a shot, I bolted along the path in the other direction, securing my jeans as I ran. Bobby and Gary were yelling at each other, probably about me. My feet were moving faster than my body. There wasn't much time to put distance between myself and my captors.

Chapter 5

Present Time

I opened my eyes. There was no moon, no light, only blackness and the chilling cold. I rubbed my arms and legs to stimulate circulation and warmth.

Marion, you'd be so proud of me. I escaped my captors and avoided sure death. I became empowered. Yes. What were the words you said? Life only hands you what it thinks you can handle? So losing a husband to a pregnant girlfriend and finding yourself alone and pregnant wasn't enough? Let's get kidnapped, threatened with death, lost, cold and alone in the wilderness. Of course.

Marion—bite me!

I wanted to scream out, *What am I doing here? Still, I'd done it. Escaped.*

A few fitful naps and a lot of cold later, a hazy light filtered through the trees and I pulled my cramped body upright to move on. I stretched my limbs and found a spot to relieve myself. Everything looked so different from the night before. A light snow started to fall, making me anxious. If a storm came, I'd need to find shelter. I looked up and down the trail, not sure which way to go. It didn't make sense for my kidnappers to waste time looking for me. But nothing about those two creeps made sense anyway. Besides, another fact needed to be faced: I was lost.

With no idea how to find my way back, I decided to follow the track in the other direction, forcing myself to believe it was the safest choice.

The snow came down heavily for a few hours. I wouldn't let myself stop walking and concentrated on counting one step in front of the other.

One and two, three and four. One and two, three, and four.

A sharp wind blew the snow all around and I shielded my eyes in order to see. The dampness chilled me to the bone and my feet felt numb. The path ended abruptly on the bank of a stream. I waded across in my socks and shoes, still wet from yesterday. "Oh, shit . . ." My feet might have felt numb, but that cold water still shocked the hell out of me.

A well-used game trail followed the stream.

One and two, three and four.

The track moved through a tight line of trees and up an incline. I struggled to the top, spying a clearing ahead, and continued across the open field with limited visibility. A dark structure loomed up ahead. The structure began to take shape, and then, I saw it.

"A cabin … I've found a cabin." Hesitation stopped me from moving forward. *What if this is my abductors' cabin?* A furtive glance around told me otherwise. There was no visible road to this cabin, no sign of activity. A recent memory of a conversation between my captors reminded me that a logging road led straight to their uncle's place. *No, it's not the same cabin.*

I climbed onto the porch to see a padlocked door, and the windows shuttered and locked on the outside. "Hello … hello?" I pounded on the door until I was exhausted, and then sank down to my knees. I sat with my back pressed against the cabin wall, staring at the storm.

"Can't go back out there … just can't."

A swaying sensation rolled through my abdomen like waves on a shore. My hands flew to my torso. "Oh … sweet baby." The tears streamed down my face as I experienced my baby moving for the first time. "You're alive, and you're moving." Determination filled me once more. I went from window to window, shaking the wooden shutters to see if I could break them. *Fat chance. They're built to keep animals out.* Long nails protruded from the slats of the shutters and I had to be careful to avoid them. Obviously, they were there to discourage bears from breaking in, and they, also, stopped me from getting a grip on the slats. Once again I sunk down onto the porch, accepting my total helplessness. I shook my head from side to side in disbelief. "I'm so sorry little one … so sorry."

My head rolled backwards and all hope faded. In a matter of minutes, all feeling left my body. I let go of my reserve with a sigh. Nothing seemed to matter and soon everything began to fade away. I closed my eyes and slipped into blackness.

"Georgia, you can't give up."

My eyes shot open. *What?* No one there. I leaned back against the door. *Wait … there … someone spoke again.*

"You must get inside the cabin."

At that moment, I realized that the voice came from inside my mind. A woman's voice, although soft and gentle, it startled me. The hair rose up on the back of my neck. *So weird.*

"How? I don't see how." I felt stupid, talking to a voice in my head. But then, it really wasn't my voice I spoke to.

"Go to the back of the cabin."

Exhausted but compelled, I pulled myself up to my feet. I labored my way around back, struggling against the fierce wind. An eight-foot wide overhang extended from the back wall and ran its full width. Stacks of cut firewood were piled under the roof. A narrow path between the stacks provided access to another door. It too was padlocked.

"Great …" My hopes diminished once again.

"You didn't expect it to be open did you? Search." I instinctively turned, looking for the person belonging to that voice, but saw no one. *I've finally snapped and lost my mind.* Still, I scanned the wood in spite of my thoughts.

A small space gaped between the wall and wood stack to the left of the door. I removed my glove and squeezed my fingers into the tight crevice. Something cold and metallic feeling hung on a hook. My numb fingers shook as I retrieved a key and fumbled with the padlock. The door creaked as I pushed it open, and with a sigh of relief, I entered.

Blinking, my eyes adjusted to the dim light. I opened the inner shutters on the windows allowing some light to filter in through the outside slats. Dust particles danced in the light beams of this one-room cabin, about twenty feet square. A quick glance around the room, revealed a light switch on the wall by the front and back doors, and two wall plugs. I flicked the switches. Nothing happened. A small electrical box was mounted on the wall by the back door with wires running to the plugs and outlets up and down the walls. I went outside behind the cabin and saw a wire running from the corner of the roof to one of the outbuildings out back. *There must be a generator.* I decided to deal with that later and went back inside.

A wood-burning stove stood on the back wall of the cabin, filled with kindling and dried sphagnum moss, all ready to light.

Matches ... I need matches. My excitement at getting into the cabin, and the prospect of heat, left me shaking along with the shivering from the cold. My first priority—get dry and warm. A box of long matches sat on a shelf behind the stove.

A lit match in hand, I reached out to light the moss. My hand froze in mid-air. *What if Gary and Bobby see the smoke? They'd find me.* I blew the match out. Instead, I removed all my clothes, wet and stiff from the cold. Leaving them in a pile on the floor, I curled up under the comforters on a brass bed. It was useless. The bed was as cold as I was and the shivering continued. No way could I warm myself. *To hell with this. Take a chance, girl. The kidnappers won't be out in this. They're probably long gone.*

Flames shot up immediately. Feeling returned to my icy hands as I held them over the heat, and with it, pain. Tears stung my eyes, mixed with relief. The throbbing confirmed I was still alive. A cardboard box of kindling with firewood stacked in front of it sat to the right, and I placed more wood in the stove.

Wrapped in a comforter from the bed, I curled up in a rocking chair. It didn't take long for the warmth to make my eyes flutter shut.

Some moments later I jumped up, choking on wood smoke. "Oh shit." The damper was closed. Tears stung my eyes, and bile rose up in my throat. *Carbon Monoxide. How could I be so stupid as to not check the damper?* I soon fixed that and flung the back door to the cabin open until the smoke cleared, then slammed it closed again, shivering. Both doors opened into the cabin. When shut from the inside, a wide wooden bar fell across the centre, locking it in place. I felt protected from the elements for the moment, and settled back into the chair. If my abductors found me, it would be because they came looking for me. It seemed unlikely with the raging snowstorm outside.

My body warmed and sleep claimed me, only to wake up some time later sweating from the heat. I stepped backwards to the front door and took toll of the interior. A picture window on my right looked onto the porch and across the clearing. A long, wooden table and four chairs sat under the window, with a kerosene lamp in the centre.

A counter ran the length of the sidewall, centering a window with a view of a stream. Cupboards lined the wall on either side of the window. The sink, fit into the countertop, made me smile. The pipe sat open and drained into a bucket sitting on a shelf under the counter. The rest of the shelves contained pots, pans, and dishes.

I sank onto a couch on the opposite side wall, flanked by matching bookcases, lifting my bare feet onto an old wooden trunk serving as a coffee table. A large round rug lay in the centre of the room. My gaze caught sight of men's clothes hanging on hooks beside the table. A winter jacket, a pair of brown corduroy pants, and a jack shirt. In a dresser, one drawer contained socks, jockey shorts, and a couple of sweatshirts. I put on a pair of the jocks and an oversized sweatshirt, finishing with a pair of wool socks.

As the night grew dark and the light faded, I attempted to light the kerosene lamp. It seemed simple enough. After fumbling around with the wick, success was mine. *Yay!* My search through the cupboards revealed plenty of tinned goods: ready-to-serve soup, vegetables, fruits, fish, and various meats. Labeled storage bins of various sizes contained coffee, tea, baking supplies, dried fruits and some spices. I picked up the bin of raisins and sniffed, and then stuffed a handful into my mouth. *Mmm, delicious.* My stomach growled, reminding me that a bag of chips and a bottle of coke over two days wouldn't satisfy the needs of a pregnant woman. My hands massaged my stomach. "Oh, sweet pea, let's eat." I grabbed a can of tuna, quickly opened it, and devoured the contents.

One last stoke to the fire and the bed beckoned me. An instant later, I got up and moved across the cabin to the counter. My eyes scanned the shelf, searching for one particular item. I tried to stay awake, listening for sounds outside the cabin. Too exhausted to fight my need for sleep, my heavy eyelids closed, the butcher knife safely tucked under my pillow.

Chapter 6

My eyes popped open. I bolted up, unsure of my surroundings. It was morning and my lengthy sleep surprised me. A chilled cabin greeted me, and I scurried out of bed to refill the box. My warm, dry jeans were a joy to put on. A ring of keys hung on a coat hook and I went outside to remove the padlock off the front door, which gave me easy access to the creek for water. Four inches of snow covered the ground and snowflakes still fell. Trembling with cold, I unlocked the window shutters to let in the morning light, and hurried back to the warmth of the cabin. Thoughts of the kidnappers filled my thoughts as my eyes scanned the meadow through the picture window.

Where are you, you bastards? Are you out there? Are you coming?

I shuddered and turned away. The stream beside the cabin was the obvious source of water, and armed with two pails from under the counter, I trudged out once again. A thin film of ice had formed over the stream, but one easy bang with the bucket broke through. I stared at a cup of water that I raised half- way to my lips. *Was the water safe to drink? How could I tell? Better boil it first.*

Cooking on a wood stove proved to be more difficult. The heat couldn't be turned up or down with an instant flick of a switch. Within minutes, the porridge boiled over and burned on the bottom. I ate the sticky mess anyway. It was wonderful to have access to this food but the supplies would only last so long. The longer I stayed, the more likely the weather conditions would prevent me from leaving.

I stood by the window watching the continued snowfall and one thought came to mind. *I escaped one hostage only to be trapped by another—Mother Nature.* The irony of this filled me with despair. My eyes searched the sanctity of the cabin. It would be hard to leave but I must. *Or maybe the owner is a hunter and will be back soon.*

Certainly, the well- stocked woodpile and food supplies indicated the cabin was being used. *Girl, you can't be sure anyone will return to the cabin until spring or summer.*

The battle of whether to go or stay was decided by logic. I was a long way from civilization, but I needed to leave. If I could find my way back to the dirt road, I could make it out.

"That's it, sweet pea. Once the snow stops, we're leaving."

A couple of out buildings stood behind the cabin, as well as an outhouse. The smaller of the two structures contained tools, an axe, more pails, a knapsack, fishing rod, an awl, some shovels, a tarp and various fishing gear. The larger one was a workshop equipped with small hand tools. They were old but well maintained. A late model Honda 3000 Series Inverter Gas Generator stood in one corner. Nosing around, I could see it had an electric start. *Looks easy.* I checked the gas tank and saw it was full. *How long would a tank last?* Newer generators were quieter than the old ones, but fear stopped me from trying to start it. *What if my abductors were still around and heard it?* There were some five-gallon kerosene cans stored in the shed for the kerosene lamp, but I didn't see any more fuel for the generator. The generator seemed to be overkill for two light switches and two electrical outlets, especially since I didn't see any electric kitchen appliances to plug into them. I decided to be cautious and forget the generator.

I found some paper and a pen back in the cabin and made a supply list of what I should take. On a duplicate copy, my name and telephone number were added to leave for the cabin owner. A sudden thought hit me. *What if my kidnappers found this cabin and my note advertising my name and phone number?* The second list was thrown into the stove. If I found my way back to civilization, there were other ways to find the owners.

I spent the afternoon gathering items and added a sleeping bag from the bed. That night I fried some bannock, a heavy bread and a diet staple to Indigenous people. It didn't resemble any bread I knew, but at least it wasn't burnt. I, also, cooked up some rice and placed it in a plastic storage container mixed with canned baked beans. Preparing some plastic bags of dried fruits, nuts, and raisins was a simpler task.

I decided against taking any of the fish products in case I came across a bear. *Don't want to smell like dinner.*

The next morning, the sky was overcast. The distant horizon promised a clear day.

"This is it! We're leaving!"

My knapsack was soon filled with the previous day's gathering of food supplies, some matches and a first aid kit. On the outside of the pack, I tied the axe, a small shovel, the sleeping bag, a bottle of water and the tarp. By eight o'clock the fire was down to coals, the cabin relocked and the key replaced on the hook.

I took one last glance at the cabin, then walked across the clearing and headed back down the trail that brought me here.

The snow changed the appearance of the terrain, making the woods unfamiliar. I plodded along on what appeared to be a main trail. The morning wore on and I knew I'd never find the way I came in. The old game trails were no longer visible. Sometimes fresh animal tracks led me for a time until they disappeared into thick brush. I stopped to look around. *Lost again.* Dease Lake had to be south-east. But when the sun disappeared behind the clouds and the trail veered off, my directions were turned around. I tried to follow the creek, knowing water usually led to civilization. This wasn't always easy to do. Tripping over hidden debris in the snow was dangerous and could lead to injury. So in the end, I chose to follow the fresh, untouched ribbons of snow that filled the trails. *Keep moving.*

I stopped at noon to rest and eat, and then pushed forward, singing a hearty rendition of Michael Buble's, 'Home', to create noise for any animal life nearby. But I promptly stopped, fearful that Bobby and Gary were searching for me. I shuddered. It was highly unlikely they were still in the area, but my fear became stronger than my reasoning.

Dusk came, prompting me to make camp for the night. A hollow between two fallen trees caught my eye. Half of the tarp covered the hole nicely on the ground, with the rest pulled over the edges of the two trees and tied down. My sleeping bag lay over a bed of evergreen branches inside the tarp. I dug around in the snow to retrieve some twigs and debris for a small fire.

Some dry sphagnum moss scrounged from the woodpile helped to get it started.

I was proud of my little camp set-up. *Pat yourself on the back, girl. You did well.*

A dinner of rice and beans, followed by some dried fruit, quelled my hunger. By now it was dark. I pulled some branches across the opening of the tarp to protect me from the wind and hopefully from the dangers of the forest at night. In spite of my apprehension about sleeping outdoors again, I fell asleep quickly from exhaustion, warm and cozy in my little nest.

The sound of snapping twigs woke me. Something or someone was out there. I listened and held my breath as the noise moved closer. My throat constricted. *Oh God, here we go.* A large shadow loomed on the trail. A smaller shadow passed on the outside. A partial moon illuminated the snow enough for me to make out a doe and a yearling. I breathed a sigh of relief and let my muscles relax. They stopped to feed on the bushes beside the path. I silently watched them, feeling privileged to be so close to two of nature's majestic creatures. They eventually moved on, oblivious to my presence.

This time, sleep evaded me.

Every noise kept me on edge. I managed to doze off shortly before dawn. The call of nature, finally, forced me up.

"Today willl be the day, sweet baby. Today we'll find our way out."

I kept moving from path to path throughout the morning, never once seeing the creek. What I did see sent chills throughout my body. Bear scat. *Fresh bear scat.* My bones ached at the thought. The fall was a bad time to run into bears. My grandfather was a hunter and told me stories as a kid about the dangers of bears when they were in hyperphasia. Bears need to reach a certain body weight to trigger an enzyme that leads them into hibernation. Females were especially dangerous because they can be pregnant and give birth during the hibernation phase. With trepidation, I moved on, pushing the thought of bears from my mind.

Again, the sun hid behind cloud cover, hindering my judgment. All the paths and trees looked alike. Faced with yet another fork in the trail, a lunch break seemed appropriate. My final decision took me to the left. Thirty minutes later, rounding a bend, I came within twenty feet of a grizzly bear. We both stopped short. He looked as startled as me.

My heart pounded in my ears. My mind worked overtime.

Should I run? No, never ever run from a bear, black or grizzly.

The animal let out a roar but stood his ground.

Okay ... should I yell, appear aggressive and large? No, that's for blacks not grizzlies.

He started to paw at the ground. *Is it a he or a she? A pregnant she?* For no logical reason or prior knowledge on the subject, other than sheer size, I decided on a male.

The bear lowered his head and moved his shoulders from side to side. *Uh-oh ... this is definitely a bad sign. Maybe I should drop to the ground and play dead. But what if he drags me away and buries me?*

My mind turned to mush. Too many questions, not enough answers. In truth, it didn't matter if I did know what to do. My body felt frozen to the spot. My breathing became shallow. All time felt suspended as I stood perfectly still and watched. I knew that you should never stare a male gorilla in the eye; he would think you were challenging him. Without a clue as to whether this worked with grizzlies, I lowered my eyes to the ground and waited.

The bear let out a deafening roar and charged. I stifled a scream and closed my eyes tight. Sucking in my breath, I waited with taut muscles. Nothing happened.

I opened my eyes and watched him retreat to the same spot on the trail, but once again with lowered eyes, using peripheral vision to watch his movements.

He was only sending me a warning. *Maybe, I should back away slowly.*

I placed one foot behind me slowly, then the other. He started to move his shoulders back and forth again.

Oh my God!

The huge animal charged again. My heart pounded so hard, I thought it would burst through my rib cage. This time my eyes stayed open, but he only came a few feet. A half-hearted attempt and once more he backed away. All feeling was gone from my body. Images flooded my mind of the bear dining on my broken, bloody body, and the bear curled up in his den amongst my ripped clothes and scattered bones, deep in winter slumber. *Would I be the last meal that took him into hibernation?*

While I stood my ground trying to decide if I should attempt to back away again, the grizzly gave a short snort and turned his back on me. He lumbered off down the trail. Backing away slowly, I turned the corner behind me and sank to my knees. My breathing was raspy and my whole body shook.

Okay, girlie, this is no place to suddenly go weak. Get your ass out of here before he decides he wants a piece of it for lunch.

I tore back along the path, and when I reached the fork in the trail, I turned right and kept moving. I'd been lucky. Thank God it wasn't spring. I wouldn't stand a chance with a mother bear and her cub.

Mid-afternoon approached and I finally stopped for a rest. I felt a little discouraged, knowing that I should have reached the dirt road by now. After my bear encounter, I didn't relish the idea of spending another night in the woods. I perched on a stump and stared around me, noticing that the path reached a stream. My heart pounded in my chest as I raced to the water, searching for a spot to cross, rushing through the shallows and up onto the other side. The trail took me to an incline.

Oh, no.

Pushing myself up the hill, I followed the path to the edge of the trees and a clearing.

"No!" I yelled, falling to my knees. "It can't be … no … no!"

I pounded the ground with my fists until the wet snow seeped through my clothing. My body shook from hysteria and the chilling dampness. The cold finally forced me up. I dragged my weary body across the clearing with a heavy heart and circled to the back of the cabin. The key was right where it should be and once again, I let myself in. The wood stove roared to life when lit. I stripped off my wet clothes and collapsed into the bed, not allowing myself to think about what this meant, or chastise myself for my stupidity in circling back. I wouldn't allow myself to feel! When dusk came, so did a deep sleep.

Chapter 7

Early November - Georgia's In-Laws Home, Vancouver

Alice snapped at her husband. "Oh for God's sake, turn that thing off."

Frank Charles glanced at his wife and picked up the remote and hit the mute button. "What are you so upset about?"

Alice gave her husband a condescending look. "Don't be stupid. What do you think? Story after story. When are they going to let this thing die down? And, then there's that Marion person, blabbing her mouth off all over the place."

"How can you be so cold? Georgia was a member of our family for many years. I for one was very fond of her. It's a tragedy what's happened to her."

"Well of course it is, dear. But there's nothing any of us can do about it. The more they talk about it and that Marion woman tells all our family business to God knows who, it reflects back on us."

Frank moved over to the wet bar and poured himself a scotch. "I see. So this isn't about a beautiful young woman who meets a tragic end and the devastation it's caused her family, but about you saving face with your friends."

"Don't be cruel."

"That's your job, not mine."

Alice bristled. She sat rigid on the edge of the couch. "How can you not see my point here? Our son impregnated two women within weeks of each other. If the mistress disappeared no one would have cared. But no, the wife disappeared and everyone's sympathy is with her. The wronged wife, the unborn child—a great travesty. And do you think any of those news people really care? To them it's a great story."

"You certainly have a perverse way of looking at things. Marion said nothing about our family in all of this. Besides, this is Colin's mess and it reflects on him, not you."

"Oh Frank … don't be so naive. The sins of the son always reflect back on the parents, which affects the status of our name."

At that precise moment, Colin Charles walked into the room. "Mother, whatever are you talking about?"

Alice was taken back. "Colin, dear … we didn't hear you come in," she drawled in a syrupy voice.

"No wonder, with the intense conversation I overheard. What do you mean by the sins of the son?"

"We were talking about all the news reports about Georgia. I was saying how they've made Georgia out to be a victim here …"

Colin cut his mother off. "Of course she's a victim. She was abducted and murdered, for Christ' sake."

Alice rolled her eyes. "You're as naive as your father. I'm not talking about that. I'm talking about her being pregnant and separated from a cheating husband, and how it affects our family name."

Colin seethed. "Sometimes I don't believe what comes out of your mouth. You never accepted her in this family. Now the poor woman is dead and you still blame her for what you think are attacks against the family name. Can't you even let her rest in peace?"

Alice stood up in a rage. "Don't you talk to your mother in that tone. If she hadn't run off to that ugly, uncivilized northern outpost, none of this would have happened to her."

"Alice, I think you've said enough. Calm down," Frank said.

She glared at her husband. "Don't you tell me what I can and can't say."

It was Colin's turn to rage: "And if I hadn't left her for Julie, she wouldn't have felt the need to go up to the Yukon. So why don't you blame me instead of her?"

"Oh, don't think I've let you off the hook in all of this. You should have been more responsible before you thought with the wrong head."

"I'm out of here." Colin turned and marched out of the room. A few seconds later, the slamming of the front door could be heard.

Frank took another sip of his scotch. "That went well."

"Oh shut up."

"You know what your problem is, Alice? You're a snob. You think you're above everyone else and you can't stand it when they stand up to you.

"I am not a snob. And I accepted Georgia into this family as Colin's wife."

"But you always treated her like a servant who was invited to sit down for dinner with her owners."

"Georgia was a nice enough girl, but I believe people should stay with their own kind. She wasn't one of us."

Frank downed the last of his drink. "Come on. Both of your grandparents were indentured servants from England. They spent their lives as struggling farmers once they paid off their debt."

"And my father made a fortune. He gave us status and respectability, of which I am proud, and I'll do what it takes to protect our name."

Frank stared hard at his wife. She hadn't taken his name when they married, a fact he supported. It was the thing to do these days. He never gave it a thought until now. The realization came to him that she hadn't felt his name as worthy as her father's. He rose from his chair and headed to the bedroom. "Be careful of what you sacrifice for the sake of your good name. Good night."

Chapter 8

The next few days were a blur, as I fell in and out of consciousness. My body had never been so cold. Concerns about hypothermia forced me to drag myself to the stove to rebuild the fire, making sure to drink water before I passed out again. Thoughts came back to me of looking out the window at the never-ending snowstorms, further trapping me here. I was plagued with dreams and nightmares.

The fire in the wood stove flared with each stoke of the iron poker, my body soaking up its warmth. Sudden whispers from the front porch caught my attention. I crept across to the window and peeked through a slat. My heart raced as recognition took hold.

It was them.

Oh dear God. What'll I do? I backed quietly away from the window, my eyes glued to the front door. The handle began to wiggle and the sound of someone's weight pushing against the door pounded in my ears. "Uh!" My hands flew to my face, covering my mouth to stifle a scream. My breath caught in my throat.

I turned and ran to the back of the cabin, unlatched the door and rushed outside. A fierce wind swirled snow all around, chilling me to the bone. Blinded, I raced behind the sheds. I saw an old water tower. A wooden ladder led to the top. My focus became that platform.

"There she is," Bobby yelled.

The climb took away my breath and filled my lungs with cold air. Gary and Bobbie stood below, laughing at me. I wrapped my arms around my body to protect me from the cold ... understandable with one glance at my socked feet, bare legs and oversized sweatshirt.

Gary waved an arm. "Come down, bitch. Don't make us come up there and get you."

Tears stung my eyes and froze when they reached my cheeks. "No ... no."

He reached into his pocket and pulled out a gun. "Maybe I'll use you for target practice from here." He laughed and pointed the weapon at me, pretending to shoot. "Pop ... pop ... pop."

A voice bellowed from behind the cabin. "No, you don't. Not yet anyway."

"Colin?" I couldn't believe my eyes, as my husband walked towards Gary and Bobbie. "How did you get here?"

Gary spun around. "Who are you? Gary asked. "What do you want here?"

Colin stared up at me, but spoke to Gary. "Not what I want, who I want. I'm her husband. Georgia, what are you doing? Come down this instant."

My body was numb from the cold. I couldn't comprehend his words. *Colin wants me? No, I didn't believe that.* Still, I asked: "You came for me?"

He started to snicker. "You? No, not you." He turned to Gary and Bobbie. "I want my baby.

Then, you can do what you want with her." They all stared at me and laughed cruelly.

"But, it's not time. She's not ready to be born yet." I stared into the sky full of stars, trying to sort my thoughts and then, looked down at this man who became a stranger. "Why, Colin ... why?"

Colin just shrugged. "I grew up and you didn't ... you live in a fantasy world."

My eyes searched the sky again and focused on the Pleiades Constellation, home to the Lemuroids, higher souls who came to live in Lemuria before Atlantis according to mythology. *I want to live in their world, to float free, and know their wisdom.*

"One way or the other, you're coming down, bitch. Hard or easy, it's up to you," Gary said.

"No ... no," I cried. "You can't have her. She's mine." The edge of the platform pressed under the edge of my toes, and one push forward propelled my body into the air. The freedom of flying like a bird overtook me and I shrieked with laughter at the shocked look on their faces. The ground loomed closer as I began to tumble and fall, with my body plummeting faster and faster.

My light-hearted cries turned to screams of terror.

The mournful cries of the wolves jolted me
awake. "Yuk!" My bedding and clothes were
damp. My fever had finally broken. Combined
with the chilled air and the lasting effects of my
recent nightmare, I shivered under the blankets.

My watch revealed that four days had passed.
I forced myself out of bed and scurried over to
the stove to restart the fire. A change of clothes
came next. Moving to the window, I was amazed
to see a clear sky, stars shining. The Pleiades
Constellation caught my eye, like in my dream.
It's believed the Lemuroids went home to the
stars when Lemuria sank into the Pacific Ocean.
And that today, they are reborn, bearing our
world a new generation of enlightened children.

For the first time since returning to the cabin,
the snow stopped falling. In a hollow way, I
felt comforted. At least something changed. The
clearing in front of the cabin was blanketed with
three feet of untouched snow. The evergreens of

the forest beyond stood as sentinels, protecting the cabin from harsh winds and the world beyond. Filtered moonlight through the trees cast dark shadows across the clearing.

The wolves howled again.

"Oh no, those damn wolves … please … please stop." My hands covered my ears and my legs shook. It wasn't so much fear of the wolves that I felt, but the feeling of loneliness and extreme isolation that their cries accentuated. When Colin had left me, I'd experienced loneliness for the first time in my life. Surrounded as I was with loving family and friends who cared, I didn't think anything could make me feel worse than I felt then.

What a joke compared to this!

Thoughts of death were in my life for a while. Five months previously, when Colin left, I had wished for it. The day of my kidnapping I thought I'd be killed. And now? Now, I didn't want to die. But who was I to think I was in control? My tracks to the cabin were well covered. My enemies would never find me. That meant my rescuers might not as well—if there were any. Was this a sanctuary or a tomb? Stay or leave? I had no idea in which direction to head. Here at least, the cabin provided warmth and water, but not enough food. So—stay and eventually starve to death, or leave and possibly freeze to death. Some choice!

As I thought of those closest to me, tears wet my cheeks. What a wimp I'd been—selfish and self- pitying. I'd tried to cling desperately to my old existence during those six months. Having never lived alone, my present situation was a reality check compared to the fantasy world I'd been living in. This past week, my shattered world tumbled down around me, with no experience or life skills to deal with the challenges facing me.

The sky suddenly came alive with light, rolling back and forth across the horizon like waves on the shore. Normally an exhilarating experience, this colorful display of the Northern Lights left me feeling overpowered by its raw energy. I was a mere speck surrounded by a daunting universe.

Standing by the window, I made my decision to stay. Better to face the small world inside the cabin than face the unknown world outside with its wolves, bears, and who knows what else. Now

... did I base this decision on sheer logic or because I was a coward? Whatever my motivation, it was a definite decision and it felt good. I'd been indecisive for so long, running blindly from crisis to crisis. My whole world had been based on sheer emotion instead of rationale.

Yes, the past eight days were hell.

My time in the woods and at the cabin were filled with tears, fears, and self-absorbed despondency. One moment I was fearful that my enemies would find me; the next I wished they would come and put me out of my misery. I felt tired—tired of crying, tired of fearing the unknown, and tired of being tired.

Feeling a decisive kick from within, my hands moved to my abdomen.

"Oh my God! You're moving. You're alive." For the first time in days, the baby moved. *Look at me. I'm laughing and crying.* But this time, they were tears of joy.

A definite reminder that there was more to consider than my sorrowful life. I knew I must take control. Since my situation wasn't about to change, and since my future was unknown, the only choice left was to take charge of the present, one day at a time.

I sat down by the warmth of the stove. Relaxing into the hypnotic sway of the rocker, I thought back to the circumstances that brought me to this place— at this time and in this state.

Why do I think I'm a coward? I've survived a marriage break-up, escaped my kidnappers, survived my encounter with a grizzly, and found shelter and some food.

I think all the tears and fears I'd been experiencing for so long, right back to the day Colin walked out on me, were accentuated by my pregnancy. *Hormones.* Through all my suffering, physical and emotional—my baby survived. Her strength and endurance amazed me, and I drew from her strong will to live.

Her? Yes—her! I knew my baby was a girl.

I didn't know how, but at that moment it became clear that we would make it. I wouldn't give up. I looked down at my abdomen and felt another wave of movement.

I'm not alone. You're here with me. I rubbed my stomach and smiled. "Maybe you're one of the enlightened ones, sweet pea."

Thoughts of family saddened me. With no way to let them know I was alive and sheltered, their grief would be all consuming. *Were they looking for me? Was anyone looking for me?* Probably, I concluded, but there were a lot of miles between where I was now and where I was last seen in Whitehorse.

As the days passed, my concerns of being discovered by my captors lessened. A daily routine developed. Mornings were spent doing cabin chores. Afternoons were spent fishing in the stream for rainbow trout with a rod and tackle found in one of the sheds, adding to my larder. I wrote in a notebook found in the bookcase, keeping a careful record of each day. My evenings were spent reading the selective choice of titles. One book, which became my bible, was on survival in the outdoors. There was a short section on childbirth in the wilds with instructions about cutting the cord and the afterbirth. I reread that section over and over. There were books on the gold rush, similar to Marion's, and an assortment of fiction books. A set of three books in a series of thrillers by Sean Dixon, an author I never heard of, was particularly exciting.

All I had for clothes beside my one set were the ones hanging on the hook by the door. Another wooden trunk used for the coffee table contained bed linens and towels. "Oh dear, baby girl. This reminds me of your needs when you arrive. I'll cut up the towels for diapers and figure out some nighties for you." I let out a snort. "This should be fun, sewing has never been my strong suit."

There were some doilies, tablecloths, and knickknacks that I placed around the cabin, adding a feminine touch. The routine became important because it gave me a focus and a purpose to each day. When the day ended, I told myself to be proud of surviving another sunset.

The one constant that nagged at me on a daily basis was hygiene. Daily showers and long soaks in bubble baths didn't exist here. An old metal washtub from under the bed served as the only thing available for washing clothes and for stand-up baths. There was no soap, no shampoo, no hairbrushes, blow dryers, or hair curlers, only a bottle of bleach, which I used sparingly. My biggest chore was constantly boiling water, to wash dishes, clothes and myself, and for drinking water.

Using an outhouse did not appeal to my delicate senses, including my sense of smell, but that was my only choice. I felt grateful that at least at this time of year, the pungent odour of this necessary outbuilding was not enhanced by excessive heat. At night an old metal bucket served the purpose. No way would I go outside in the dark or the cold for relief.

As the days passed, my long hair suffered from lack of grooming. I felt unclean. An old mirror hung on the wall with the silver scratched off a lot of the back. But I could still see a broken reflection and my hair looked pretty wild. With a pair of scissors I found under the kitchen counter, I chopped it all off to chin level. Luckily, the water in this area was hard water, meaning it had a lot of minerals in it. My curls and waves all but disappeared, leaving my hair hanging straight. I used a fork to comb my hair and control the tangles. Over time, I became quite adept at this new grooming feat. I used the scissors meant for cutting paper to cut my nails and shape them. It seemed there was always dirt under my fingernails, so a small paring knife served to clean underneath them.

One day I stood on the outside porch looking in the picture window. I caught my reflection in the glass. My hands flew to my mouth as I exploded in a fit of the giggles. This woman with no make-up, chopped stringy straight hair, oversized sweatshirt and men's jeans held up with twine, did not resemble the woman I knew.

If they could see me now.

If I hadn't looked so ridiculously funny, I probably would have cried. I gave my head a shake.

Get a grip, girlie. Make-up and clothes won't help you here. This is survival.

It was now the end of November, and I decided to drag the throw rugs and carpets outside to air and beat with a broom. Pulling the rug that ran along the front of the counter, a new discovery stopped me in my tracks.

"No way, sweet pea … a trap door." I talked to my baby constantly. She became my focus and my comfort.

I stared at the door, compelled to open it, but afraid of what might be down there. Some cabins had trap doors in the floor as a means of escape. However, this cabin was close to the ground with a log skirting. If it opened to a crawl space, it was anyone's guess as to what would be down there. I envisioned rats, spiders and other undesirables. In the end, my curiosity overcame my overactive imagination, and I leaned down and pulled the door open, revealing nothing but blackness. A blast of cold air hit me in the face, along with a cloud of dust, making me cough. I lit a lamp, and lying on the floor, dropped my head and arm into the dark hole.

*... you cannot run away from a weakness,
you must sometime fight it out or perish,
and if that be so, why not now, and where
you stand*

Robert Louis Stevenson

Chapter 9

The lantern light revealed a root cellar with a ladder. There were rows of shelves lining the wooden walls.

"Oh shit!" My language skills had narrowed since I arrived at the cabin. Talking out loud was normal practice for me. Hearing my voice reminded me I wasn't dead—yet. My expletive outburst was twofold. One for discovering the root cellar, the other for the pain in my swollen, tender breasts. The pain shot through them as I leaned down to peer into the dark hole.

I placed the lamp on a higher shelf and descended carefully into a six-foot square room with support beams. The room was about seven feet deep. Wood slats lined the floor. Jars of home-canned fish, vegetables and fruits filled the shelves. There were boxes of potatoes, onions and carrots —all well- preserved in this cold storage.

A huge smile lit up my face. "Jackpot, sweet pea." I danced a little jig and fist pumped the air, thrilled with my discovery. The necessities to survive were at hand. This well-stocked cabin, closed for the winter, was a mystery, but one for which I was grateful. A sudden thought overwhelmed me. *Maybe, the owners are coming back for the winter and I'll be found. Or a mad trapper, someone like my kidnappers.* Fear took hold as my mind short-circuited on all the negatives. With a deep sigh, I sat on the bottom step of the ladder and looked at my stomach. "There I go again, little one, fearing things that may never happen." Instead, I planned a festive night of feasting on my newfound goodies.

As the days passed and November with them, more negative thoughts surfaced. The extreme loneliness for one, tugged at my heart, especially after dark. I tried to meditate and build my positive reserve. Other fears tore away at my spirit. My growing body, ripening with pregnancy, reminded me that I would be alone during childbirth. So much could go wrong. The thought of giving birth without a doctor stressed me out. What if it was a breach birth? What about the pain without drugs? And after the birth, what about infection? These were only my fears about myself. Then, there was the baby and the medical needs she might require. That really scared me.

The unknown factors were just as frightening. I worried about the extreme cold of winter—envisioning hungry wolves attacking me when I went for water, or grizzly bears breaking into the cabin for food. My sense of hearing intensified. Every unexplained sound made me jittery. In a state of nervous exhaustion, my mental condition deteriorated to the point that I began to question my sanity.

It was now early December, and the voice in my head from that first day at the cabin came to me in a dream. In the dream, I slept. A voice as soft as the gentlest breeze willed me to waken.

"Wake up, Georgia. It's time. Time for us to meet," she whispered.

I opened my eyes. Her face filled my field of vision: an aged face at best, but one marked with such peace that she appeared timeless. She sat in the rocking chair by the cook stove. She wore a long ivory dress of eyelet lace and her feet were bare. Her long grey hair hung in waves past her shoulders, a shade of rich smoky grey with a blue tinge. What held my gaze were her eyes; they were the palest of grey with an iridescent shine that was love itself. In her hands, she held a white crystal, its light projecting like a star burst. A shimmering mauve aura glowed all around her. It was a mesmerizing sight, and one that filled me with peace and comfort. It never crossed my mind to fear her or to doubt the reality of the situation.

"Who're you?" I asked.

"My name is Kaela."

I stared at her in silence, digesting the beauty of her delicate features. She rocked slowly back and forth, her face alight with a serene smile.

"How do you know my name?"

Kaela rose from the chair and came to sit on the bed beside me.

"I've known you for a short time and I'm here to help you."

"Help me how?"

"To know yourself and to know your destiny," Kaela said.

At that, I chuckled. I was thirty years old and knew so little about myself. Destiny was something I'd only read about in fiction books.

"Then you have your job cut out for you. So far, I've been a bad life student. I hope you're a good teacher."

"You'll be a student for life. In order to grow, you must change; in order to change, you must learn; and, with knowledge comes choice. Understand I'm not here to teach you, only to guide you."

"That's too bad. I thought you might teach me to be wise." I heaved a deep sigh.

Now it was Kaela's turn to chuckle. "Wisdom cannot be taught. Wisdom is acquired from experiencing life—good and bad—and connecting with your higher self."

"Well, what I thought was good turned out to be bad, and I certainly do not feel any wiser for it." *Wow, did I sound bitter?*

Kaela rose from the bed and returned to the rocking chair.

"When you start to see from within, through your inner self and not through your eyes, it'll all make sense," she countered. "And that's why I'm here. But enough for tonight—sleep and I'll return."

I woke up in the morning to bright sunshine streaming through the cracks of the window shutters and looked at the rocking chair, recalling every word of my dream.

How strange.

I wasn't sure what the dream meant, but somehow it made me feel less alone. I hoped to dream of her again.

It looked like a good day to shovel a proper walkway to the stream and around the back to the outbuildings. The snow was about ten inches deep. The sun shone brightly, the sky was clear. As I fell into the rhythm of the shovel, I thought about my dream. A sudden rustle in the brush to my left stopped me in my tracks. "Uh …" My head shot up and I listened. Time to get back into reality.

"Hello," I yelled, my legs running on their own accord. "I'm going inside now."

The rustling became more pronounced, and having made my presence known, I took off under the overhang and through the back door of the cabin. With a slam and a bang of the bar falling in place, I hurried to the front window in time to see a doe run out from the right of the cabin. She sprinted across the clearing, stopped, and turned to look at the cabin. I experienced a sudden kinship. I could feel her caution and vulnerability. Only moments before, I had feared her. It suddenly occurred to me that I, always the fearful child, carried my fearfulness into adulthood. With this came the realization that most of what I spent my life fearing was the unknown ...

Settled in the rocking chair, a cup of tea in hand, I gave thought to the word fear and stood up to retrieve a dictionary I'd seen in the bookcase. The definition read, 'anxious anticipation of danger.'

Hmm ... what a waste of time and energy to anxiously anticipate something that we know nothing about, or that might never happen.

I grabbed pen and paper and proceeded to write down everything I feared in life. My list wasn't that long. As a child I was afraid of strangers, thunder and lightning, garden snakes and bugs. *Was that so unusual?* As an adult, I was scared of being alone. "Huh." A sardonic laugh turned to a snort. *Under my present circumstances, what choice did I have?* I felt anxious making decisions by myself and was fearful of violence. *Was this learned behavior or genetically based?* With nothing but time on my hands, I had no shortage of opportunity to figure it out.

That night I slipped into an easy, peaceful sleep. I awoke a short time later and rose to build the fire. Turning from the stove, I was startled to find Kaela sitting in the rocker.

"Oh." I jumped. "You startled me."

"I'm sorry. Please know you have nothing to fear from me."

"Somehow, I know that," I said. "But I don't understand. Last night you were in a dream but tonight I'm awake."

"We manifest in many ways. This evening you see me as a vision."

I huddled under the warm covers, propped up against the headboard, my hands on my belly. Again, I felt a calmness and ease in her company.

"You told me I had to go within and see with 'Self'. By 'Self' do you mean 'soul?'"

"Soul, higher self, or spirit."

I gave her a pensive stare. "How do I know if I'm seeing with 'self'? I don't think I know the difference." "Seeing only through your eyes comes from a place of emotion, usually negative emotion. When you see from 'within', through the eyes of your soul, you're like an observer, detached and unemotional. You see things as they truly are, not as you think they are, or sometimes wish they were. You do know the difference."

I let out a big sigh. "I'm not so sure about that."

"This morning you experienced fear. Outside where you felt unsafe, you contemplated the worst. You felt protected when you came inside and realized you need not be afraid. Going within can provide you with a similar security, allowing you to truly see. The realizations you achieved today came from within. You began the journey." The soft silkiness of her voice comforted me. The simplicity of her words made sense, and instead of sounding like a lecture, they came across as common sense.

At that moment, the howling of wolves startled me. I cringed and stared hard at the window.

"Tell me why you fear Mother Nature so."

"Well … I'm not used to nature, especially this raw. I'm frightened by strange noises." *Oh come on, you're frightened of everything.*

"So it's the fear of the unknown and the unfamiliar you're experiencing then?"

I smiled and nodded. Here it was again, slapping me in the face.

"You know, child, you and nature have a lot in common." She pointed to my stomach. "You both bear life; you both fiercely protect that life. You both nurture and heal. At this point, I must tell you, you are a healer. Should you choose to follow the path of the healer, you could help humanity. One day, when you are ready, you will remember this conversation. But your path at this time is to heal yourself, so I will not confuse your thoughts."

She paused and paced the room before continuing. "You're a kindred spirit with Mother Nature; she's your sister. Don't fear her. Respect her power and when you find your own power, you'll bond."

I wondered how she knew about my happenings earlier that day. Perhaps she was a figment of my imagination? Maybe, I had gone mad. "Last night I asked, 'Who are you?' but I think I meant 'What are you?'"

A serene smile formed on her lips as she answered my question: "I'm a native spirit, an elder of the Tahltan Band. My mother was from the Crow family and my father from the Wolf family. Native spirits come to help family when needed. I'm with you always, helping when I can."

"But I'm not from your family."

"You're on Tahltan lands, living in an elder's cabin. I believe your needs warrant my presence."

I stared at her in silence, her words hard to digest. "Am I mad—insane?"

"Heavens no! Madness is born from fear and you do have your fair share of them. But do you feel afraid when in my presence?" she asked.

"No, the complete opposite."

"Then I 'm not madness and you're not insane," she said.

"Your eyes—they're grey."

Kaela's laughter rang out with a gentle vibration that echoed around the cabin, a sound I likened to the delicate tinkling of expensive wine glasses.

"It was tradition for the son to be raised by his uncle and if he died, the nephew would marry his uncle's wife and take care of his family. The uncle died while hunting one day but the nephew was still a boy. The uncle's wife, my mother, lay with a white trader. I was born. One day the trader left never to return. When the nephew grew up, he married my mother and became my father."

Kaela's eyes glazed as if she were remembering past memories. She shook her head and focused on me.

"We're of a higher vibration level than humans, which is why you normally cannot see us. Your science has proven some animals and insects have highly developed eyes and see things humans cannot."

I shifted my position, stretching my legs. "Then how is it possible for me to see you?"

"When it's necessary, we slow down our vibration and appear before you."

Kaela disappeared into the lavender mist around her. The mist dissipated and I was alone once again, left with lots to ponder.

It was now the third night since I'd first seen Kaela, and I opened my eyes to see her sitting on my bed. I knew what my first question would be. "Tell me, why do you only come to me in the dark?"

"Because that's when you need me most."

"But how do I know I'm not dreaming? Perhaps if I saw you in the daytime, I wouldn't doubt your existence."

"I've come to you many times in the daytime. You never saw me. I gave you energy to run from Gary. The day you found this cabin and slipped into darkness on the front porch—I spoke to you."

I twisted my hair around the fingers of my right hand, and tried to remember. "The voice. You told me to come to the back of the cabin." I sat up straighter and pulled my left arm out from under the covers, grabbed a hold of my skin with my thumb and the forefinger of my right hand, and pinched as hard as I could.

"What are you doing?" Kaela asked.

"I'm pinching myself," I said, clenching my teeth. "If I have a mark there in the morning, I'll know I'm awake and I'll be a true believer."

Kaela's laughter rang out. "You silly girl, I'll leave you a sign if that's what you need."

Something bothered me here and I found myself frowning at Kaela. "How come I don't fear you? Me— who has always been afraid. Do spirits have some kind of control over us?"

"No. We cannot control your will or your ability to make choices. All of our messages are filled with positive energy and words of love. A spirit encounter leaves you feeling calm, and you most likely experience a change for the better. You turn inwards and learn acceptance and love of self, until such time as you can turn outwards and love the world."

"What about people who don't learn and change, or ones who do bad things. Where are their spirits?"

"If they're not ready to receive our message, there's nothing we can do for them. Such people have spirits who try to reach them. But we're not always successful," she said somberly. Smiling, she continued. "But you are ready. Know that you and your baby are protected. If you choose to believe that is so, you'll be safe here."

The next morning, I addressed the fire and donned my clothes. I was zipping up my jacket to retrieve water from the creek when my eyes fell on the rocking chair. A white object rested in the hollow of the seat, reflecting the light. I walked over and picked it up. It was Kaela's crystal, the one she held in her hands during her first visit. This was her sign to me. I suddenly remembered last night's vision. Stripping off my jacket, I pulled up my sweatshirt sleeve. There in all its glory, sat a purplish bruise the size of a quarter on the inside of my arm, stark against my white skin. It was the mark left from pinching myself the previous night.

"She is real. Kaela's real."

I sat in the chair, rocking back and forth slowly, the crystal cupped in my hands. It was undoubtedly the best gift I ever received. At that moment, I believed.

Chapter 10

My thoughts were of Christmas, and that old feeling of loneliness welled up from deep in my chest, leaving a lump in my throat. The date on my watch read December 16th. Memories of home reminded me that this was the day we would start to decorate our tree, making sure it was finished for my brother's birthday on the eighteenth. My mother's birthday was the day after New Year's, and the tree would come down the day after that. A family tradition followed for years, the reasoning of which had long been forgotten and no longer mattered.

I thought of the unique purchases that I had made this year in Whitehorse for Christmas. My eyes stung with tears thinking of the tremendous sense of loss my family would feel this holiday season. A time for good food, family fun and renewal of spirit would be ruined for them. I reminded myself that it would be harder on them because they thought me dead.

I decided to cut down a tree. Embracing this practice in my world of isolation should give me plenty to do over the next few days and take my mind away from negative thoughts.

A sudden kick in my abdomen brought me back to reality. I placed my hand on the little foot pushing against its protective cocoon. Many nights recently, I dreamed of birthing my daughter. Smiling, I talked to her.

"Okay, sweet pea, I know what you want. We're both hungry. Time for food."

I bustled around making lunch, thinking how ironic my situation was. I always wanted a Christmas in a setting like this. I remembered a conversation with Colin last year about going away for the holidays.

We were driving home from his parent's place after celebrating Thanksgiving with a family gathering of thirty people.

"Honey, why don't we go away this year?" I suggested.

Colin glanced at me with a frown. "Away? Where?"

"I don't know. A cabin somewhere. A place with snow covered trees and a wood stove. We could cut down a tree and drag it back to the cabin. Drink hot wine by the fire."

"Are you nuts? You know I hate snow. I like the heat you get from turning up a switch, not a place where you have to cut firewood. That's too much like work." He stole a quick glance my way. "Why in the world would you want to do that anyway?"

I stared at his profile for a moment. "I thought it might be good for us to get away from everyone else. You've been working so hard lately, so many late nights. It could be romantic. Just the two of us in the woods."

Colin silently concentrated on the road. I waited. "It's not a time for romantic getaways. It's a time for family and friends, parties and such. Besides my parents would be really upset if we broke tradition. You know that. Let's not upset them."

He scolded me like a child.

"We celebrated the biggest family gathering your family ever had tonight. Surely they wouldn't take offence at our missing one holiday with them."

"Well, the answer's no. Change the subject! I'm too tired to get into it with you."

Discussion closed. When Colin said no to something, I knew better than to argue. Of course, later I came to realize that one of the friends he didn't want to miss at Christmas was Julie, his lover. Upon reflection, I believe I knew something was wrong. I was blind, seeing what I wanted to see.

Now, one year later, I'd get my Christmas in the woods but not in the best of circumstances. The strange thing about it was, back home, I'd dreaded my first Christmas without Colin. My thoughts were clouded with visions of family parties where everyone felt sorry for me being single, especially New Year's Eve with my coupled friends.

It was absurd that I'd been so in need of Colin. Why was it necessary to be seen hanging onto his arm during those times deemed important to be a couple? I'd always believed men and women were only halves waiting to become whole together. *What a ridiculous responsibility we place upon ourselves, with such a limiting philosophy. No wonder I never truly knew Colin or myself. What great things could be achieved when two individuals came together as one, but were capable of maintaining their individuality!*

The realization hit me that I could be happy all alone. I'd never have chosen my present circumstances, but it made me all the more determined to make the best of them by acknowledging the season with nature. It might not be romantic in the conventional way, but it would be spiritual.

I bundled up and went outside to one of those rare December days when it wasn't snowing. Some small trees, rooted in the open where they received enough sunlight to grow even and healthy, sat near the tree line at the rear of the cabin. A spruce tree about three feet tall caught my eye. *Perfect.* One swift cut with the small axe downed my tree. I shook the snow off of its branches and took it inside. A bucket of nuts and bolts in the shed caught my eye. Too heavy to lift in my pregnant state, I dragged it into the cabin and placed it by the stove to warm up, a perfect stand to hold the trunk in place. "Phew ... time for a rest, babes."

My pregnancy state began to take a toll on me physically. Afternoon naps became a daily addition to my routine. In late afternoon, a search began for objects to put on my tree. I found some blank paper in a drawer. "Oooh ... look at this stuff, sweet pea." An old wooden cigar box full of old dusty pens, pencils, and some colored pencils, sat on the shelf under the sink. I spent the next hour cutting out squares from the paper, coloring them red. With slots cut in the paper, I folded the paper back and into the slots to form red cylinders. A Santa's head drawn on white paper and scalloped along the bottom of the face to represent a beard served as a template to cut eleven more. A face drawn with a black pencil completed the effect. There was nothing to hold the faces onto the cylinder. A trip to the tool shed produced some fishing line which was threaded through a hole in the face and a matching hole in the cylinder. The result was twelve Santa ornaments with movable faces. *So cute.*

With the tree planted firmly in the pot of 'heavy metal', I tried to lift it onto the end table beside the couch. "Uh-oh … this friggin' thing is heavy." Two attempts later and up she went. It added a cozy dimension to the cabin. The smell of the pine needles filled the room. I quickly added my newly made treasures and stood back to admire my handiwork.

"So sweet …" My hands came together. *Clap clap.* I bounced on the balls of my feet like a child.

A new day dawned and I awoke with a sense of purpose. My morning chores kept me busy. I hurried through them like an impatient kid, anxious to get back to my tree decorating. Aluminum foil molded into the shapes of stars and balls completed my ornaments. An old box of cotton balls were pulled out of shape and spaced onto branches to look like snow.

My tree needed a garland. After naptime, I decided to make one of popped corn strung on fishing line. A difficult feat soon abandoned, leaving my lap full of the delicate, broken pieces. Popping corn on the wood stove proved to be a new challenge as well, creating a string of multi-shaded morsels shaded from white, to tan, to black. Sleep came with the mixed smell of pine tree and burnt popcorn.

The sun streamed through the shutters onto my little tree. Today was December 18th and my Christmas tree decorating was nearly complete. Using bolts, washers and fishing lures on threaded fishing line, a unique replacement garland was born. I set out to find a tree top ornament. My search yielded nothing and, in the end, I placed a lace doily over the top protrusion of the tree and tied it a third of the way down with fishing line to form a head. The rest of the doily flared out like a skirt. My make-shift angel completed my Christmas project.

I retreated to the rocker to examine the fruits of my labor.

I giggled and then snorted, "I wish you could see this, sweet pea." *First graders could have done better.* Regardless, I was pleased.

Today was Kris' birthday. The tree was finished on time. My thoughts wandered back to our childhood. We were inseparable then. We grew up in the still undeveloped area of North

Vancouver, close to Lynn Canyon. Our home boasted of two lifestyles. From the front picture window, the city of Vancouver sprawled before our eyes.

This urban view saw many changes and we watched the skyline grow as ageing buildings gave way to hi-rises, giving a flattering defining edge to the green acreage of Stanley Park. Gastown was born; a shopping district that allowed the turn of the century landscape and buildings to be refurbished.

The back of our home sat at the base of the North Shore Mountains and presented a sharp contrast to the urban offerings of the city below. We had a stream running through our property. My brother and I spent many a day wading in that waterway and chasing the abundance of frogs that springtime provided. There were blackberries, salmonberries and wild raspberries to gorge on. We had cougars and bears visit on occasion. As a teenager, whenever I got bored with nature and my brother's company, a twenty-minute bus ride would place me in the middle of civic excitement. But this controlled encounter with nature as a child did nothing to prepare me for what I was experiencing here.

Kris joined the forces when he grew up, and was stationed at the Comox Navy Base on Vancouver Island. Remembering the words he used to sing to me on my birthday, I rocked back and forth in the chair, and sang them to him.

"Happy Birthday to you, You belong in a zoo. You look like a monkey, And you act like one too."

I closed my eyes and slipped into a meditative state, trying to connect my mind with his. *Happy Birthday, Kris.*

The remaining days to Christmas passed quickly. I had a routine in place. With daily chores finished, I wrote in my journal and followed that with exercises. I walked in a circle around the clearing on sunny days, ending with a stroll beside the steam on the game trails worn by moose and caribou. A black bird joined me on many of my walks, flying overhead and circling the meadow. "Hey, Mr. Crow, why are you always alone?" Many times I found him sitting on the porch railing, watching me through the window. At first, I believed him to be a crow, but I soon realized that he was a raven.

Decorating the cabin continued. A wreath of pine branches adorned the back door. An aspen log from the wood pile centered the coffee table. Over the winter-white bark, an arrangement of pine branches, sphagnum moss and some pinecones, scrounged from the wood pile, sat creatively.

December 25th dawned and I arose to find it snowing. "Merry Christmas, sweet pea."

I rocked for a time, singing carols and hymns, not allowing myself to dwell on my family. Feeling powerless to help them with their pain, I resolved to stay positive.

A lot of effort was taken in preparing my Christmas dinner: a canned chicken rubbed with spices warmed in the oven, canned beets soaked in vinegar, raisin and cinnamon bannock with raspberry compote, and rice cooked in the juices of the chicken. I lit a storm candle in the centre of the table and sat down to eat. Most certainly, my feast would feed more than one, but on this day I refused to ration myself. The leftovers would feed me for a few days, and would keep well in the root cellar.

I gave thanks for the protection that this shelter had provided for my baby and me, and with a sip of tea, I toasted my family: "Merry Christmas, everyone." An image of them sitting around the dining room table became too much to bear.

My heart felt heavy. "Damn." Tears sprang to my eyes. *You can't shut them out completely. You're not superwoman.* I gave in to my despair.

"Kraa … Kraa …" I looked out the window and saw the raven sitting on the window sill.

This was my first chance at seeing him close up, and to my amazement he wasn't pure black. An iridescent blue and green shone through his feathers.

"Why are you still here with me … hmmm? Are you a spirit? A messenger? Maybe … my protector?" The raven cocked his head on an angle and blinked his golden eyes.

"Merry Christmas, raven. You need a name … how about Feathers?"

"Toc, toc, toc," he said.

I laughed and toasted him. "Feathers it is."

Later that night, I sat propped up in bed and looked around the cabin. Even though the dwelling was rough, all the feminine touches and decorations I had added these past weeks transformed it from a house to a home—my home.

"Mom, you'd be proud of me. You would not believe how domestic I've become—or how crazy— talking out loud with no one to answer back."

I leaned over and turned up the lantern. Settling back against the pillows, I began reading yet another book from the bookcase. A crime story by an author called Sean Dixon. "Okay, Mr. Dixon, take me away into your world."

My lack of concentration kept me from getting into what appeared to be a great thriller. Before long, I put the book down and gazed around my one-room abode. Household chores, even pleasant ones, were never on my list of favorite things to do back home. Now, I treasured them as a means to deal with the ever-increasing boredom, and to keep from thinking about my impending childbirth.

There were moments of sheer joy when I would talk out names for my child. "How about Sandra after my mother, or maybe Raven after Feathers. That's a pretty name. If Colin were a part of this, he'd insist on calling you Alice. Huh … never," I chortled. *Divorce was good for some things.*

The past two months, talking to my baby came naturally and gave me great comfort. But, the thought of her arrival had been pushed to the back of my mind. My increasing girth, however, reminded me that she would soon be here. "Oh, sweet pea." I took a deep breath and let it out slowly. *Distraction. Distract yourself. Don't think about it. Get a grip, girlie. It's just those old pregnancy hormones acting up again.*

"And where are you, Kaela?" I yelled. "You haven't been in a while. Today is Christmas. I could use a spiritual visitation."

Chapter 11

The New Year arrived and my body felt cumbersome as I entered my eighth month of pregnancy. I stood by the stream, exhausted from my fourth trip to fetch water. Each day started with cutting a hole in the ice. It was getting harder for me to swing an axe and to haul water from the stream.

Feathers sat on a tree branch, watching me. "Hey blackbird, wish you could help me pull these buckets out of the water. My back sure hurts." I could only fill the pails half-full, which forced me to make more trips. Although it was only a matter of minutes between each trip, a thin layer of ice always formed over the hole, and I needed to break through again. My bulky frame slowed me down—a fact I found frustrating. The bucket handles were tethered with long strands of rope used to lower them into the water, to compensate for my inability to kneel down and fill them.

My concern didn't lie with my physical welfare. From all I had read in my book, I was progressing normally. My mental condition bothered me. The euphoric state I experienced before Christmas had fallen flat. It had snowed every day since the holiday, a daily reminder of my extreme isolation. New Year's Eve and Day came and passed. I saw nothing about my situation to celebrate, and slipped into a depression.

Returning from one of my numerous jaunts for water, the sound of a jet caught my attention; it was the first plane I'd seen. It headed northeast. I cupped my eyes with my hands to keep the large snowflakes from blinding me. I jumped up and down, waving my arms. "Hey, down here!" Soon, all that remained was the white jet trail. *How could I be so stupid? As if a jet that high could see me.* Watching it dissipate, I compared their fate with mine. "Who're all those people, sweet pea: students returning to school, visiting family members returning home after the holidays?" *People living ordinary lives, oblivious to what was happening in mine.* My body stiffened and without thinking I spat out: "I hate you all."

Within the confines of that plane, a tiny spec in the vast sky, were 300 or more passengers. This moving vessel, carrying them to their destination, was capable of catering to all of their needs—food, beverage, entertainment, conversation, companionship, comfort, and, if necessary, a captain who could communicate with the outside world. In contrast, I was one person alone in a remote land, surviving day by day with the barest of essentials. High above me, they were experiencing modern day life while I felt trapped in a world equaling that of our pioneering settlers. I returned to the cabin, completely despondent.

Another realization hit me: "Oh my God, today is Mom's birthday." I couldn't stand the idea of my family suffering under the mistaken belief of my death. Pacing the cabin, I ranted and raved about how unfair it all was—their pain, my feeling of entrapment. My hands dropped to my swollen belly, "Oh babes, maybe I should have left when there was still a chance. I'm so messed up."

Then, I 'crashed'.

I removed my outside clothing and kicked it around the floor. My final explosion triggered when my eyes fell on the Christmas tree.

"Who am I kidding? Carrying on as though my life is normal. I can't do this anymore."

One by one, I grabbed ornaments and threw them. Decorations flew in all directions.

"I'm never going to leave here." I screamed. "I'm going to die from starvation, childbirth, or in some other disgustingly painful way."

In a fit of temper, I threw the treetop angel across the cabin, and with one swift movement, the ravaged tree sailed through the open doorway into the snow beyond. I slammed the door shut and spun around to see what else I could vent my anger on.

"Oh no." I grabbed a hold of a chair as my eyes saw spots, and waves of colored light blurred my vision. "Whoa—not a dizzy spell." I worked my way to the bed and collapsed onto my side in a fetal position—as much as my impregnated body would allow–and fell asleep.

When I awoke, Kaela sat in the rocker. "I didn't think you'd ever wake up." She smiled.

I searched the room and felt my face turn red. Amongst the disarray of the cabin, my ornamental angel lay upside down against the far counter.

"I know what you're looking at," Kaela offered.

"I feel so stupid. I don't know what came over me," I said, weakly.

"Look at me, Georgia … please."

My eyes met hers and my unease left me. Her face was so full of compassion and love, my whole being felt warmed.

"You're only human, remember that. No one is perfect. The hormonal changes your body is experiencing from the pregnancy are having a big effect on your emotional state." She chuckled before continuing, "Adding this to your present circumstances, I'd say you were acting pretty normal."

"It's been a while since you came. I missed you." I knew I sounded like a spoiled child, but I wanted her to feel bad, to cover my feelings of guilt for my temper tantrum.

"You haven't needed me until now. You must look back at the last two months you spent here. You've come a long way." Kaela stood up and walked over to sit with me on the bed. "You must draw your strength from all you learned. Perhaps if you read your journal, you can find the key. Do you know what brought on this little outburst?"

"Yes … I do." I nodded. "Today, I came face to face with my frailties and self-doubts. I was reminded that childbirth is approaching and I'd be alone."

"… And?"

I pushed myself up and leaned back against the headboard. "Today's my mother's birthday. I can't stand the thought that my family is suffering. It's hard enough dealing with my own. I wish I could see her and let her know I'm all right."

Kaela stared at me pensively for a moment, and then frowned. She started to say something and then stopped. I could sense it was important, and remained quiet while she stood and paced the cabin. I sat on the edge of the bed and waited.

"I want you to listen to me carefully, and keep your mind open to what I have to say.

"Okay."

"The Tahltan believe that everything has a spirit and only ones with power can see a spirit. We also believe our Peoples have two souls. A day soul and a night soul. The Peoples believe dreams are really the night soul travelling without the body. They can soul travel wherever they want to without physically leaving."

Kaela sat in the rocker and leaned forward, staring at me intently. "You have that power. If you so desire, I'll help you to see your mother." She paused, but her eyes never left mine. "Do you understand what I'm saying?"

"I've read articles on the subject. But I haven't mastered the art of meditation yet. Nine times out of ten, I fall asleep."

"There are reasons for that. First of all, you lie down to meditate, perhaps you should try sitting up. And try meditating in the daytime, not at night when you're tired."

Again, I nodded. "That makes sense."

"Another reason may be that you aren't ready to see your inner truth. It'll come if you persist, and happen when you're ready."

I remembered having a similar conversation with Marion. It frightened me then as much as it did now. The thought of seeing my mother felt exhilarating, but the old fear of the unknown reared its ugly head. Reading about such things was fascinating; experiencing them would be quite another. It was my turn to pace around the cabin while rubbing my hands together.

I turned to Kaela and pursed my lips, feeling apprehensive: "How do I know when to come back and how do I find my body again?"

"You will receive a signal when it's time to return. As you travel, no matter how far, you're still connected to your physical body. When you receive the message to return, think of your body and you'll be back."

"What kind of signal?" I sat on the edge of the bed and stared hard at her.

"You'll hear me call you back. There are some important elements required for a successful trip. The first is relaxation, and the second is clear imagery or visualization. I'll take you through this before you begin your journey. This will keep you from falling asleep. The third element is concentration and control. Again, I'll help you, and when you're ready, you'll go beyond."

"I still don't understand how it works—" I said, my voice trailing off. Panic started to take hold. That old 'fight or flight' feeling had a strong grip on me.

She sat beside me and patted my hand. "Everything is in a state of matter which takes many different forms. Think of matter as the lowest vibration of spirit and spirit as the highest vibration of matter. Remember when I told that I lower my vibration so you can see me?"

My eyebrows flew up. "That's so simple but makes perfect sense. I understand."

"So—are you ready?

The image of my mother took shape in my mind. In spite of my reluctance, I knew I must do this. But what about my baby? Maybe she comes with me.

"One more question. What happens to my baby during all of this?"

Kaela took my hand into hers. "She'll be fine. This is your journey not hers. Your physical body will continue to function normally. She'll be safe, I promise."

With a deep breath and a long sigh, I answered, "Okay—let's do this."

"Prop yourself up against the headboard and cover yourself with the blankets to keep your body warm." Kaela rose and sat in the rocking chair. "Now take yourself through your meditation exercises, first the breathing control and then the muscle relaxation. I'll know when you're ready. From then on you'll listen to my voice and follow my instructions."

My heart was racing and I found it hard to concentrate. I focused on my breathing. Once it became shallower and the tension released from my body, Kaela began.

"Your breathing is slow and rhythmic, your body relaxed. Any noises you hear around you will not interfere. You know they do not affect you. The only sound you'll heed is my voice. You'll follow my instructions and know you're safe."

She spoke so softly; her words caressed and soothed me. She encompassed my whole being and my mind let go.

"I want you to visualize a white light all around you, Georgia; a warm, healing light to protect you on your journey. See the inside of the cabin with all its doors and windows. Now I want you to visualize a door you never noticed before. When I tell you to open it, you'll find yourself in a dark tunnel. You won't be afraid."

Kaela paused and I released a sigh. "Open the door and step through," she said.

A gasp escaped from my lips when I stepped through the doorway. My body filled with excitement. I could see daylight at the end of a dark tunnel, and I started to move towards the brightness.

"Keep moving, child. You'll be there soon."

My body became lighter and lighter. Halfway to the opening, I experienced the feeling of floating effortlessly. I no longer felt my physical body and flew through the air. Exhilarated, I approached the light—so bright I was blinded.

"Imagine a beautiful place; a place where you would feel safe and at peace. When your eyes adjust to the light, you will pass through it. I want you to use all of your senses. Through them you will experience the beauty and peace awaiting you. I'll wait for you at the opposite end of your vision."

My eyes focused and I caught my breath. "Wow … this is paradise." I'd envisioned a beautiful garden. A dirt pathway meandered back and forth across the garden. A multitude of flowers lined the edge of the trails. An array of sparkling rainbow colors emanated from the abundant blossoms of roses, carnations, daisies, dahlias, mums, and irises. Their sweet, floral fragrance piqued my sense of smell.

I floated aimlessly along, a foot above the ground, until reaching the centre of this Garden of Eden. Here, a pond teemed with life. Small fish hit the surface, feeding on the water bugs skimming across the surface. Frogs jumped from lily pad to lily pad, croaking their songs. The heat of the sun warmed my face as I tilted it up to the sky. White, fluffy clouds drifted lazily across the azure expanse. Birds sang their songs, and hovering like a hummingbird to watch them, I giggled with delight at my aerodynamic feat. Butterflies flew along beside

me, and I felt as one with them, knowing their freedom. Not wanting to miss anything, and wanting to experience it all, I made many stops. All of my senses were heightened, filling me with feelings of joy, peace, and contentment. Finally, reaching the end of the path, I found Kaela sitting on a bench under a magnificent willow tree.

"There you are. You have chosen your spiritual place well."

"Oh Kaela, it's so beautiful here. I feel whole."

"I'm pleased. You've experienced all I hoped for."

She patted the seat beside her. "Join me for a moment."

I sat down on the bench, but with no sensation of body, it was more like floating beside her. We silently enjoyed our garden. My mind cleared, my thoughts experienced the moment and nothing else. It felt wonderful.

Kaela interrupted my euphoria. "It's time for you to continue on your journey. Follow this path behind me into the open meadow. It will take you where you want to go. I'll wait here for you to return. Enjoy."

I found myself floating along a pathway through a meadow of wild flowers towards a small incline. I travelled faster and faster still, until I flew up and over the hill, and soared into the waiting sky.

"Unbelievable—"

Looking down, a blue-green sea stretched as far as I could see. Waves rolled up onto a white sandy beach. *I should be scared. But if that were the case, I wouldn't be smiling. Feathers, you should be here with me. Now, I know how exhilarating it feels to fly.* Higher and higher I went until I flew straight through the clouds. Glancing below, there was nothing to see but a bed of white billowing pillows.

The most incredible sight of my life took my breath away. Instantly, I slowed to a stop, suspended in mid-air. Forever etched in my memory, one would have to see this phenomenon to believe it happened. To the east, a black night sky completely filled the horizon. Dead centre sat a full, yellow moon. To the west, a sky full of pinks and purples emanated from a red rising sun. "I wish you could see this too, sweet pea. I'm suspended between night and day." I don't believe I'll ever see anything so spectacular, at least not in this dimension.

I started moving upwards again. Faster and faster, I rose until I left the planet and found myself racing through the blackness of space. I entered the galaxy over the North Pole, and circled the earth from the north to southeast. Greenland and the British Isles appeared below me. In seconds, Europe followed, and my course was set towards the Middle East. The west coast of Africa sat to my right. My path took me towards the Southern Hemisphere. Ahead was the South Pacific, to the north, Asia. Australia soon followed, and my direction changed north. Over Hawaii I flew and up the Pacific Rim until the west coast of British Columbia came to view. I re-entered the earth's atmosphere, and everything grew larger and larger until I found myself hovering over the city of Vancouver.

In an instant, I stood in my parents' darkened home in North Vancouver, save for a night light in the upstairs hallway. I took in the familiar sight and smells of my childhood home. My mother came out of the bathroom, and I followed her across the hall to her bedroom. She moved around to the left of the bed. My father lay curled up in sleep. My heart warmed to see that he looked healthy and peaceful. My mother took off her housecoat, and to my surprise, she wore the nightgown I'd bought her in White-horse for Christmas. She sat on the bed, lost in thought, rubbing her hands with lotion from a jar on the bedside table. She looked a little older and frailer to me. Mom turned towards the door, where I leaned against the jamb. Her facial expression changed. She stared, unblinking, her chin dropped, and her mouth opened.

Can this be possible? How could she know I'm here?

My body straightened, and without thinking, I started talking to her. "It's me, Mom. My baby and I ... we're okay."

Her face relaxed and a slight smile touched her mouth.

"Happy Birthday ... I love you."

"Georgia—" Mom stood and started to walk towards me.

I heard Kaela call my name. The connection broke.

Just as quickly, I stood on the path back to the garden. I sat beside her but couldn't talk. Emotion overwhelmed me. We sat silently together, staring into the garden. After a time, she spoke. "Was it everything you expected?"

"Oh yes ... and so much more." "But you're troubled?"

My forehead creased into a frown. "It's, well … I didn't expect she'd see me. She did see me, right?"

"Yes, she saw you."

"I'm worried how she'll react. I don't want to make things any worse."

"It can only be good. Your mother suffered dearly these past months. She saw you because she is a believer. Regardless of what her take is on this, it will help her. Now, tell me, did this journey help you?"

"Absolutely. Knowing my parents are okay lifted a tremendous weight off my shoulders. I'm filled with renewed strength and hope. I can't thank you enough for this."

"It's time to return to your physical being. Continue your meditation and writing in your journal. Know you can return to this garden anytime you wish. It's yours alone." Kaela stood and looked down at me. "And now you've found a sense of peace and strength once more, you must think of your baby's birth. The time is soon and you must be prepared. You're doing well with your breathing exercises, but you must plan for the birth day."

"Will you come and help me through the birth?" I asked.

"I'll be there."

With that she was gone. My thoughts turned to the cabin and, instantly, I found myself back within its walls. I floated above my body. It looked different from the outside looking down. It wasn't the same as looking into a mirror. My hands sat folded across my huge belly. *Hmm … so that's how I look in all my pregnant glory.* As soon as my thoughts turned to how to re-enter my fatness, I felt a rush and in an instant, the distance between my soul and my body disappeared.

It was dark and the air chilled me. My body felt stiff and cumbersome. Tears streamed down my face. But this time, I cried from happiness, not from despair. *Did I really see my mother, or was it a dream? What was it Kaela said? Dreams are the night soul travelling. Who knows?* All I know for sure is that I changed somehow. My resolve came back. I lit the lamp and set about preparing for bed. Lying quietly under the covers, I listened to the creaking and cracking of the log walls from the cold. I'd clean up the cabin tomorrow and retrieve the decorations from the broken tree. I must put them away and keep them. Then, I would write all I experienced in my journal. No detail would be spared. One day, I'd talk with my mother about this night, and that would be my proof.

Chapter 12

Mid-January - Vancouver

Sean Dixon walked into his agent's office and sat down at the conference table beside his publisher, John Richards. He looked from one man to the other, grateful to have them both on his team. After eight years as a freelance, Sean had decided to try his hand at a novel. Seven years ago, when Sean decided to publish his first book, mutual friend had recommended him to Trent Matheson, now his agent. A tall, slim man with brown hair and warm brown eyes, Trent looked more like an accountant. His quiet, laid back nature usually fooled the aggressive businessmen he dealt with. Sean would label Trent as passive-aggressive. His personality was a definite advantage when deals were being made. He loved to play the game, and he was good at it. At thirty-three, he had a successful business with numerous clients. However, he always made Sean feel like he was his only one.

His publisher, on the other hand, was the complete opposite of Trent. John Richards, graying at forty-five, was outgoing, with a quick, loud laugh that came from deep within his stocky frame. His sparkling blue eyes were usually full of mischief, but they could turn to 'glaring' anger in a flash, and his deep laughs to a commanding boom. With a little persuasion from Trent, John decided to take a chance on publishing an unknown author. This led to a powerful union between the three over the years. Sean called them 'Mutt & Jeff'. Not only did they enjoy a strong relationship as business associates, but they had also become personal friends.

"Congratulations, Sean," Trent said. "The last word from marketing is you have surpassed the sales of your last three books and the numbers are still climbing. You took on quite a load these past few years, and it paid off."

"Thanks," Sean replied, absently.

"It was a great tour, wasn't it?" John reflected, helping himself to a sugar doughnut.

Sean smiled. If John's wife were here, there would be no doughnut. Kelly considered it her job to monitor his food intake. John said he appreciated her 'nagging,' as he called it, knowing that his middle would be a lot more than a little thick if she didn't. But that didn't stop him from taking liberties when she wasn't around.

"And," Trent added, "I spoke with L.A. an hour ago. Looks like we have a few interested parties from the movie world. One wants to negotiate the rights to this book, and the other one is talking a mini-series with rights to all four books."

"You're kidding!" Sean straightened in his chair. "W...what? A movie deal?" John sputtered, choking on his doughnut.

Sean leaned forward on the table towards Trent. "Where do I sign?" They all laughed.

His agent slouched back in his chair, crossed his arms across his chest before replying. "We'll sit back, if you'll pardon the pun, and wait to see who..." Trent stopped talking and stared at John who was still coughing from his doughnut. "Are you all right?"

"Yeah, yeah ... don't mind me, carry on." He waved his hand at Trent.

"A long distance intervention from Kelly," Sean said. They shared another laugh.

John stood, placing one arm across his abdomen and the other behind his back and bowed to Sean like he was royalty. "This is it, Sean my boy—you have arrived." He beamed like a proud father.

"It's overwhelming … a little surreal," Sean confessed, shaking his head.

"Are you going to negotiate that Sean write the adaptation, Trent?" John asked, as he sat down.

"I don't know the first thing about adapting book to screen. I don't know if I could write one or if I wanted to," Sean said.

"Hmm," Trent pondered, "An adaptation contract would certainly sweeten the pot. At the very least, we could ask for a consultant contract on the script and filming. But you have lots of time to consider the alternatives. We don't have a strong offer yet, and it will take a few more months after that to work out all the details."

John turned back to Sean and asked, "What's next? Do you have any ideas for a new project?"

"Sort of ..." Sean paused. Looking quickly from Trent to John, he gazed down at the table and started picking chocolate from the Long John in front of him. Laying the pieces in a neat pile beside it on the napkin, he continued, "I want to do something completely different, a new genre perhaps. Maybe even a non-fiction book."

Trent sat straight up in his chair, scratching his chin. "As I was saying, we'll wait to see who else pops up. Then we'll let it be known we have offers. It won't hurt to let them compete. We'll negotiate the best deal."

Trent frowned. "Non-fiction? Do you think that's a good idea right now? I mean, you're hot, and non- fiction isn't quite what your readers will be waiting for."

John picked it up here. "I suggest if you go for a non-fiction project, you use a pen name."

Sean shrugged and continued picking at the doughnut. "I've lived with these characters for four years. I can't think about anything else right now. I need to put them to rest. I'm dried up, tapped out." Sean started breaking off pieces of doughnut now and piling them beside the bits of chocolate.

"I must say, I'm really disappointed in your behavior," John said.

Sean jerked his head up at John, eyebrows raised. John continued, "I mean, doughnuts are for eating, not dissecting. What you're doing to that Long John is blasphemy."

Laughter eased the tension in the room.

"I'm sorry you had to watch me murder this poor, defenseless doughnut," Sean said with a chuckle. He covered up the mess he created with another napkin. "The truth is, I was thinking of taking some time off. It's not only the characters in my books that need to be put to rest."

Sean caught the glance exchanged between John and Trent.

"I mean, whether I write non-fiction or fiction, my true fans will wait. I certainly can afford financially to take some time off. I thought I'd go back to Dease Lake in a few weeks where all this began, and spend some free time at the cabin. I love writing; you both know that. I can't see myself ever retiring from writing, but now I can create for the love of it, not because I need to make a living."

"Trent and I both know you pushed yourself hard since Laura left. You never allowed yourself to deal with your emotions. Obviously, you're ready now."

Trent picked up the conversation: "I'm with John on this one. We'll take care of business at this end. Please check in with us on a regular basis. We can conference call anything important as it comes up."

"You bet. I'll be spending time in the Dease Lake house for a number of weeks before I head to the cabin. You can reach me there. I'll be out of touch for a couple of weeks at the cabin. But after spring break, I'll be installing a satellite phone since there's no cell service out that way."

The three men stood and shook hands.

... nothing in life is to be feared. It is only to be understood.

Marie Curie

Chapter 13

The night was still as I sat rocking, with daylight at least an hour away. The only sound to be heard was the crackle of the wood in the fire. Every once in a while, a loud crack resembling a rifle shot rang out, breaking the silence. It took me some time to figure out that these thunderous claps were trees cracking from the extreme freezing conditions that had enveloped us these past few weeks. Sometimes, the ice on the stream exploded with a loud boom.

The baby, unusually active, kicked me awake each time I made myself comfortable. I finally gave up trying to sleep and rose to practice my birthing exercises. I had attended classes with a girl friend when her husband was away in the service, so the breathing exercises came easy. Two weeks previous, I started a list of things that needed to be done for the birth. Divided into four sections—chores, linen needs, medical needs, and miscellaneous items—I studied this list daily. I washed towels and linens, storing them in plastic bags in the trunk to keep them sterilized. My watch read the twentieth of January. I became determined to be prepared and to pull this birth off. My baby's survival depended on my cool head and control. Pioneer women birthed in the wilderness, and so would I. I felt encouraged, also, by the fact that Kaela said she would come.

I rubbed my stomach as the baby kicked harder. "Okay, sweet pea, it's time to read about the pioneer women again."

I found a copy of the same book Marion had lent me in Whitehorse. It chronicled the courageous lives of pioneer women in the Yukon. Some of them travelled the Chilkoot Trail into the Klondike during the gold rush days. These tales gave me hope and courage in my moments of weakness.

One story was of Martha Brown, a married woman from Chicago who travelled to Seattle with her husband, Joe and her brother, Bradley. Joe decided they would have more luck if they went to the Sandwich Islands. But Martha had her sights set on the Klondike. So husband and wife went their separate ways. Her brother tried to send her back to Chicago to their parents—she refused. She travelled by steamer to Alaska with Bradley, and walked the Chilkoot Pass into the Yukon. It wasn't until the rivers froze over that she discovered she was pregnant.

Even though she, Bradley and his partner did not have enough food for the winter, she had a healthy pregnancy. Cut off from civilization, she gave birth to a normal, healthy baby. Martha became my inspiration. Whenever I doubted my ability to be my own midwife, I read her story and those of other strong-willed women. "We'll do this, sweet pea. You and me."

One of the items on my miscellaneous list was an object to serve as my focal point during labor. According to my prenatal book, I would need an item to focus on when the contractions and pain increased, to control my breathing and my emotions. I decided to make a happy-face doll and call her Martha.

I remembered the doily used for my tree-top angel. Turning the kerosene lamp up, I found the doily and stuffed the centre with crumpled paper, forming a round head, and tied it off with fishing line. A felt pen completed the face with big eyes and lashes, a tiny nose, and a happy smile. I sat in the rocker with my new- found friend in my hands. "I christen thee, Martha."

A single, shrill scream broke the silence. I lifted my head and listened. All was quiet. Then, pandemonium broke out. Screams of terror filled the silence outside the cabin, mixed with growls, snarls, and snapping.

"Night hunters, Martha," I said aloud. "Wolves."

I waddled over to the front window, and opened the shutters. Only pre-dawn, I could see enough of the clearing to know that they weren't out front. But the clarity of sound, from all the noise, told me they weren't far away. On the other side of the stream to the left of the cabin, a shoulder of trees opened up to another clearing. My guess was that the wolves downed an animal in that field. From the ruckus, it could only be a large mammal: a moose or caribou.

The poor animal bellowed in the final throes of death, a stark contrast to the fierce frenzy of the wolves. Returning to the rocker, I covered my ears with my hands. Shivers ran up and down my spine. "Oh God," I cried out, "you poor thing, hurry up and die."

Then, it was over.

I could still hear the wolves growling at each other. Protecting their share of the kill, no doubt. Thirty minutes later, silence. Either they had their fill and moved on, or were resting, waiting to gorge themselves again. This was a part of nature I hated. Only the strongest survived. It reminded me of how precarious and violent life could be in the wild.

I recalled my conversation with Kaela last month when she asked me why I feared nature. It occurred to me that Mother Nature and Human Nature have strong parallels. Both have a fine balance of weights and measures. In both worlds, the strong control the weak, beauty struggles against devastation, and we see love versus hate. The two constantly cross paths; an experience that can be either disastrous or spectacular. I had begun to lose my fear of this overwhelming entity who we call Mother Nature. The more time

I spent at the cabin, the more a bond grew between us on a spiritual level.

My thoughts returned to the wolves and their full bellies. I had rationed my food supplies to last into early spring, but I knew I was lacking nutritionally. All my foods were canned. I worried about my protein intake. I did have the vitamins that I'd picked up the day I was kidnapped, but they would only last until mid-February. These past two months, my baby grew, but she was small. I also had concerns about my strength and hers when it came time to give birth. I wondered if the wolves may have killed but not eaten. Sometimes, they killed for sport. It was ironic that they may have too much food and I not enough. Of course, nature would not bear witness to waste. Other predators would feed off what was left, wolverines for one. Quite capable of downing a large mammal on their own, they were also known to follow wolves on the hunt. Their turn would come once the wolves moved on. I shuddered at the thought of wolverines.

I teased myself, imagining the smell of a tantalizing roast cooking in the stove with thick herbed gravy to pour over my canned potatoes. "Mmm," I groaned, "Stop torturing yourself."

A sudden thought popped into my head. I looked up at the window. Daylight crept up on me. The meat was fresh and the extreme cold would have chilled it quickly. I could be one of those predators. Why not? If the wolves were gone, I could salvage some of the meat and add to my larder. I crossed to the window and opened the shutters. All was quiet. The sky was clear and I knew it would be cold. The sun wouldn't be up over the mountains for another couple of hours.

"What would I need, sweat pea? A saw, the small axe, a knife, rope and the plastic tarp."

I started to pace the room. It wouldn't be easy. I would have to keep on guard against other marauders. In my condition, I certainly couldn't move fast.

"Oh, sweat pea, can I really do this? Should I?"

My eyes landed on the pioneer book, and my happy face doll.

"All right, Georgia, you're being a chicken shit, letting that old fear of the unknown sneak back in. You can do this, you can, and you know you can," I said, determinedly.

The frost line was well up the inside of the door. January was considerably colder than December, and I learned to calculate the temperature from how high or low the frost line sat on the wooden door. "It's definitely under minus thirty Celsius, babes." Checking the thermometer, it registered minus forty Celsius. These were days to spend sitting up close to the woodstove. I used the last of the tin foil on the wall behind the stove to reflect the heat out into the cabin.

I decided that a long, thin carving knife would have to do, and gathered up most of the other items. Dressing as quickly as I could muster, I layered my clothing and donned my coat. I wrapped a scarf around my face, pulled my wool hat down to my eyebrows, and topped them with my hood. I was almost out the door when I remembered a pair of rubber gloves on a shelf. I didn't relish the idea of handling the bloody meat with my winter gloves.

The tool shed provided the saw and the tarp. Following the path around to the front of the cabin, I turned towards the stream. I walked face first into the wind and shivered. My clothing wasn't adequate for such low temperatures. I'd have to work quickly and return to the warmth of the cabin as soon as possible. Ice fishing had become a thing of the past. It was far too cold to stand on the little bridge. When hauling my daily buckets of water, they were frozen into solid blocks of ice before I made it back to the cabin, forcing me to thaw them on the stove before I could go for more. I had learned the hard way about touching metal or wood without my gloves on. At these temperatures, a simple touch burned the skin like fire.

Reaching the bridge over the stream, I paused to look at the uneven flows of ice in the centre of the waterway. They'd piled up and over each other, being pushed by the strong current beneath. I crossed over and into the protection of the trees. It was only minutes before I stood at the edge of the clearing.

My eyes searched the open field and found the carcass, a caribou. The wolves were nowhere to be seen. But I remained cautious. I once read you couldn't always see wolves, as they blend in with the snow. They may be resting close by.

"Hey ... h-e-y!" I yelled, letting my presence be known. There I stood, waiting, listening, and watching. "Ya ... hoo!" I screamed.

Suddenly, a red head popped up from behind the caribou. It was a fox, and I had undoubtedly disturbed his breakfast. He stood his ground while he watched me trudge across the field. He backed up when we stood about twenty feet apart. He ran a short distance, turned, sat down and stared at me. With his thick winter fur, he was pretty, although his head looked bigger than his body.

"Sorry, little fellow, I'll be out of here shortly, and then he's all yours."

One look at the caribou and instantly that old gag reflex kicked in. "Oh my God ...," my hand flew to my mouth. His throat was ripped apart and his belly was open wide, his inner organs pulled out and shredded. The poor thing had bled to death, leaving the snow all around him stained red. Pieces of bone extruded from the open wound of a torn shoulder, and his face was disfigured with a missing nose.

A few deep breaths controlled the urge to vomit, and I inspected him to decide the best place to dress him. He had been a magnificent bull with impressive horns. Choosing the back hindquarter, I moved closer to the caribou and struggled down to my knees. No easy feat for a near term pregnant woman. "Oh shit ..." Instantly the smell repelled me and my throat constricted for a second time. The taste of bile burned my throat and I lost control. I twisted sideways, and retched over and over, until lack of oxygen made me dizzy. Pushing myself up, I walked a short distance from the caribou.

"I can't do it ... I can't." My voice resonated around the clearing, ricocheting back.

Something had to be done soon, as my body already felt chilled to the bone. The red fox sat in the same spot. His head tilted to one side.

"Right. You can't figure out this crazy woman, can you? The great hunter, that's me."

Please, give me the strength and courage to do this.

The animal was only partially frozen; this would help with the sawing. The blood had frozen into ice crystals. The job wouldn't be as messy as anticipated. Glancing at the fox, I grabbed a frozen piece of flesh off the ground and threw it to him. He backed off for a moment, came forward and sniffed at it. He picked it up in his mouth and ran off.

My eyes passed up and down the hindquarter, wondering where to begin. The only thing that came to mind was to cut above the knee to eliminate the scent pads that would taint the meat. This seemed like a good place to start. Taking a deep breath, I bent down and sawed the leg off above the knee. I girdled the skin with the knife, peeled it away from the leg and flank, and continued to the centre of the back, stopping at the spine. The knife went through the skin past the inside of the flank.

The extreme cold, combined with bending over in my condition, made it difficult to breathe, and forced me more than a few times to stop and catch my breath. With the frozen flesh exposed, one swing of the axe cracked the pelvic bone. The sound of breaking bone intensified my nausea, and I moved away to gulp in fresh air. An intense sense of being watched came over me, and cautiously, my eyes scanned the field. The red fox had resumed his original position. I threw him another chunk of flesh.

"You buried your bounty, didn't you?" I yelled. "Well here's another piece for you to cache."

He ran off with his prize for a second time. *We could keep this up all day.* He'd have to wait for me to leave to get any more. Concentrating on the carcass once more, I took the saw and cut through the rest of the hindquarter, using chunks of frozen snow to scrub the flesh clean. "We're all done, sweat pea. A butcher would be appalled."

The leg joint and tools were rolled up in the tarp, leaving an excess of rope to pull the thirty-something pound joint. The plastic tarp slid easily over the frozen snow.

I worked my way across the clearing to the edge of the trees. My body ached and my bones were chilled. "We'll be inside soon, babe." My breath hissed as it passed through my lips and froze. Again, a feeling of something watching washed over me.

A growl behind me caused the hair on the back of my neck to bristle and confirmed my sixth sense. Slowly, I turned.

My eyes were blinded by the whiteness of the snow. Searching the field once more, there she was, standing about twenty yards in front of me. I guessed a female by the smoothness of the hair on her legs. The grey timber wolf blended into her surroundings. Her winter coat thick between her shoulders, she looked about eighty pounds. Another growl, exposing her gums and sharp teeth, sent a chill through me. But she wasn't looking my way. Her stare centered to my left. I heard a snarl and shifted my gaze to the far side of the clearing. My knees almost collapsed. A wolverine crept slowly and low to the ground towards the caribou. The scene unfolded before me, my feet frozen to the spot. The wolf charged across the field in the direction of the wolverine. With a long, sleek body, her feet were huge. He stood his ground, snapping and snarling.

Circling each other warily, the wolverine stopped facing towards me. There was a moment's hesitation as he caught sight of me. He appeared to be assessing his position, and sidestepped the wolf, moving cautiously towards me. I gasped and looked to the wolf in desperation. She observed his retreat from the clearing. There was no escaping the wolverine. One swoop over and my hand freed the axe from the tarp. I prepared to back away from the joint of meat. The wolverine would probably leave me alone, if he took possession of my hindquarter.

Before my plan could be put into action, the wolf suddenly let out a loud snarl and charged the wolverine from behind. She placed a good bite in his hide and the wolverine yelped, taking off in the direction from which he came.

Relief washed over me. I turned my attention back to the wolf. An unbroken stare held us both motionless for what seemed like an eternity, although, it was probably seconds. A tear in her left ear, possibly the remnants of a previous fight, reminded me that she might challenge her right to the caribou joint as well. There was no time to examine this instinctive feeling.

Moving quickly through the trees to the stream, a wolf cry echoed behind me across the field. The bridge came into view, and I crossed it without looking back. I'd reached the bottom of the steps to the cabin when a series of snarls stopped me cold. One glance towards the bridge revealed that the wolf had just crossed it. Behind her, two other growling wolves crept across the bridge low to the ground. The three of them inched forward snarling and snapping their jaws.

My race from the opposite side of the stream left me breathless, my heart pounding against my chest. The scene unfolded in slow motion. My legs felt like jelly. The wolves spread out and realization hit that they were circling all around me. *What are you doing, girlie. Move it.*

My wobbly legs took the stairs and I pushed the door open to the cabin, pulling the tarped meat in the door behind me. I turned just in time to see one of the wolves, teeth barred, jump onto the porch and charge the open doorway. My reflexes kicked in and I slammed the door shut in the face of a snarling, snapping male. The bar fell into place and I collapsed into a chair at the table. The wolves moved about the porch, still growling. Two of them stood up on hind legs, placing their front paws on the picture window glass. I was up like a shot, closing the shutters across the window. Each window in the cabin was shuttered and locked. Only then, did I feel safe.

Chapter 14

My work wasn't done yet. I tried to ignore the wolves while washing the hindquarter down, and cutting it into roast-sized chunks. I placed them all in the root cellar. When it was safe, I'd move most of them out to the tool shed where they'd freeze.

I stripped off my clothes and washed down my body with water warmed on the stove. The rest of the day was spent in the confines of the cabin. Eventually, the wolves moved back across the bridge but I could hear them at times during the day snarling over the carcass. *Thank God I've got enough water and wood inside the cabin.* At dusk, I snuck out the back to stock up more wood and empty my pee bucket. *No visits to the outhouse today.*

Last, but not least, I discarded my bath water, which left me chuckling. It hit the ground already frozen, tinkling as it broke into tiny shards of ice scattering over the snow like broken glass.

"Don't throw the baby out with the bath water," I yelled, hurrying back inside with a laugh.

I sat in the rocker in front of the warmth of the stove and told my baby a story. "You know why I was laughing, sweet pea? Having to preserve water, the settlers only bathed once a week and the whole family shared the same tub of water. Can you imagine? Gross. First Dad bathed, then Mom, who were followed by the children. Before the bath water was discarded, the baby was bathed–and that is where the saying originated from."

Snuggled in my warm bed for the night, I rubbed my abdomen. "You're quiet now, little one. I guess you're as worn out as me." Sleep came easy but not for long.

The wolves returned to my side of the bridge. I could hear them running on the porch and sniffing at the door. I listened until the quiet returned. As soon as sleep claimed me, they started to fight with each other. This lasted another thirty minutes. They returned to the cabin during the night off and on until I was jerked awake by their yips and howls. I was so physically and mentally tired from exhaustion and fear, that I lost my temper. "Go away," I yelled. "I need sleep."

A voice to the side of me spoke. "No wonder, you've had a busy day." Kaela sat in her favorite place, the rocking chair. "You should be proud of what you accomplished today."

"I was scared to death," I said, grateful she'd come.

"Yes, I can see that. We've talked much about nature and your fear of it. The Tahltan Peoples know that the land is a provider of food, medicine, and shelter. They are close to the land. Nature is like a mother to our Peoples—and to the animals. The animals must feed as do we. Do you understand this?"

"Yes." I got up to get a glass of water and returned to sit on the bed.

"How much do you know about the wolves and their culture?"

"Very little."

"Let me tell you a little about the female wolf's role. She's a leader of the female pack in their social structure, and could outlive the male leaders to become a pack leader. She decides on where she will pup, dictating where the rest of the pack hunt. There is no question of her place in her world. She's respected as a hunter, a mother and a leader. Wolves are intuitive, concerned with their young, their mate and their pack.

You and she are both trying to survive in nature and the land can provide for you both. She is coming into her mating season, and soon like you, she will birth. Her role will change from hunter to nurturer and protector. You are sisters. Do you see that you are the same?"

I nodded my head. "You make it easy to understand."

"The wolf does not want to be around people. You threatened their survival instinct when you took part of their kill. Otherwise, you would never encounter them. If you can understand this, and respect the parallels between you, and respect the mother for providing for you both, your fears will lessen."

"You're very wise. I hold your strength and wisdom in high regard. You've shown me perspectives that are different from mine, and yet they all tie together. Tell me about your life. Were you a mother?"

"Yes. I was married and had a son. When the white man came to our land, they brought sickness. Small pox almost wiped out our Peoples. I lost my mother, my husband, and my son."

My hand rose to my mouth in shock. "Oh, Kaela. I'm so sorry."

Kaela smiled. "It was my destiny. My father was Nonnock, the leader of the Tahltan Peoples. He, also, died. As the only living member of my family, I became Nonnock. My white man name. Kaela was discarded and I adopted my Indian name of Nonnock. I became the mother of the Tahltan and spent the remainder of my life leading my Peoples."

She disappeared into the lavender mist around her.

Sleep came and stayed this time. I drifted off, snug and proud, to dream of floating across the fields with my wolf sister.

The next day, all was quiet. I stepped onto the porch to enjoy the warmth of sun shining from a clear sky. A movement to my left caught my attention. The female wolf stood on the bridge. An unspoken connection hung between us, and with it, a feeling of mutual respect and understanding. Perhaps she knew she had nothing to fear from me, as I her. We had a common denominator. My hands rested on my abdomen. "She's our sister, sweet pea."

A long wail echoed from the opposite side of the bridge, breaking the silence. She tilted her head and answered back. She turned and ran with majestic grace, the fluidity of her movements symbolizing the appearance of a floating specter. Almost out of sight, she took one last look at me over her shoulder.

Then, she was gone.

Chapter 15

February 10th - Dease Lake

Sean sat down in front of the pile of mail and newspapers on his desk. He stretched his long, lanky legs underneath the table, and surveyed the paper chaos in front of him. This would definitely take a while. He let out a sigh and rubbed his temple.

It was his first trip back to his cottage in six months. His next-door neighbor, Sarah Brown, collected his mail and kept an eye on his place in Dease Lake. Sean sorted his correspondence into three stacks: newspapers, bills, and personals. Then he sorted the personal pile into letters from family and friends, what appeared to be solicitations, and fan post. Most of his fan mail went to his publisher's office, but people always seemed to find his private addresses, here in Dease Lake and in Vancouver.

It was hard for him to think of this cottage as home anymore. He had spent little time here in the last four years. But then, that had been his choice. He opened the bills first and compared them to his statements he'd paid online in Vancouver.

Sean sat back and took a sip of his coffee. His lips puckered. *Cold coffee–yuk.*

Reflecting on his life as a writer, he thought about the routine he'd followed the past several years. People assumed he was a free spirit, writing when he chose to, travelling the world at leisure, doing exciting book tours. They were envious of his lifestyle, believing him to be rich and wanting for nothing. Certainly, he felt grateful to be self- employed and not tied to a nine-to-five job working for someone else. He also appreciated the fact that he could do something he loved and make a living at it. But this was a business, and like all other businesses, it needed structure and focus to make it successful.

He chuckled at the rich part. He could now consider himself financially stable, but it had taken him fifteen years to find himself in this comfortable stage of life. The last four years had been extremely demanding. He'd taken on a four-book contract, accomplishing one book a year—a series of thrillers with the same main character.

The doorbell rang and Sean smiled. He felt sure it was Sarah from next door. He'd only returned the night before, but she wouldn't waste any time coming over to say hello.

"Hey, neighbor. What took you so long?" Sean winked at her.

She smoothed her silver hair, her eyes crinkling as she laughed. "Good to see you too, love." Sarah handed him a parcel. "I picked this up yesterday. Hadn't brought it over yet."

"Come on in. Coffee?"

"No time today, I'm afraid. Off to an appointment. Come over to my place tomorrow and we'll have a good talk."

"Sure thing. See you then and thanks for this," Sean nodded at the parcel.

He chuckled on his way back to his study. 'A good talk' with Sarah meant an opportunity to catch up on local gossip. *I can always count on her not to disappoint me on that score.*

His neighbor, a 68-year-old widow, made it her business to know everyone and everything that happened for miles around. Sarah was never malicious; it kept her lonely life busy. Everyone loved Sarah and recognized that she had a heart of gold. Over coffee and her famous cinnamon rolls, Sean's education was upgraded on local politics, business and social life.

He read his fan mail and placed the writer solicitations in a large envelope to send to Trent in Vancouver.

Sean stood and moved to the window. His study faced north to the Cassiar Mountains. They provided an incredible backdrop to the white-blanketed fields in the foreground. There had been a heavy snowfall this year. It had been a number of years since he'd been here at this time of year, so it was a different kind of beauty that he was enjoying. His thoughts turned to the cabin, a three hour drive northwest of Dease Lake into the Tahltan territory, and a five kilometer hike into the little log home he'd inherited from his grandfather. This was the roughest, most undeveloped area in British Columbia. He looked forward to the tranquility and promise of spring.

The ringing of the telephone broke into his muse and he returned to his desk. "Hello?"

"Sean? Trent here. Listen, I know you just arrived up there, but I really need you to return to Vancouver."

"You must be kidding. Today is my first day here, Trent. What's up?"

"We have a strong deal on an adapted mini-series. The producer wants to meet you next week for discussions."

Sean was silent. "You there, buddy?"

He released a sigh. "Yes, I'm here."

"Hey, I know you wanted some time off, but this is a big deal."

"Of course it is. It's important and what I pay you for," he said, with a chuckle. "I'll leave in the morning and be home the day after."

"Good, call me when you're here. That'll give me the weekend to go over the details with you before we fly out on Monday."

"Will do, catch you later."

Sean felt disappointed and excited at the same time. *A movie deal! Isn't that what every author dreams of?* He pulled his attention back to the private mail on his desk. *Best to finish with this mail at least.*

That afternoon, he took a drive around the town and drove a short distance to a lookout. He gazed down at the town and soaked up the snowy view beneath him. This land spoke to him and always drew him back. And when it did, he felt like he'd come home. When he returned to the cottage, he packed his bag for the morning and called his neighbor.

"Hi, Sarah. Thought I better tell you, I have to go back to the city in the morning on business."

"But you just got here. What a shame."

"Actually, it's exciting business. I'm happy about it. It's all about timing, I'm afraid. But I'll try to be back in a couple of weeks on the outside."

"Well … we never got our chat and you won't get a cinnamon bun either."

Sean laughed. *Hmm … let's see, movie deal or cinnamon bun? Sarah's cinnamon buns were a def-*

inite contender, they were that good. "I'll hold you to a couple when I get back."

"You drive careful, now. See you soon."

The next morning, Sean was off at dawn. He looked up the road that led to Telegraph Creek as he passed the turnoff.

It beckoned him to turn right, but the cabin would have to wait.

Chapter 16

"Ooh … ouch."

I bent over the kitchen counter and sucked in a deep breath as the pain coursed through my abdomen. The big moment had come marking the beginning of the first stage of labor.

My contractions were a steady thirty minutes apart. The time was 10:30 a.m. A cramping sensation in my lower abdomen joined the back pain that had pulsed since early morning. They were getting stronger, but not to the point that I needed my breathing exercises.

Preparations for the birth kept me busy all morning, following the instructions written out in January. Going through the motions, enforcing only positive thoughts, gave me a feeling of confidence and a sense of purpose.

Stacks of firewood filled a third of the cabin. I knew it was imperative to keep the stove fire going, and easy access to the wood would be essential. The floor of the cabin became my focus with a good sweep and scrubbing with bleach. I'd saved most of the one bottle of bleach I'd found for this day. Sterility was foremost on my mind. The counters were washed down with hot water and bleach. After more trips to the stream, every pot and bucket was filled with water and covered to keep clean. I reheated the large soup pot. These chores took me into the early afternoon.

"Okay, sweet pea, time to ready the bed for us." She hadn't moved the past few days, another indication that the birth grew closer, as she rested for her birth. "I should be resting too, little one." *No. Have to keep busy so my mind doesn't wander where it shouldn't go. Too scary.*

I scrubbed a tarp down with bleach and placed it on the bed under a clean sheet, with a towel set over that. The wall mirror was secured to the bars on the bottom bedpost with some twine. Extra blankets and pillows were placed at the top of the bed. The time would come when I would have to watch as the baby left the birth canal. The only way to see this was to prop myself up high enough to view the birth in the mirror. I placed some other bags on one side of the bed to deal with shortly. My happy face doll took a spot beside the mirror.

"There you are, Martha. All set to do your thing." I stared hard at the doll, reminded of her purpose to keep me focused when the pain became unbearable. My chest constricted, and that old feeling of fear crept in. I rubbed my aching belly and talked to my baby. "Stay focused, right sweat pea?" I took a few deep breaths and pushed them out hard.

My contractions were down to fifteen minutes apart. The pain increased and took my breath. I crossed to the window and looked across the meadow. It was snowing. To my surprise, Feathers sat on the wooden railing of the porch.

"What are you doing out in this storm? You should be in your nest."

He stared at me with his head titled sideways. A low guttural rattle emanated from his throat. It wasn't his usual manner to speak to me.

"I don't know what you're saying, but thank you, friend. I truly think you're here to protect me. See you soon."

The shutters were closed to block out the cold and ensure my safety. The kerosene lamp beside the bed sat filled and lit. The contents of the two bags placed on the bed came next. My efforts included towels, a plastic bag for the placenta, sterilized scissors, surgical tape from the first aid kit, and customized terry towel pads (made from a towel) with a belt made from twine for vaginal bleeding after the delivery. An extra large towel was laid out to wrap the baby in after the birth. I placed a pot of hot water with some sterile cloths on the chest beside the bed and a bucket of drinking water with a soup ladle on the floor next to it. Weeks of planning for this day, trying to prepare for every possible necessity paid off. Truly, my tools for this birth weren't traditional, but they were sterile and would do the trick …
I hoped.

Timing my contractions, my pains were down to ten minutes apart, forcing me to concentrate on my breathing. I inhaled a long breath through my nose and counted. "One." Exhaling through my mouth slowly, I counted again. "Two." A third bucket by the bed reminded me to frequently empty my bladder. My last chore on the list, a body wash, followed by five minutes of scrubbing my hands like the book said, paying particular attention to my fingernails.

Then it happened—my water broke.

"Oh my God, this is it," I cried, hearing the panic in my voice. "Where is Kaela? She said she'd be here." I made my way to the bed, propped myself up with pillows and covered myself with a clean sheet. There was nothing left to do but wait for the next contraction. I checked my watch and noted the time was 3:10 p.m. It came with excruciating pain. I grabbed hold of my hair with my hands and cried out.

"Oh Jesus, it hurts!"

The second stage of labor had started, and it scared me to death. Doubts crowded into my thoughts. "I can't do this alone." The contractions grew stronger, coursing through my body like a knife, and when the pain temporarily subsided, the feeling of being ripped apart took its place. Breathing exercises went by the wayside, and my body tightened up with each pain, adding to my discomfort.

"Please help me," I cried, full of pain and anger. "Where are you Kaela? I need you." My teeth clenched and rage shook my body. "I hate you Colin. Bastard."

My scalp hurt as I squeezed my hands into tight fists with my hair entangled through my fingers.

Then, I saw Martha, smiling from the mirror's edge, and my list came to mind. "Use a point to focus on when the contractions are too hard to bear. Remember to pant." *Calm yourself girlie, concentrate.* My eyes never left that doll, and visualizing Martha giving birth during that cold January in the Yukon, my breathing became controlled.

The desire to push felt strong. I raised my bent knees and pulled the sheet forward to watch in the mirror. When the next contraction hit, I started to pant, and with my stare fixated on Martha, I inhaled and panted. "Wha, wha, wha." Inhale. "Wha, wha, wha." Inhale.

This was repeated over and over until the pain stopped. The feeling to push overwhelmed me, but one look in the mirror told me to wait. The contractions were so close. Soon the bulging of the vagina and the crowning of the baby's head should appear.

My mouth was dry! My tongue felt like a rock. I grabbed the ladle of water beside the bed and took a few sips, wetting my face with my other hand.

Collapsing back onto the pillows, waiting for another contraction, the pushing urge became almost uncontrollable. But I held back.

Time ticked by. I repeated my routine over and over. And still no Kaela or baby. I could see by the slats in the shutters that darkness had come.

Finally, a contraction came and with my next set of pants, the bulging could be seen.

"Wha, wha, wha." Inhale. The pattern continued.

Exhaustion was close.

"Where are you, Kaela?" I couldn't believe she hadn't come. Panic welled inside me.

Then, I saw the head, covered with a mass of wet blond hair. My eyes filled with tears. "Oh…sweat pea…soon," I whispered, my voice hoarse from screaming. Trying to focus my tired mind, I pushed with the next contraction.

"No, Georgia! Don't push." Kaela's voice echoed in my mind. "Remember to wait for the contraction to peak first. You don't want to force the baby too quickly. When the contraction peaks, remember to take a deep breath. Then push your chin onto your chest and push as hard as you can while slowly releasing your breath."

Relief flooded over me. She'd finally come. I raised myself up on my elbows and pushed hard, repeating the thrust a second time before the next contraction.

"Good girl." Her calm and relaxed voice soothed me and helped me to concentrate on her words. "Now—take fast, shallow breaths and pant. Wait for the next peak."

"Wha, wha, wha … Wha, wha, wha."

The baby's head became more visible. Then it was time to push again. "Urr—gh."

Collapsing against the pillows, I slipped my hand over the bed and into the cold water, running my wet fingers across my dry lips and over my hot face.

My contractions built and peaked. I panted and pushed until finally with one last effort the baby's head slipped out of the birth canal. All pain was forgotten.

"Oh my God! Kaela, look … the head is out."

"I see it, child. Now remember, don't push. Look in the mirror. Can you see the cord? Is it around the baby's neck?"

"No, the cord isn't there."

"Good. Let the baby move itself onto its side so the shoulders can push through. Check the baby's face to see if there are membranes over the baby's mouth and nose," she urged.

It was difficult to see the baby's face in the mirror because of my position, but squirming a little sideways, the face showed clear.

My contractions continued. Finally, the baby's shoulder came through the canal, then the other shoulder. After a couple of weak pushes, the baby slipped out quickly.

"Oh Kaela, she's a girl. I knew she'd be a girl. Look at my beautiful baby."

Tears streamed down my cheeks. Though exhausted, my job wasn't over yet. I collapsed onto the pillows to catch my breath first and gather my strength.

"You must sit up now and help the baby breathe. You can do it, child. Up you get." Kaela, gently, but firmly coaxed me.

The baby looked blue with a white, waxy coating. Her head rested against my arm and my other hand slipped underneath her body, slightly tilting the head downwards to drain fluid, like the survival book said. I wiped the baby's nose and mouth to clear the fluids with a cloth dipped into the warm water pot. She started to cry right away, her skin turning to pink almost immediately. She was so tiny, but perfect in every detail. The cord stopped pulsing, so I wrapped her in the large beach towel to keep her warm. Checking my watch, it was 10:02 p.m.

Had I really been in labor seven hours?

A glance in the mirror to see if there was any bleeding revealed a tear from the birth. Lying down, I placed her on her side in my right arm with her head down to assist drainage, and waited for the afterbirth of the placenta.

"She's beautiful," Kaela whispered. "You should be proud of yourself. You came through this courageously."

"I couldn't have done it without you. Thank you for being here."

"You're welcome. But you did all the hard work."

My free hand massaged my abdomen to help stimulate the afterbirth. About twenty minutes later it came, prompting me to open the towel around the baby. I tightened surgical tape around the cord in two places, one close to the body and the other about four inches along the cord, and picked up the scissors. My hand shook and I froze.

"What's wrong, child?" Kaela said.

"I'm afraid to cut the cord. What if she keeps bleeding?"

"Cut the cord about an inch outside of the second tape, leaving a total of about five inches of cord attached to the baby. She'll be fine."

I took hold of the cord and put the scissors in place. *Here we go!* I closed my eyes and cut through the cord. There was a minimum of blood at the tip of the cut, and then it stopped. *Thank God.* The placenta went into a plastic bag to be saved for a doctor. Sometimes they send them to the lab for testing if the baby has any problems. I pushed the thought from my mind.

It was time to feed my daughter. As hard as I tried, I couldn't coax her to latch on. Several tries later, I gave up in frustration. A section in my pregnancy book covered this problem. It was called 'suck training'. I inserted my index finger up to the first knuckle joint, into her mouth, palm up. The tip of my finger gently stroked the roof of her mouth to encourage sucking. Once I felt her begin to suck, I straightened my finger and applied pressure onto the back of the tongue to encourage her to flatten it and extrude it over the lower gum. I pulled her bottom lip down. The sides of her tongue wrapped around the sides of my finger. I let her suck for a minute and decided she was ready to latch on. I leaned back and brought her to my breast. She latched on just fine. "Oh Kaela, look. She's feeding."

Every few minutes I massaged my lower abdomen—this and the breast-feeding would help contract the uterus and control my bleeding, according to the book.

Mother and daughter dozed for the next hour. "Ooh … sweet pea, it's chilly in here. Time to refill the stove." Dizziness came and went after a few moments of sitting on the edge of the bed, and still exhausted, I moved slowly to the woodstove and added more wood. The remaining water on the stove was still warm enough to wash the baby and myself.

"Your first bath, little one, and then we'll change the bed." Tears streamed down my face uncontrollably and my limbs shook. Relief and weariness took hold.

"Finally, we're free to snuggle under the covers." The fresh, warm bed calmed my nerves and my body started to relax. Howling wind blew frozen snow against the window. The only other sound came from the crackling fire. In my drowsiness, I felt content for the first time since arriving at the cabin. We were safe and secure, my baby and me. The time was 11: 32 p.m. The date ... an ear-splitting grin spread across my face: "Sweet pea, it's February 14th. You're my Valentine, a special baby on a special day."

Staring at my baby's sleeping face, another first came to mind—I was at peace for the first time in nine months.

"Kaela, are you still here?"

"Yes, I'm here."

"I've decided to call her after you. To avoid confusion, may I call you by your Indian name?"

"I am pleased and honored by your request. Of course, you may call me Nonnock."

"Then her name is Kaela Anne Charles," I whispered, as sleep claimed me.

Sometime during the night my eyes opened to see Nonnock sitting in the rocker. She was watching baby Kaela and me, a silent smile on her lips.

Chapter 17

The days passed quickly now with always something to do. Baby Kaela dictated my routine and my pace. Initially, there was no semblance of a schedule, her routine irregular. Drained from her constant needs and my cabin duties, I worried over her feedings like a mother hen, never knowing if she was receiving her proper share of milk or if my body was producing enough. But in the past few days, an order had appeared to her sleeping and eating patterns. My milk was plenty and I noticed some weight gain on Kaela.

My pregnancy book said that mothers' milk is devoid of Vitamin D, unless the mother was on supplements. My fears that she would be deficient prompted me to add some homemade formula to her diet from saved cans of evaporated milk stored in the root cellar. We settled into the rocking chair and I decided to feed her the new formula with an eyedropper before her regular mother's milk. I placed the dropper in the side of her mouth and squeezed.

"Oh sweet pea, you have to help me here." The liquid dribbled out of her mouth and down the side of her face. "Let's try again." This time it went down her throat and she started to choke. "Oh baby, I'm sorry." I lifted her up to my shoulder and patted her back. "Okay, one more try. There you go ... that's it. Mmm ... good, all that enhanced Vitamin A, C and D. Good girl." I had no idea if adding a small amount to each feeding would be sufficient, but it made me feel better.

Kaela was a good baby. Once a need was met, be it feeding, changing, or affection—she responded immediately with instant contentment. I filled the sink with warm water. She looked shocked as the water crept around her body and then she appeared to smile. They say babies that young don't smile, but you couldn't convince me of that. "Look at those big eyes and that smile. You love your baths, don't you, baby girl?" I tapped her nose with the wet cloth, and Kaela's eyes crossed as she looked down her nose, sending me into fits of giggles. Her arms and legs splashed about followed by squeals of joy. This was our playtime, and my heart soared. "Oh baby girl, you have rejuvenated me." A new love, never felt before or known by me to exist, grew inside me. For the first time in a long time, I felt truly happy.

The temperatures warmed considerably and the snowing stopped. Sunny days ensured that going outside to get water was a pleasant diversion. With Kaela sleeping a full four hours, there was plenty of time for my baby chores. Washing diapers became a daily occurrence, as my home-made supply made from old towels was limited.

One beautiful afternoon, I stood out back at a makeshift clothesline, hanging wash while Kaela slept. The birds were singing, prompting me to stop and listen. I whistled and they stopped. Another whistle ... and they answered back. Feathers sat on the edge of the roof with his head cocked sideways. "What, Feathers? You and I talk, why not them? Are you jealous? You know you're my favorite."

"Kraa! Kraa!" he answered.

Laughing, my thoughts turned to my new status. Motherhood. A tiring and exhilarating role.

It evoked feelings of protectiveness, nurturing, and needfulness. The last time I felt this happy was on my wedding day. *Whoa!*

These were the same feelings taken into my marriage with Colin, seeing this as my role in our union. Thoughts came to mind of fights with my mother-in-law. As overbearing as she was, I considered her a threat, and expected her to back off and let Colin go. *Not to grow up and become a man, but so that I could take over mothering him.* No wonder she and I could never get along. We were vying for the same role. *Colin wanted a partner, not a second mother. Or did he? Well, okay, the woman is still a bitch. We probably wouldn't have gotten along anyhow.*

Feathers flew overhead as I headed to the woodpile and picked up the axe. My first strike with the axe knocked me sideways. *Whoa! I'm weaker than I thought.* The axe felt heavy. With each stroke of the axe, I thought about the roles played by men and women in relationships, and my perceptions of them. Traditionally, the men in Colin's family were taught to be protectors, the providers, and our knights in shining armor. We women were taught it's okay to show fear and uncertainty, and to have it acknowledged but not our men.

"So tell me, Feathers, are bird relationships as complicated as ours?" I swung again. The axe slipped off the side of the log. *Pay attention, you'll hurt yourself!* I spread my feet far apart, in case the axe slipped again and swung with all my strength. *Crack!* Silence. "Okay, don't answer. I think you're still pouting 'cause I spoke to the other birds. Hmm …?"

Colin was taught to hold in his insecurities, to not be 'wimpy'. Closing off feelings, the myth of the 'knight' in shining armor is perpetuated. *Crack!* He was taught to be an achiever and that 'work' was the place to accomplish this. Unfortunately, in our society, success is measured by monetary and material gain. Colin was a prime example of this, an excessive workaholic. He'd been groomed well.

"Poor Colin, you were truly living the myth."

Did all families believe in this, or just mine and Colin's? Certainly, his father, grandfather, and great grandfather, generations of lawyers were workaholics and believed the woman's place was in the home. My grandfather, an army Colonel, believed the same. Another thought popped into my mind, as I leaned on the handle to catch my breath, and stared off into the woods. I'd left the protection of my father and placed myself in Colin's hands when we married. The dutiful daughter became the dutiful wife. The needy, fearful child became the needy, fearful wife, afraid of the world and its unpredictability. My dreams and my happiness became tied in with Colin's dreams, which were centered on his work and material accumulation. His values became my values.

"Marion was right, Feathers. I built my life around his, giving up my friends and activities for his, carrying the mistaken belief that we were all halves until we found our mate and we became whole." The lyrics from an old sixties song about being 'half, now I'm whole' came to mind. *Romantic yes. Realistic–no.* I swung hard and the axe made a loud, resounding connection with another piece of wood. *Crack! Such drivel!*

I should have woven his life into mine. *A little hard if you have no idea what your life is. Colin was my life, and I surrendered my power to him.*

Why hadn't my parents prepared me for this? Why had they allowed me to leave their protection so naively unprepared, and destined to make so many mistakes? Surely, they knew.

I felt cheated by this lack of knowledge. My mother wanted my brother to go to university so he could get a good job with good pay and live a good life. She wanted me to go to university to find a husband who could get a good job with good pay to keep me in the life I was accustomed to—to being looked after.

"Cinderella looking for her Prince Charming. I lived in a fantasy."

I married the 'myth,' not the man. I didn't even know who the man was—neither did he.

"Sorry old man." *Crack.* "You still acted like an ass. After all, you didn't even try to work it out or discuss it with me. You ran away, coward."

Crack! The axe hit a knot and slipped off the wood, knocking me off balance and hitting the side of my ankle. "Ow ..." I yelled and fell to the ground. "Oh, shit ... that hurts." I rocked back and forth in pain as blood poured from the gash. Pulling myself up, I hobbled into the cabin and grabbed a towel and the first aid kit. I applied pressure to the wound. With not much flesh in that area, the gash was open to the bone and ran about five inches long. My worst fear had just become reality.

A serious injury. What should I do?

Chapter 18

March 15th - Dease Lake

Spring thaw usually occurred in April, but it would be earlier this year. Sean decided to return to Dease Lake and proceed to the cabin before it started. All the melted snow would turn the roads to mud. It was the perfect setting for him to come to terms with his demons, and he wanted to share the beginning of spring in the isolation of the cabin.

His business trip was successful and he and Trent had returned from Los Angeles with a movie deal in hand. Sean was contracted as a consultant on the script and filming whenever it was scheduled to begin. It had taken longer than he expected to get back to Dease Lake. They'd spent a week in L.A. and then flown back a couple of weeks later to meet with the screenwriter.

Finally, his time was his own. His neighbor, Sarah, had been away the few days he'd been here at the cottage. Sean spent his time alone spring cleaning the cottage and doing odd repair jobs. A commotion outside brought him back to the present, where he stood at the window of his study. Overhead, he watched as a formation of Canada geese flew north towards the Cassiars. The return of the geese was a sure sign that spring was on its way. His gaze shifted to the pools of melted snow in the yard and he realized that the thaw was well underway. *Better leave for the cabin in the next few days.*

Sean returned to his desk to finish clearing it off. Gathering up the newspapers, an old headline caught his eye.

SEARCH CALLED OFF FOR MISSING WOMAN

He picked up the paper and read the article dated November 18—four months previous.

After a two-week search, the Royal Canadian Mounted Police, Dease Lake Detachment, called off the search for Georgia Charles, the kidnapped victim of two Whitehorse bank robbers. The two men robbed the Klondike Savings & Loan in White-

horse on October 31. They fled the scene, taking the victim with them in a stolen vehicle. A few miles south of Whitehorse, they then switched to a stolen cargo van. The bodies of Robert Alan Smith, 22, of Prince Rupert and Gary William Chambers, 21 of Prince George, were retrieved from the wreckage of the van 40 km south of Dease Lake on November 3rd. Police believe they lost control of their vehicle during the sudden snowstorm that hit the area November 2nd. Speed and road conditions were a factor.

The body of Mrs. Charles was not in the wreckage. Police scoured the area, but found nothing. Staff-Sergeant Leo Pratt of the Dease Lake Detachment issued this statement.

"We do not believe that Mrs. Charles was with the two men when the accident occurred. We've been working closely with the Whitehorse and Watson Lake Detachments. We believe foul play was involved. Unfortunately our search was hindered by days of blizzards. The resulting snow has covered any evidence we may have found. I speak for all of the detachments involved, when I say we are all saddened by this case and send our deepest regrets to Mrs. Charles' family."

Most of the money stolen during the robbery was recovered in the wreckage.

Sean stared at the photo of Georgia Charles, printed beside the article. The black and white photo was a headshot of a woman who appeared to be thirtyish. She had long, dark hair and dark eyes, with full lips. Her smile was devastating. But it was the eyes that held his gaze. They were like deep pools of water, warm and inviting, innocent, yet containing a hint of sensuality. Sean had never felt so drawn to a photograph before. Perhaps it was because he knew she'd died. He sat quietly, soaking up the details of her face. *Recognition–that's it.* He sat forward. *No, I don't know her but ...* It hit him. She reminded him of a girl he'd known in college. In fact, they could be sisters. The girl had been his roommate's girlfriend. He'd lost touch with them both years ago. He threw the newspaper into a refuse box with a sigh. *Life could be so cruel.*

Sean strode up the front walkway to his neighbor's door. At forty, he had lost that pretty boy look. His dark hair, graying at the temples, framed a handsome, youthful face. He was 5'11" and his well- built frame completed the picture of an attractive and virile man.

Sarah answered his knock and led him into the kitchen. Seated at the kitchen table, Sean surveyed the room, noting the freshly painted, two-tone beige walls, with red printed curtains, and the new cherry wood cupboards.

"You've redone your kitchen. It looks great," he said.

Sarah poured him a cup of coffee. "Except for the cupboards—did it all myself this winter. Gave me somethin' to do during all them cold days. Your timin's perfect Sean. You musta smelled them cinnamon buns; just took 'em out of the oven. Here, help yerself."

"Mmm…. Sarah, one day I might marry you," Sean said, stuffing his mouth with more of the bun.

"Oh be gone with ya. A handsome man like you could have the pick of any woman. You needn't be bothered with an old crow the likes of me,"

Sean studied the woman sitting opposite him. She was small, but wiry. Her short straight hair, now totally silver, framed her thin face. At 68, she was still an attractive woman.

"You shouldn't talk about yourself that way. Any single man in these parts should be proud to have you for a partner. Which reminds me, are you still seeing Roger?"

"Nope," Sarah answered with an air of authority, "I sent him packin'."

He smiled. "I guess I shouldn't have asked."

"Not at all. I don't mind talkin' bout it. He started tellin' me what I should and shouldn't be doin'. That was bad enough, but then he asked me to marry him," Sarah offered, rolling her eyes to the ceiling, "Said he wanted to take care of me. I said I don't need anyone lookin' after me. More like I would be carin' for you, I said. At my age, I don't need any man I gotta cook for when he's hungry. And I sure don't wanna be washin' his dirty socks and underwear."

"Dare I ask what he said to that?" Sean tried to keep a straight face.

"Can you believe he accused me of leadin' him on?" she said, refilling Sean's cup. "Said he

194

thought I knew he was lookin' for a companion to grow old with, and he wanted to make an honest woman out of me."

"And you said?" Sean interjected with amusement.

"I told him he didn't need to marry me to have me as a companion. And as for leadin' him on, I told him I was only human; I get lonely too. But a companion to me is someone to talk to, play cribbage and laugh with; and once in a while a good roll in the hay to keep me joints oiled." Sarah snorted. "And that's as honest as I need be. So he left and I haven't

seen him since."

Sean exploded with laughter. "Sarah, you're incorrigible." Sarah sighed.

"Uh-huh, and one day I'll find me a man who appreciates that. Truth is, since my husband, Tom's, passing; I've become too independent. We had a great marriage, don't want to tempt fate. Now, young man, let's talk about you. What's on your mind this sunny day?" Sarah sipped her coffee.

"Well, I'm leaving today to go to the cabin. Break-up's already started and I want to get in before it gets too bad."

"Hope you haven't left it too late. You know, I'm glad you've decided to take some time off. Everyone around here's been worried about ya these past years," Sarah said.

"I appreciate that, Sarah, I really do. We both know why I kept myself busy, too much anger and too much pain. But now, I'm ready to take a good look at what happened and why. I've stopped blaming it all on Laura."

Sarah placed a hand on Sean's arm. "Sometimes things have a way of happenin' and it's nobody's fault. Life still goes on and you find your place in it. You do, that is, if you want your life to have some meanin'."

"I guess you know all about that, Sarah, with Tom's passing," Sean said.

"Loss is loss, whether it's death or someone leavin'. The grievin' process is the same. From what I can see, you're about to lay yours to rest. Welcome back," Sarah said, with tears in her eyes.

"Thanks, Sarah. You've been a good neighbor and a good friend," Sean whispered, his hand squeezing Sarah's.

"So, how long you plannin' on stayin' out there?"

"Three weeks, I would guess. Break-up should be over by then. I'm not taking my lap top for this short trip in. I'm cutting myself off from the world...and looking forward to it. My agent knows I can't be reached until mid-April. Hopefully, my satellite radio for the cabin will be here. I may have to make a short business trip or two this summer, but my plan is to spend as much time at the cabin as I can until September. And on that note, I'd better hit the road," Sean stood.

Sarah walked him to the door, and with a big hug, saw him on his way.

"You take care of yerself out there. See ya in three weeks."

... shut your eyes and you will know what I mean by thought entombed in darkness. Light comes through the senses, and not only through the sense of sight. Awareness requires the use of your entire being as an eye.

Charles A. Lindbergh

Chapter 19

The towel was soaked with blood. I stood and grabbed another along with a basin of hot water from the stove. After cleaning the wound I could see that the bleeding slowed. No major arteries had been severed. My concern was that the wound needed to be stitched. *Not much chance of that here.* The survival book was sitting on the coffee table beside me. I found the section on treating open wounds in the wilderness. *Okay, let's see. Hmpff...*

The book suggested the wound not be stitched up because if it got infected, it would need to drain. If it couldn't drain, there would be worse consequences. I skipped over those not wanting to scare myself. *Okay, what do I do?* I read the instructions twice and got to work. Using the sterilized eye dropper used to feed formula to Kaela,

I squeezed hot water into the wound to cleanse it. I winced. "Oooh … that hurts like hell."

Then I took pieces of surgical tape cut into two inch lengths. About a half-inch from each end, I cut out a strip on either side of the tape, leaving me two half-inch square ends with a l/4" strip between them, resembling a butterfly suture. Holding the wound together on either side, I clenched my teeth and placed my suture tape across the wound to keep the two sides together, continuing the length of the open cut until it was closed with sutures about l/8" apart. A sheet of gauze went over that, held in place with a tensor bandage wrapped around the leg. The book said to clean it three to four times a day to keep out infection. The pain was excruciating. *Suck it up, girlie. No pain meds here.* My chores still needed to be done. In addition, I had to attend to the needs of my baby. There was no time to feel sorry for myself and I limped around the cabin as best I could.

Cuddled with my daughter in my bed that night, I tried to forget the throbbing ache in my ankle and concentrated on my thoughts earlier in the day about my relationship with Colin.

"Oh, baby Kaela. Don't ever believe men are knights. They are humans with human frailties." I laughed, with my obligatory snort. "Listen to me, sweat pea. Only a few weeks old, and I'm teaching you about men."

It wasn't fair of me to condemn Colin for something we were both guilty of.

I'd created a tidy, unchallenging life for myself with Colin, and allowed him to bully me. I was a mere appendage to him. As an observer to my life, I silently suffocated. We both defined ourselves by what we were instead who we were. For the first time, I was ready to admit my contribution to the demise of my marriage.

I surprised myself with a twinge of understanding as to why Colin felt it was his 'duty' to go to his pregnant Julie. She needed him more than me. He was perpetuating the myth. Towards the end of our relationship, I had tried on occasion to assert my will. After ten years, Colin wasn't comfortable with me challenging what became habit and his perception of marriage. More of Marion's wisdom came to mind. *You have to realize something, Georgia. Colin's leaving had more to do with him than it did with you.* What she meant was that I'd stopped fulfilling Colin's expectations. That didn't mean that there was something wrong with me. Our biggest problem was lack of communication. Once I started to believe it was Colin's way or no way, I accepted it. I wanted peace not constant confrontation. That was wrong. Maybe the marriage would have ended sooner or maybe he would have come around to my way of thinking on some of the issues. Bottom line, I didn't try. Communication would have gone one of two ways, we either would have communed or we would have realized we shouldn't be together. I allowed Colin to think that his behavior was okay. It dawned on me that once it started to go wrong, and I accepted it, it escalated to the point of no return. My ego blamed Colin. His ego blamed me. The simple truth is the marriage failed, not me.

A sudden sense of freedom came with this acknowledgement. Lost and alone in the wilderness with my baby, I was, for the first time in my life, free.

With a new sense of confidence, I kissed Kaela on the forehead. A new threshold was crossed this night. "Good night, sweet pea." Sleep came with a newfound sense of peace, even if my ankle was consumed with heat and pain.

A tickling sensation on my face woke me to my spirit guide sitting on the bed beside me. She smiled and waved a feather under my nose.

"You were sleeping so soundly, I took measures into my own hands," she said.

I laughed. "I'd have thought a spirit would have more sophisticated ways to wake up a human."

"This seemed like the gentlest way. Now tell me, how is my namesake doing? She appears to be a good sleeper."

"She is, and she's gained some weight these last few weeks."

"And how is mother doing?" she asked.

I pushed myself up, aware of the agonizing tenderness in my leg. "Not too good. I had an accident today with the axe and the pain is killing me."

"That is one of the reasons I chose to visit tonight. Be careful of infection. You must go to the evergreen tree in the forest. Gather the pitch blebs off of the trunks of the pines. They will be hard. Chew them to soften the pitch and place on the wound like a poultice."

"Will it numb the pain or is it only for infection?"

"Pitch is anti-bacterial. Do you have some cinnamon and clove?"

"Yes, in the spice jars."

"Then sprinkle some ground cinnamon and clove on the wound, and that will numb the pain."

"Cinnamon, clove and pine pitch. You're sure they'll work?"

"These are but a few of the ancient healing ways of the Tahltans. There are many more but at this time of year, the plants are not accessible. These are some of the ways that the mother looks after our Peoples."

I shifted my leg to ease my discomfort, reflecting on her words. "Respect and understanding. Another step closer to losing my fear of nature."

Nonnock smiled and reached forward and patted the tip of my nose with the feather.

"In the morning, I'll find some pitch," I said. "And what of your insights today. Tell me of them."

"I saw myself for the first time as I really am; now that was true enlightenment."

"And did you like what you saw?"

"Not at first. I saw some of my faults and then my mistakes. But I realized that I lived in a belief structure I took at face value, without ever questioning its role in my life."

"Where did you learn this belief structure?" I pondered this a moment. "From society?"

"So 'society' taught you these ideals," Nonnock stated.

"Not entirely … I guess my parents played the most important role."

"Yes, that's right. Your parents did. Now tell me why you're angry with them."

"What?" My eyebrows shot up.

"Is it not your feeling that they left you ill-prepared for your marriage to Colin?" she pushed.

She was right. I felt some anger, but this was the wrong word for it. "Once again, you know me better than I know myself. I expected my parents to have all the answers, and yes, it disappointed me to find out they didn't. Probably, I needed to find someone to blame for my shortcomings."

"You placed Colin on a pedestal, and you know that was wrong. Don't make the same mistake with the elders. That is falling prey to another erroneous belief. There is no one handbook on parenting to teach you all you would like to know. Raising children is the hardest job in the world, and one that is done by trial and error. Your parents drew on what they were taught. As your teachers, they did the best they knew to guide you."

I sighed. "I'm beginning to see how destructive having expectations of people can be."

"Sometimes parents get caught up in what they would like you to be, instead of who you really are."

"But as little kids, we don't know who we are yet. And if we did, how could we convey that to two adults who believe they know what is best?" I asked.

"You've answered your own question. When you are small, the responsibility lies with your parents. It is their obligation, as children lack maturity and knowledge. It is up to you to take on that responsibility when you're an adult. You must become your own parent and discover for yourself what your reality is. Do you under-stand?"

"Yes. You know, I tried to emulate my par-ent's relationship in my marriage to Colin. But the biggest difference was my Dad always let my mother be her own person and he always val-ued her opinion. Because I never expressed my-self, Colin assumed I didn't have any opinions. Towards the end, whenever I tried, he couldn't handle it."

"You seem to have learned a lot since my last visit." Nonnock rose to stand by the wood stove.

"My whole life came together, and for the first time, I can make some sense of it. But I couldn't have done this without you."

"You've done well because you were ready to learn. I merely guided you. You accomplished a lot these past months and you have a lot to be proud of."

Sleep took its time returning once she left. I watched my daughter sleeping, her face lit up in the filtered moonbeams. My spirit's shared in-sights of parenthood played a two-fold role for me. On the one hand, I was happy to be so in-formed, while on the other, scared to death of the responsibility. There was one true thing that became apparent to me. My parents' ideals and teachings came to me straight from their hearts and from a place of love. This much I knew I could pass on to my child.

Not only had I taken back my power, but I began to understand all that it meant.

The next morning, I waited for Kaela to go down again and headed out back to the pine trees. The pitch krebs were easy to find and before long I had plenty. My wound was swollen, hot, and quite red but I couldn't see any formation of pus. After cleaning it out I sprinkled cinnamon and cloves on the open wound while chewing on a piece of amber pitch. It tasted–piney? I placed the softened morsel on the wound and grabbed another piece. "Blaagh ..." I spat it out in disgust. "Oooh ... that was gross, sweet pea. Tastes like turpentine." I got up for some water. Comparing the pieces of pitch, I gingerly picked up an amber colored tidbit and sampled it's flavor. "Hmm ... same as the first bit." The chunk that I spat out was a dark brown. Into the garbage went the dark ones. Distracted by all of this sampling and spitting, it suddenly occurred to me that the pain in my leg had lessened. "Huh! This stuff works." I felt completely amazed and laughed.

"Look at me, a true survivor."

It was mid-March, and the minus twenties days and minus thirties nights were long gone. The days were sunny and the snow began to melt. The sudden appearance of swallows full of song, busy building their nests, filled me with anticipation of an early spring. Last week, I placed a stick in the snow notched at one-inch intervals. It appeared to be melting about an inch per day. This morning, I removed the aluminum foil from behind the wood stove and dampened down the fire, as it was too hot in the cabin.

As nature began her thaw, so did the remainder of my caribou meat.

"Well, sweat pea, today we make caribou jerky. Don't want to lose the last of our meat." Baby Kaela was propped up at the top of the bed with pillows all around her. She gurgled and cooed like she understood my ramblings. "Let's open my trusty survival book and get the recipe."

The process was fairly simple, and I spent the morning drying cut strips in the oven. A major staple in my diet, it would be nice to taste something new. Months of caribou stew, caribou steak, and roast caribou, had become a little boring. *Was I complaining? Me bad.*

Looking through the picture window at the majestic snow-capped mountains standing stark against the clear blue sky, I reflected on the past year and my time at the cabin. So much had changed, time, place, priorities—me. The old Georgia was no more, and I marveled at the emerging one

The raven was sitting in his usual spot on the deck railing. "I like me, Feathers."

"Toc ... toc ... toc," he replied.

With a laugh, I talked back. "I know ... you like me too."

Supplies were running low and soon I'd have to go. Leaving the security of the cabin scared me, but after all I'd come through, the courage would come. Kaela's needs depended on it. But not right now. Not yet. Only after the snow melted and the ground grew hard. There was still time to enjoy the warmth and peace of Mother Nature in the spring, and watch her nurture new life.

My thoughts were interrupted by the faint sound of voices coming from behind the cabin. The sounds increased in volume and came closer. They sounded like excited children trying to out-shout each other. Louder and louder, closer and closer they came, until the cabin filled with their noise. Stealing a glance at my sleeping daughter, I threw open the front door and limped out onto the porch. To my amazement, a string of Canada geese flew overhead, heading north towards the mountains.

"Yes! Yes!"

Thrusting my fists into the air, I hopped out into the clearing, whooping and hollering like a crazy person.

"You're back and I'm alive to see it. I love you, you big beauties."

The geese continued north. Once in awhile, the lead would change with one from the line. Their constant chatter never stopped. They seemed as excited to be back as I was to see them. This was my first day of spring!

I limped as best I could around the meadow, while Feathers, an agile, aerial acrobat, soared and tumbled in the sky. And later, with Feathers back on his railing perch and me sitting on the porch stairs, I knew—a change was coming. How, when, what—that I didn't know.

"But it's coming, Feathers."

That same low, guttural rattle I heard the day Kaela was born escaped from deep in his throat.

"My protector." I gave him a big smile and blew him a kiss.

Chapter 20

March 17th, Dease Lake

Sean headed out of town on the unpaved Telegraph Creek Road. Travelling west for about 50 km, he spiraled down twenty percent grades and maneuvered around single lane hairpin turns with no guardrails. The going was rough. The usual potholes kept his attention focused on the road, but it was the frost heaves that made his progress slow. As the day warmed up, the road turned to mud. Sean switched his truck wheels to 4-wheel drive to help compensate for the slippery surface.

Reaching the turnoff that would lead him down into the Tuya Valley, Sean stopped to stretch his legs and take in the view. Far below, he could see where the Tuya River met the Stikine River. It was at this junction that he would follow the forestry road north though the valley along the Tuya River. The spectacular snow-covered Mount Aziza towards the southeast stood tall, forming a breathtaking backdrop to the Stikine Valley. Still an active volcano, small eruptions left it surrounded by flat-topped cinder cones, aptly named Coffee and Cocoa Craters.

Still takes my breath away.

Sean inched his way down to the junction, awed by the raw beauty of nature. This part of the journey never failed to stir up his emotions and make him grateful for the experience of a small glimpse into the past. Still untouched by the modern world, this land held many historical memories. Sean made his way through the valley. He turned off the main forestry road and began the final stage of the journey that would lead him to the cabin trail.

He could see about two feet of snow in the shaded areas of the trees. As he slid down hills and inched slowly back up in low gear, Sean was starting to doubt his decision to reach the cabin today. He contemplated putting on chains, but he was almost at the trail to the cabin and kept going. His truck bogged down in the mud a few times, but he managed to rock himself out. About one kilometer from the spot where he usually parked his truck, the worst of his fears happened. The truck slid down a small hill. There was no straight road to gain momentum up the incline ahead. The truck couldn't climb and when he tried to back up, his wheels bogged down into the thick mud.

"Damn...damn it, anyway!" Sean pounded the steering wheel with his hands. "Why didn't I turn back when my gut told me to? *Because you're bloody pigheaded and stubborn.*"

Sean exited the truck to survey his situation. It only confirmed what he already knew. The truck was stuck here until the grader operator came to level the road after break-up. The chains wouldn't have helped him in this situation any- way.

"Guess I'm hiking the rest of the way".

Climbing back into the cab, he wrote a note for the grader operator, Jack Hill. Sean wanted Jack to know that he was all right and headed for the cabin. He placed the letter on the dash with his keys so that Jack could pull the truck out and park it off the road at his turnoff. He worked his way to the back of the truck. He decided to take his backpack filled with some fresh meat, vegetables, and fruits. Everything else he needed was already at the cabin. What was left in the pickup could be transported later. He went back to the cab and reached in behind the seat for his rifle. It was a sawed-off shotgun nicknamed, The Defender. He wouldn't travel without it.

Walking the road was much worse than driving. The mud became deeper as he progressed. In some spots, Sean sank into the mud up to his knees. With each lift of a foot, pounds of thick, clinging mud followed, glued to his boots. He plodded forward, knowing that the snow-covered path to the cabin was up ahead. Sean had almost reached the path when he heard a pair of Whiskey Jacks whistling behind him. He turned in time to see them swoop across the road, missing his head by inches. Startled and thrown off balance by his pack, he fell face first into the mud.

"Son-of-a-bitch!" He sat up and wiped the mud out of his eyes. Smearing his mud caked face with the sleeves of his jacket; he noticed a large group of Whiskey Jacks sitting in a line on a tree branch. They stared at him in silence.

Sean started to laugh; all the frustrations of the day built his laughter into a deep gut-wrenching howl. He struggled to his feet and moved to the side of the road. He washed his face and hands as best he could with snow.

He worked his way to the pathway and the going became easier. He left his snowshoes in the truck, because the snow was too soupy to use them effectively. There was still two feet of snow in the trees, but this path was a game trail. Caribou and moose had worn it down. *Should reach the cabin by dusk.* As Sean moved along the path, he thought of Laura and smiled. She hated the cabin. If he thought things went badly today, it would have been a lot worse if Laura were here. She'd only visited the cabin half a dozen times. Then, she refused to come. *A city girl through and through.* He was surprised she stayed with him in the Dease Lake cottage as long as she had. His thoughts wandered to the last day they'd spent together at the cottage. It had been four and a half years ago, in the fall. Laura had been edgy for days. He realized later that she had no intention of spending another winter in the north. Sean didn't own the Yaletown condo at that point. That came with the advance on his book deal four months later. He'd come out of his study midday to find Laura pacing around the kitchen.

Sean poured himself a cup of coffee and observed Laura. "What's ...?"

Laura cut him off. "We have to talk."

"Okay, let's sit." He pulled a chair out from under the table.

Laura continued to pace. Sean instinctively knew he wasn't going to like what she had to say. Whenever she was edgy and withdrawn from him, she had something major going on in her mind. She stopped and faced him, "I'm leaving."

Sean stared at her, his coffee cup halfway to his mouth. They held each other's gaze for a long moment and then Laura turned away. "What do you mean? You want to go to the city for a while and visit your folks?"

Facing him again, Laura held herself rigid. "No, Sean. I'm leaving and I won't be back. I want a divorce."

"A divorce? What are you talking about? I know we've had some problems lately, but talking divorce is ridiculous."

"Let's be honest. I haven't been happy here for a long time. You know that ..."

"I know you hate going to the cabin, and I haven't pressured you on that score. I also know it was hard for you when we came to the cottage three years ago. But you've been sub teaching at the school; you've made some friends and gone to the city when you wanted. I guess I thought you settled into life here."

"I hate it here." Laura yelled. "I've been pretending for the sake of our marriage. I'm a city girl. I hate small towns, small town people, and small town politics. Everybody knows our business and I hate that too. I'm a private person. And what they don't know, they make up. Sean, I have to go."

"Why didn't you discuss it with me? I mean ... maybe we can go back to the city and start over."

"You love it here. This cottage is part of who you are. It's part of what you do as a writer. I couldn't take that from you," Laura added, lowering her voice. "I'm leaving on the afternoon flight to Prince George; connecting with the evening flight to Vancouver."

"For God's sake, stop pacing up and down. You're driving me crazy. Please sit and talk to me," he yelled.

Laura stopped and faced Sean while he continued.

"So that's it. You're not willing to discuss this? You've made up your mind for both of us. What gives you the right to decide what is best for me? What gives you the right to decide for me, whether or not I should compromise in order to save our marriage? Laura, I love you, I want us to work this out. If I didn't notice how unhappy you were, I'm sorry. But you had a responsibility in this marriage too, to open up to me, and let me know what you're feeling. Tell me it's not too late and we'll work on this," Sean pleaded.

Laura lowered her eyes to the floor, "I'm sorry. It's too late."

"Too late ..." Sean echoed.

Laura glanced up at Sean, and looked away quickly. Something in her eyes turned his stomach over.

Then he knew. "Laura?"

Laura continued to stare at the floor. Sean stood and asked the question he dreaded: "Who is he?"

Laura looked up at him and held his gaze. "You don't know him, Sean," she answered.

Sean's body stiffened and his head started to spin. He grabbed Laura by the arm and screamed at her. "Who is he, Laura—who is he?"

Laura began to cry and tried to pull away. "You're hurting me … you're hurting my arm."

Realizing what he was doing, Sean let go and backed away. "I guess it doesn't really matter, does it?" With a dull voice of acceptance, he continued. "You've made all the decisions here. You've worked it all out, including replacing me with another man."

"I'm sorry," Laura said, weakly.

Sean strode out of the room. Without turning around he addressed Laura for the last time: "I want you to leave. I want you out of this house right now."

He slammed the door to his study and shut out the world.

Sean felt chilled. The sun disappeared behind the hills to the west. His feet were sloshing around in his mud-filled boots and his pants were damp from his tumble in the mud. Rounding the bottom of a hill, the path started to rise up to the left. He knew once he made the crest, the cabin clearing was only fifty meters away. He'd left the Tuya River one kilometer back and followed a stream that emptied into the river. That stream ran beside his cabin.

Almost there.

Sean felt excited. For the first time in years he was retreating to the cabin without a work schedule. He thought of his woodstove all set to light. He could smell the coffee and feel its warmth when he cupped his mug. It'll take a while for the cabin to warm up. He envisioned himself wrapped in a blanket, curled up in the rocking chair close to the woodstove, engrossed in a good book. Sean loved to read by kerosene lamp. The smell of the oil and the shadows it cast brought back familiar memories of times spent at the cabin with his grandfather.

He stopped to catch his breath at the top of the hill, and thought he could smell smoke. A quirky smile curled the corner of his lip. His little fantasies were playing a reality game with his senses. Sean could see the clearing through the trees and hurried through them to the open meadow. The cabin sat beyond. He stopped short in his tracks. *What the ...?*

Smoke swirled from the chimney. It was almost dusk. Sean could see a kerosene lamp burning on the table in the picture window. A well-used path led to the back of the cabin. Sean crossed the clearing quickly. He noted a notched tree branch standing up in the foot of remaining snow. He stealthily followed the path around to the back of the cabin. Most of his hard-earned firewood was gone from the overhang, with the reserve in the woodshed completely gone. All of this indicated to Sean that whoever was in the cabin had been there a long time. The chopping block with the axe leaned against it drew him closer. *Is that blood splattered on them? What the hell is going on here?*

He'd heard of squatters moving into cabins for the winter. They usually left them in shambles in the spring. He circled back to the front of the cabin cautiously, and held himself back from storming in the door. He didn't know what to expect or how many people might be inside. *They might have guns and are laying in wait.*

Sean dropped his backpack and grasped the defender tighter and snuck up onto the porch to peek through the window. He slowly raised his head and peered inside. The cabin appeared to be empty. He stretched his head to look into the corners of the one-room cabin. *Nobody.*

He felt like a pepping tom. *Give your head a shake. This is your cabin.*

Sean noticed the cabin interior. It was decorated with curtains, doilies, and tablecloths, giving the cabin a feminine touch—Laura's touch. Whoever the intruders were, they'd taken liberties with personal belongings that weren't theirs. Filled with a sudden rage, Sean jumped up and raced along the porch. He threw open the door and burst into the cabin.

What he saw next stopped him cold.

Chapter 21

March 17th, North Vancouver

"Hmpff ..."

At the sound of his wife's voice, Robert Carr looked over the edge of his newspaper. Sandra peered through the living room curtains. Other than the slight raise of her eyebrows, her face remained expressionless.

"What are you looking at, honey?" The doorbell rang as he spoke.

"We have a visitor," she said dryly.

He watched his wife walk to the front door and open it. "Hello, Sandra."

Robert recognized the voice of his ex-son-in-law immediately and put down his paper.

His wife nodded. "Colin."

"Uh ... may I come in for a moment? I would like to talk with you and Robert."

Sandra stood back from the door and gestured him into the foyer. She led Colin into the living room. Robert couldn't believe Colin would come to the house, especially without calling first. He had talked to Colin on the phone a couple of times after their daughter, Georgia went missing, but hadn't seen him since before Colin left Georgia the previous May. He stared for a moment at Colin and stood up.

"Robert," Colin said, moving towards him, extending his hand in greeting.

Robert ignored his hand and gestured towards an armchair. "Sit down, Colin."

"Thank you."

Sandra joined Robert by the couch and they all sat down. He felt the tension in the room, but stayed silent, waiting for Colin to talk.

"You've both been through a lot, how are you doing?" Colin asked.

"We're coping," Robert said. Colin's words sounded stilted, completely insincere.

Colin nodded. "I would like to offer my help to you both in any way I can."

"Help? In what way?" Robert asked.

"Well, to start, my lawyer's services to help settle Georgia's legal matters," he stated, uneasily.

Robert stared hard at Colin for a moment, searching for the right words. "That's kind of you. However, the only legal matters of Georgia's that may concern you are the condo and furnishings, which she has left in a will to her brother. You signed the condo over to her in the separation agreement. My own lawyer has that well in hand." Robert noted the change of color in Colin's face.

"May I ask whether your lawyer has applied for a certificate of death?" Colin asked.

Sandra let out a gasp and Robert felt a sudden anger, but he repressed it. "As a lawyer, I'm sure you know it takes seven years to obtain a death certificate for a missing person."

"Under normal circumstances ... yes. But these are special circumstances. Since, uh ... foul play is suspected, an application can be presented to the courts now. Georgia's legal affairs can't be settled without a death certificate."

Robert was well aware of this from talks with his own lawyer, but his family had no intention of pursuing it at this point. It was all too fresh, too raw, and Sandra still hadn't come to terms with the loss of their daughter. No one in his family felt the need to deal with such finality this early on. It had only been four and half months. He stole a glance at his wife. He could see the tears forming in her eyes.

"I really do think it would be best for everyone involved," Colin continued.

"How so?" Robert asked.

"This has been hard on all of us. I think we need to move forward with our lives."

Sandra sat stiff and silent, as she had the whole time. Robert gave Colin a steely-eyed glare and responded in a quiet, but firm voice.

"Somehow, I get the feeling what you really mean is that you need to move forward with your life. I don't see what Georgia's personal affairs have to do with that."

Colin shifted uneasily in his chair, glancing from one to the other.

"I really am sorry for all that has happened and I know this is a delicate matter. This situation has been hard on my family as well. However, the fact remains that I have a new family and I have to look to the future. I'm under pressure to do what is right for them." Colin paused. "I need a death certificate, so I can legally remarry and give our baby my name."

"You bastard," Sandra yelled, jumping up. "Need we remind you Georgia was also carrying your baby? The only reason my daughter ended up in a situation that cost her life, and that of our grandchild, is because you had an affair with that woman. I don't give a damn about the pressures put on you by her or your bastard baby." Sandra charged out of the room, leaving Robert to deal with Colin, who by this time was standing and shifting uncomfortably from one foot to the other.

"I'm sorry, Robert. I didn't mean to upset Sandra. I'm sure as a man, you can understand my situation."

Robert was seething, not only for Colin's tactlessness, but for his cool arrogance. Colin presented himself as though he had every right to be here making his demands. Robert stood and headed straight to the foyer.

"You're an insensitive ass, Colin. There's no way you'll gain any sympathy from this family."

He opened the door but stood in Colin's way so he couldn't leave. "I could pop you one right now, but I won't because my wife is upset enough and you aren't worth the damage it would do to my arthritic hand," Robert hissed through his teeth.

He stepped away from the door and Colin scurried out, without as much as a word.

"Goodbye, asshole." Robert slammed the door behind him as hard as he could.

Two weeks later, Robert received papers from Colin's lawyer. They stated that even though Georgia was legally separated from Colin, he was still her legal husband. He had the right to apply to the court for a certificate of death. The date was set for early May. Included with the notice of his application was a writ of claim against Georgia's will.

I knew it. There lies the real reason for your visit, you bastard.

The document stated that as Georgia's legal husband, Colin was entitled to have the condo and contents revert back to him. The facts were, he had made mortgage payments during their marriage, paid a share during their separation, and paid off the balance when they signed the separation papers.

Like I said, a fucking asshole through and through.

Robert locked the papers in his desk in the study. He didn't want Sandra to see them and experience any more pain.

I should've popped you when I had the chance.

... change is the constant, the signal for rebirth, the egg of the phoenix.

Christina Baldwin

Chapter 22

The sun fell behind the trees, and the filtered rays of light reflecting through the evergreens disappeared. I'd gathered more pitch for my wound, paying careful attention to pick only the light colored pieces. I made my way behind the cabin, favoring my sore ankle. It had been four days since my accident. But my ankle was quite swollen and there was some weeping from the wound. Kaela was down in sleep until her next feeding. With no choice but to leave her alone in the cabin, my times away to do chores such as this were timed and kept to a minimum.

My eyes took in the last of the cut wood and my thoughts wandered. Food supplies were running low. Soon, a decision would have to be made about when to leave the cabin. Once the snow melted, and the days were warmer, we'd leave. This notion and all that it meant distracted me and lost in thought; I opened the back door and stepped inside.

Instant shock took hold and I dropped my basket of pitch. The only sound to be heard was the hard blebs hitting the wooden floor, and the broken pieces bouncing and skittering around the room.

I gasped at the sight of a man standing by the open front door, his filthy clothes and rubber boots dripping mud on the floor. The worst of it was his face. His mud caked features made him look deranged. He stood staring at Kaela on the bed. The sudden appearance of this stranger shocked me to the point that the words he spoke didn't register. He could be one of the kidnappers. It had been so long since I'd seen them, and this man was unrecognizable in his disheveled state. Maternal instinct took over and I limped over to the bed swept my baby up and held her tight to my chest. I backed up towards the rear door, reaching backwards for the latch. I was about to fling the door open when his words broke through my fear. He spoke quietly, but firmly.

"Who are you? What are you doing in my cabin?"

That stopped me dead in my tracks. I stared at him with my mouth open.

"I asked who you are. And what are you doing using Laura's things?"

He stared at my hand on the latch. I let go of the latch and wrapped my arm protectively across Kaela. There was no way I could out-run him. My body shook. "Your cabin? It's your cabin?"

He stared at me, looking perplexed. "Yes ... it's mine. You ... you look familiar," he stammered. "Who are you?"

"Georgia Charles, and this is my daughter, Kaela,"

He slapped his forehead. "Of course, you're the woman in the newspaper," he said, mumbling an afterthought, "But you're dead."

Raising an eyebrow, a rueful smile tugged at the corners of my mouth, although my heart still pounded. "I ... don't think so ... unless you know something I don't."

He returned the smile and replied in a softer voice. "I'm sorry. That was a stupid thing to say. How did you get here?"

"I ... umm ..." I couldn't believe I was actually talking to an adult, and he didn't look so crazy now he'd calmed down. The words poured out of me. "I escaped two men and got lost ... well, first I was kidnapped in Whitehorse ... it snowed and ..." I took a deep breath. "They were bank robbers and stole the miner's payroll ..." Once I started, I couldn't stop. "The weather trapped me here ... see, they got a flat tire and I ran." It hit me that everything I was saying was jumbled and didn't make any sense. "... and so, here I am." I shrugged and shut up.

We stared at each other a moment. Thoughts washed over me from disbelief that he was real to maybe he was another vision. I stifled a hysterical laugh. *Why would a spirit appear in such a freaky state?* My body started to shake and tears slid from my eyes.

The stranger came over to gently place his hand on my arm. After I slightly backed away, he gestured. "Here ... sit in the rocker."

Startled by all the pandemonium, Kaela protested loudly.

"Now, that's quite a story," he said softly, smiling down at me.

"I can't believe I did that. To have a real person to talk to after all this time, I couldn't get my thoughts together." I started to rock my wailing daughter. "Poor Kaela, she's not used to this much noise."

As I sat rocking my wailing daughter, the man sat down at the table.

"Oh my God," he said, sitting forward. "You had your baby here in the cabin, all alone?"

"Yes, I did."

"That's unbelievable. You must have been scared to death."

"I was lucky. All went well," I said. I decided not to tell him about my spirit guide. "So, you own this cabin," I changed the subject. "This is so ironic. When you burst in, I was thinking about the owners and how I'd have to find them when I left here. By the way, in all the commotion, I don't think you gave me your name."

"You're right, I didn't. I was too busy establishing ownership." He smiled. "My name is Sean … Sean Dixon."

"The author?" I asked, incredulous.

"Yes, that Sean Dixon."

Looking him up and down, with his wet, muddy appearance, I started to laugh. "Who knew? You don't look much like the person on the back of your covers."

"So, you've read my books, have you?"

"Yes, but I have to admit that I hadn't read your works until I found them in your bookcase." I nodded towards the collection.

Sean snorted. "A captive audience. Now there's a new way to gain a reader."

"Tell me something, Sean Dixon. Why are you covered from head to toe with mud? And look what you did to my clean floor." As soon as the words were out of my mouth, I realized what I'd said.

"Your floor?" Sean asked with raised eyebrows. "I guess I have made a right mess of it, haven't I? To answer your question, my truck became stuck in the mud and I had to hike along the road knee-high in slime. I was attacked by a couple of blue jays and fell face first into the gooey muck."

We shared an awkward laugh.

"How long do you think it will before spring break-up is over?" I asked, soberly.

"About three weeks. My truck isn't going any-where until then."

My face clouded over in disappointment.

Sean appeared to pick up on my emotions. "I know you'd like to get out sooner now you've been found. Any other time of year, we'd leave tomorrow. I'm sorry."

"I'm just anxious to get notice to my family that I'm alive and well. Will you take Kaela and me out as soon as possible?"

"Of course. If the weather stays like this, we might be able to leave sooner. It's really all about when the grader can safely work the roads. I was lucky to make it in as far as I did."

My eyes glistened at the realization that this man was my savior. He could get me back to my family.

"Thank you," I whispered. I stood and placed a sleeping Kaela on the bed.

Sean watched me and shook his head.

"I don't know how you survived here—physically, mentally, emotionally, the whole thing. But we'll have a few days to talk about it all. Right now, I think a bath and change of clothes are in order for me."

"There's hot water in the large pot on the stove, and the washtub is under the bed. And I'm sorry I used your wife's things. I was trying to make the cabin as homey as I could."

"My ex-wife and don't worry about it. I thought you were a squatter and had a husband around here somewhere, and I felt violated. If I frightened you, I'm sorry."

"Totally understandable." I limped my way to the trunk for a clean towel.

"What did you do to your leg? You're wincing. Are you in pain?

"I had an accident chopping wood with the axe. Once you've had your bath, I'll clean it and dress it for the night."

"That's unfortunate. I'd like to take a look when you dress it."

I turned around to hand him the towel as he removed his sweatshirt. I stood there, watching him, not sure what to do or where to look. His eyes caught mine and he glanced away quickly, probably as embarrassed as I. This man was a complete stranger and I was watching him undress. I could feel my face color.

"Well, this is awkward, isn't it?" he said.

"If it were daylight, I'd sit on the porch. Uh … I could sit in the rocker and read until you're finished, if that's okay?" I stammered.

"Of course. Here let me move it closer to the stove for you."

"By the way, there's no soap."

The man headed to the front deck and returned carrying a backpack. 'I forgot I'd left this out there." He fumbled around in a side pocket and pulled out some bars of soap. "I knew I was out at the cabin." He opened one.

I stared at the bar of soap and moved closer. My eyes never left it. "Can I smell it?"

He looked surprised, but obliged me.

I held it to my nose. "Mmm … so fresh and clean. Smells like spring flowers." I wanted to kick him out of the cabin and lather myself with

242

the soap. After I handed it back to him, I could still smell it on my hands.

"I understand. Such a small thing that becomes a big issue when it's not available."

I grabbed a book and settled down with my back to him. I don't remember what I read. The odour of soap and the sound of splashing water behind me brought to mind the vision of a naked man standing in a tin basin … a clean-smelling, attractive, naked man. I found myself wondering if the real thing was as good as my image.

"Oh boy," I muttered, chastising myself for my thoughts.

"Did you say something?" he asked.

"Uh … just reading aloud." I suspected that the next few weeks of living in one room with a stranger, who was also an attractive male, could prove challenging if not a little weird.

After his bath, I watched as he pulled food-stuffs from his backpack. My mouth watered at the sight of apples, oranges, fresh mushrooms and garlic cloves. A plastic insulated pack came next with frozen steaks, pork chops, and bacon.

"Oh my God," I cried out.

Sean gave me a studying glance. "What's mine is yours. We'll share it. Here, catch." Sean threw an apple my way. I caught it in one hand. I turned it over and over, savoring the moment. About to take a bite, I was overcome with guilt.

"Maybe we should take an inventory first. I had planned on leaving in about two weeks. I estimated the last of the food would take me to three weeks. But with two of us sharing it, it will be tight."

"Don't worry about it. We can fish, and there are more supplies in the truck. I'll hike out and carry them in. I have more vegies and fruit. If we don't have enough food, one apple won't save us anyway. Enjoy it."

For the next ten minutes, I concentrated on that juicy, green Granny Smith apple, always my favorite. Every bite teased my taste buds, as I slowly chewed and depleted the goodness from each morsel, using the back of my hand to wipe away the combined juices of the apple and saliva that trickled from the corners of my mouth. Sean watched with an amused smile.

"Unless you intend to eat the core as well, I think you ate all there is to eat."

"You're right. That was the most delicious apple I ever ate," I said, wiping my mouth one last time with my sleeve.

"I know I left the cabin well stocked, but I don't know how you managed to ration the food for so long. You must have been lacking a lot nutritionally, especially being pregnant."

"I was able to fish, except during January and February, and I had a vitamin supplement until last month."

I told Sean about my adventure with the caribou. "Only last week, I made jerky to preserve the remainder.

"I'm amazed. Where did you learn how to survive in the wilderness?"

"From this …," I picked up the survival book on the trunk "… and you. Between the book and all the tools and supplies you had here, I got lucky."

"It wasn't only luck. You're one smart lady to have pulled it off."

I found myself blushing again as his admiring eyes stared at me. I turned to place the book back on the trunk to hide my embarrassment.

"I left a note with my keys in the truck for the grader operator. I asked him to tow my truck and park it by the path to the cabin. In about two weeks I'll hike back to my truck for the remainder of my supplies and tape an SOS sign to the window. I'll let him know you're here; ask him to radio the Royal Canadian Mounted Police (RCMP), as well as my friend Tom Glass. He's a helicopter pilot for the mines around here. He can fly in and get us.

"Sounds good to me." Once again, my eyes watered, knowing my rescue was at hand.

"So, what do you say we do an inventory and then I'm going to cook you a steak with fresh garlic and mushrooms?"

"Pinch me so I know this isn't a dream."

Dinner was everything I expected it to be. As I started to clean up, my new roommate insisted I sit down. My ankle was killing me and I welcomed the opportunity to sit and watch him clear the table and wash the dishes.

When Sean was finished, I heated some water and gathered my first aid items.

"Let me do that for you. You sit on the couch and put your leg up on the trunk."

A strange feeling passed over me. Not used to having someone do things for me, it felt good to let someone else take over, which totally contradicted my other thought that I'd become pretty independent these past months and could do it myself. I gave in to the pain and let Sean take over.

He carefully removed the bandages and held up a pine bleb. "What's this?"

"Pitch from a pine tree. It's supposed to fight infection." He gently removed the rest of the blebs. The swelling was worse, but the cut seemed to be healing except a couple of spots where it was moist and weeping. A whistle escaped his lips. "When did you do this?"

"Four days ago."

"There's some infection going on, but it's the swelling that's bad. I would say it's because you need to be off of this leg with it up on a pillow. You also need some ice on it."

"My daily chores and my baby's needs keep me on my feet constantly. Not much time for sitting, I'm afraid, and certainly no ice."

"You're lucky I showed up when I did. This wound looks serious. Well, I'm here now. I suggest you spend the next few days relaxing with this leg up. I'll take over the chores. You concentrate on your baby and getting this swelling down." He looked over my first aid items.

"I used the eye dropper to cleanse the open wound, but it appears to be closing up now."

Sean picked up the jar of cinnamon and cloves. "And these?"

"Those are for the pain. After I clean it, I sprinkle some on the wound. It really works."

He cleansed the wound and covered it with the spices. The whole time he worked, he'd glance up at me with a puzzled look on his face. "I think we should cover it with a piece of gauze but leave it loose to air while you're sitting. I'll be right back." He grabbed a plastic bag and left the cabin, only to return with it full of snow. He wrapped it in a towel and placed it on my wound.

"I never thought about using snow. How stupid of me," I said, embarrassed.

"First of all, you're not stupid. A stupid person wouldn't have survived like you have. And second, you've been balancing a lot of balls. You can't think of everything."

Sean put away the first aid gear and poured us each a cup of coffee. He sat in the rocking chair opposite me and placed his feet up on the trunk beside mine. "How'd you know how to dress your wound with the pitch and the spices?"

I opened my mouth to speak and shut it again.

No way would I tell him about Nonnock, my native spirit. He'd think I'd gone mad. "Uh … I think it was in a book somewhere in your library about native lore." My hand gave a half-hearted wave towards his collection.

He frowned. "Really? I don't remember having a book on native remedies. I do remember my grandfather using pine pitch for cuts when I was a kid."

In an attempt to distract him, I changed the subject. "Is your grandfather native?"

"Yes, Tahltan. My father is too, and my mother's white."

"Is he from the Wolf clan or the Crow?"

Sean looked surprised. "The Crow. You seem to know a lot about the Tahltan."

Shut up, girlie. I chastised myself for saying too much. "Not really, read that in a book, too. But, I have a question for you that's been nagging at me all winter. Why was the cabin so well-stocked with wood and supplies?"

"That's easy. For the past four years I came here every spring to write one of my series books. Usually I spend winter in my condo in Yaletown, doing research for my book. I'd come to Dease Lake in the early spring to my cottage and put the outline together. I move here to the cabin after break-up, and spend three months putting it all together. The rest of the time, while my publishers put the book to bed, I relaxed and stocked the cabin for the next spring."

"Lucky for me." I shifted my leg on the pillow. "You mentioned something about me being in the newspaper. What did they say?"

"It was an article in the local paper calling off the search for you because of bad weather conditions. They knew you weren't in the accident, but they had no idea what happened to you."

My body went rigid. "Accident ... what accident?"

"Of course, you wouldn't know anything about that, would you? They found the van south of Dease Lake, the day after you escaped. The police believed the van went off the road because of the blizzard. They suggested foul play some-where between Whitehorse and Dease Lake. With the snow storm lasting as long as it did, no one expected to find your remains until spring thaw, if ever."

I winced and shuddered at the prospect of what might have been. "And what about my kid-nappers? Did they get away?"

Sean smacked his hand against his forehead. "Oh man ... what a dummy I am. They both died in the accident. You had no way of knowing that either."

"They died?" I leaned my head back onto the couch. "When I think back to those first few weeks here. I was so scared they would find me ... and all this time they were dead." All I could do was shake my head in disbelief.

"If you had still been with them, you and Kaela probably would have died in that accident too," Sean added.

"If I'd still been with them, they probably would have found their uncle's cabin and I'd be buried in the forest somewhere. I guess when I escaped they decided to get out of here, assum-ing I wouldn't make it out."

"Either way, you were lucky to have escaped."

"It's certainly a relief not to have the worry about them when we get out of here. That would have been my next fear that they would come looking for me again."

"You won't have to worry about that now. How's the leg feel?"

"Better. Taking my weight off of it is probably a good idea."

Bedtime brought back the awkwardness we felt earlier. I insisted Sean have his bed back, but he wouldn't hear of it.

"You can't sleep on the couch. There isn't enough room for the baby and you," he said.

"I thought we could make a bed for Kaela in one of the drawers, and place it on the trunk beside the couch."

"Absolutely not. When the fire dies down in the early hours, she needs your warmth. You two take the bed and I'll sleep on the couch. I've fallen asleep on that old thing many times and been more than comfortable."

"Okay, if you're sure."

"I am, and tomorrow, I'll hang the tarp between the bed and the couch to give you some privacy."

"One more thing," I added, feeling that familiar flush rising. "There's a bucket by the bed in case I need to get up in the night. A visit to the outhouse in the dark is one fear I haven't conquered."

"With good reason." Sean chuckled.

As I tossed and turned that night, excited at the prospect that soon I'd be going home, I vowed to wait until morning should nature call during the night. The thought of peeing in a bucket behind a curtain was humiliating enough. To do so without any privacy at all wasn't something I was willing to do.

Chapter 23

The next few days passed like a surreal dream. Sean fell into the routine of doing the chores while I rested. He fed the woodstove and cut some firewood from the dead and fallen trees in the forest. He hauled the water from the stream as usual for him, and became the chef and dish-washer! I sensed his love for the cabin and how this remote lifestyle was natural to him.

Knowing that my well-being was in the hands of a knowledgeable and experienced outdoors-man, I was able to let my survival fears go. My stress level dropped and the constant tension I carried eased and exhaustion took over. Sleep breeds sleep. I found myself napping most of the time while Kaela slept. My sleep pattern eased my exhaustion and I began to relax and enjoy the spring days.

Sean made a cradle for Kaela to sleep in during the day. It was waist high, and I spent time sitting on the porch with my leg raised, watching her sleep in the warmth of the sun. We were just pre-bug season which allowed for pleasant relaxation in the warm, open air.

On the eve of the third day, he dressed my wound. "There's still a little infection, but the swelling has gone down some."

"The pain has eased too," I said.

'That's because you've had your weight off of it. I think a couple of more days will make all the difference."

We were sitting on the bench on the front porch enjoying the evening song of the birds.

"I love listening to the birds and it's a sure sign of spring when they return," I mused. "Except a raven I called Feathers, stayed all winter. That surprised me."

"Ravens stay in the north. They don't migrate south," Sean said.

"Really? I didn't know. He seemed to be alone and always around me when I was out walking or doing chores," I said, chuckling. "I called him my protector."

"The ravens are very special to the indigenous people. Some believe they can transform into other dimensions and shape shift. They're considered highly intelligent and raven spirit guides will seek out only those who they believe are intelligent enough to know their secrets," Sean paused, before continuing, "I think Feathers chose well."

Our eyes locked and I felt my face redden. I broke our stare and stared out at the meadow. "Thank you, but he never shape changed or spoke to me … at least not in a language I could understand."

"In time, he may have."

I was uncomfortable with the compliments Sean had been showering me with the past few days. I knew I was vulnerable to any kind of attention, especially male praise and it didn't help that he was an attractive, virile man. *Change the subject, girlie.*

"I noticed you have a pretty skookum generator in the tool shed. Isn't it a little overkill for two lights?"

Sean laughed. "A little. When I'm here in the summer I have a microwave and a coffee maker with me. My friend, Tom flies all my supplies in and out for me. The model I bought is an inverter generator, which I need to charge my laptop for writing."

'Ah … makes sense. So how many hours do you get out of a full tank?"

"About twenty. I'm not well-stocked for this trip in because I only planned on staying until after spring break-up and Tom's been away on a family trip back east for the winter. I think he's due back in a couple of days."

"Lucky me that you chose to come since your time here is so short."

"I'm only leaving because I have some business to take care of in Vancouver. I plan on coming back for the summer." Sean rose to sit on the railing facing me, his long legs stretched out in front of him.

My gaze followed his well-worn cowboy boots, up his skinny jeans to his narrow hips, and above to his turquoise t-shirt, snug across his broad chest and shoulders. The color enhanced his dark brown eyes and shoulder length dark hair. My stare focused on his face, taking in his strong cheek bones, straight nose and full lips. Our eyes locked and his lips curled into an amused smile. Embarrassed that he'd caught me checking him out, I shifted my eyes back to the meadow. *Good grief, girlie. You made that pretty obvious. No fear, he'd be interested in me, other than my survival story. Ratty hair, ragged finger nails, stained clothing, no make-up ... one ugly chick. At least I smell clean.* In spite of what I thought of my appearance, at least being able to wash my hair and body with soap made me feel human again. He even let me share his hair brush after seeing me comb my hair with a fork.

The end of Sean's first week arrived and the constant sunny days melted the snow. The game trails became bare, allowing us to travel a little upstream to the deeper fishponds. My ankle was healing now, the wound closed. I could walk slowly with a slight limp and minimal ache. The exercise felt great. I'd fashioned a bunting bag of sorts from an old sleeping bag for Kaela and Sean made a leather harness for me to carry her on my chest.

That night, Sean returned with water from the stream and grabbed my hand, pulling me onto the porch. "Come and see the northern lights. They're spectacular tonight."

We sat on the deck and I was comfortable with the knowledge that I could appreciate this colorful display of nature and not feel overwhelmed.

"When I first got here, everything scared me."

Sean studied me for a moment. "You'd experienced quite an ordeal by the time you found the cabin, it's understandable."

"Initially, yes. But even when I knew the kidnappers weren't coming, I was scared. The big sky, the vastness and remoteness of the area, the cry of the wolves; all of it ... even the unknown."

"You were out of your comfort zone."

"That's true. You must find it hard to understand. I mean you're so at home here at the cabin and on the land. It fits you."

"I grew up in this part of the country and my grandfather taught me a lot about the land. When I went to the city to study journalism, I remember how strange it felt. There were moments when I felt scared."

He made me smile. "Your comfort zone was challenged. Once I understood that nature could protect me, feed me, and heal me, my fears started to go. There's spirituality here." *Damn! I'm saying too much again.*

Sean gave me a puzzled look. "You've learned a lot in your short time here. You're thinking and talking like a Tahltan."

It was my turn to study Sean. He was more than a handsome man; he was intelligent, caring, and definitely spiritual. *But could I trust him? Could I tell him about Nonnock?* In spite of what he'd said about Feathers, my trust of late had been challenged too much. I'd learned to depend on myself and my own instincts. My native spirit would remain my secret. Trust came from a place I wasn't ready to visit.

I stood to stretch a cramp in my leg. "My time here alone was probably much like a young brave being sent out in the forest to find his spirit animal. A scary experience, but you either embrace it and come through all the better for it or you perish." Sean's eyebrows shot up. *Uh-oh, I might have made it worse. Shut up and change the subject.* "Since you've been here, I haven't seen Feathers."

"Perhaps he decided to turn his role of protector over to me." He reached out and brushed the hair from my eyes, warming me with a tender look. My body involuntarily stiffened. Immediately, his hand dropped and his face hardened and flushed with embarrassment. He stood and turned to face the meadow.

I stared at his back, not knowing what to say next. The awkwardness of the first few days returned and our moment of easy conversation faded. I left him standing there and spoke quietly over my shoulder as I stepped back into the cabin. "Good night."

He never answered.

A few days later, as the awkwardness eased, over dinner he asked me about my marriage. "Where'd you meet your ex-husband?"

"At the library where I worked part-time. I was in college and he was a law student. One day he came to the library to do some research because he was in a hurry and it was closer than the university law library. I helped him and after that he stopped by more often. We dated for a year and were married."

"That must have been tough, with both of you attending school," Sean said.

"Colin's parents were rich. They paid for his schooling, but nothing else. They didn't want us to marry while we were still in school. Well, his mother Alice never wanted him to marry me. I wasn't 'monied' you see.

"So how did you manage?"

I picked up our plates and cleared the table, poured us each a coffee and sat back down. "I quit school and worked full-time at the library, working my way up to Assistant Librarian. We needed my job to carry us through until he'd finished school and secured a job at a law firm. He had a trust fund from his grandfather that would kick in at thirty years of age. Just as his trust was to kick in, he left me for his pregnant law assistant."

Sean looked shocked. "Nice guy. What about your pregnancy."

"We didn't know I was pregnant at the time. I didn't learn about the baby until I went to Whitehorse to visit my friend, Marion. By that time I was five months along."

"So he didn't know you were pregnant when you disappeared?"

Now that was the question of all questions. "I … don't know. Marion knew. She must have told my family." I sat there dumb-founded. The baby could be more of a surprise than ever when we returned. "Your turn … how'd you meet Laura?"

"We met at a press conference I was covering for my paper. She worked for a politician we were following. She was tall, blond, blue-eyed and outgoing. To this small town native boy, she represented excitement and an introduction to the city night-life I'd never known before. Only, we got married three months later, way too young and miles apart in our thinking. We weren't thinking."

We moved over to the couch with our coffee and I stretched out my aching ankle on the coffee table.

"Did she like it here at the cabin?" I asked, quite innocently.

Sean laughed. "Hell no. She was a city girl. The cabin disgusted her. I thought she'd settled in at Dease Lake when we were living there. She worked part-time as a teacher, while I wrote my first novel. She took more and more trips away to the city to see family … or so I thought. One day, she said she was leaving, wanted a divorce and had a new man." He took our cups to the sink and started washing the dishes.

"You're still bitter."

He turned and leaned against the counter, wiping his soapy hands on his jeans. "Actually, I'm not. I didn't allow myself to examine what went wrong. Instead, I threw myself into a four book series. That's what this trip this summer was for. Time off and release time. But I realize these past two weeks here that it never would have worked with us. We were too different."

"Sometimes love isn't enough. It takes more than that to make a relationship work."

Sean sat down again. "That's true. We didn't know each other when we got married. We never discussed a game plan of what I wanted, what she wanted, where we were headed together. I know I had expectations of her role in my life and never stopped to ask her if she had the same."

"Sounds like our marriage. The one thing I've learned here is that I played a role in my marriage break-up. Yes, Colin cheated and then left me feeling I wasn't good enough. But it was the false expectations on both our parts that did us in."

We spent a couple of hours that evening discussing our relationships and what we hoped to have learned from them. The realization came that these were conversations I could never have with Colin. "Thank you," I said.

His forehead creased, "For what?"

"For not only respecting my opinions, but acknowledging I have some."

"Why wouldn't I? You're an intelligent woman." His eyes held mine, and I looked away shyly.

"Colin never let me forget that he finished university and went to law school, and I dropped out."

"Only to support him until his trust fund kicked in. What an arrogant ass!" Sean said, angrily. He continued, "I know someone who has their masters degree, but in everyday life and socially, he's totally inept. Being book smart is one thing, being intelligent is quite another."

Our eyes locked again, and we both smiled. "I should be thanking you," Sean added.

"Me? Why?" This sudden revelation surprised me.

"Because you're a city girl, who lacking the knowledge and skills to live in nature during the worst time of the year, adapted and, against all odds, survived. I don't think Laura would have survived and that isn't said as a condemnation. She couldn't adapt to spending the weekend here. I should have recognized our differences then if not before."

A comfortable camaraderie had sprung up between us again. My heart started to pound and I knew this man was special. He moved me, attracted me, touched my soul ... and that scared the hell out of me.

Chapter 24

Two weeks after Sean arrived; he decided to go to the truck for the remainder of his supplies. I paced around the cabin the night before he planned to leave. He leaned against the kitchen counter, watching me.

"Take us with you," I begged.

"I don't think that's a good idea. I figure it should take me four hours there and back.

"I can walk that long."

"I'm sure you can, but with your injury you'll slow me down, and it's a long time for you to be out in the woods with Kaela. I'm not concerned with the hike along the path, but what if the road is soft?"

"What's a little mud?"

"This isn't ordinary mud. It's like clay and clings to your feet. You feel like you're dragging heavy weights.

"I could wait by the roadside for you to return from the truck."

Sean stared at me. "Don't you think it would be safer for Kaela right here in the cabin?"

"I know you're right, but I don't think I could stand being alone again." I whimpered, knowing how pathetic I sounded.

His face began to soften. He came over and put his arms around me. "You've been so strong for so long. Half a day more is all I'm asking. I'm coming back, Georgia, I promise."

It had been so long since I'd felt any human touch, other than baby Kaela's that I melted into his arms. My reserve let go and I reveled in the moment, accepting his strength and the security of his embrace. His smell intoxicated me and my senses experienced something else—his maleness.

Lifting my face up, as we stared into each other's eyes, his mouth found mine. I heard myself moan, and collapsing against his chest, I returned his kiss. My body felt weak and my head spun like a teenager discovering lust for the first time. It was over as quickly as it began. Sean let go of me and backed away. "I'm sorry."

"Sorry? Why? Don't you like the way I kiss?" I threw the remark at him half teasing, half serious.

"Quite the contrary." Sean gave me a crooked grin. "I'm not sorry about the kiss. I don't want to take advantage of your vulnerability right now."

"So ... my rescuer's also gallant," I retorted, flippantly, smiling back.

"Come on. Let's go watch the northern lights." Sean grabbed me by the hand and pulled me towards the door. This time the touch of his hand sent sparks racing through my body. *Boy, am I in trouble. I knew it would be a restless night for me.*

The next morning I watched him strut across the field to the trees. Before disappearing into the forest, he gave me a big smile and a thumb up. The morning passed quickly as I took on the daily chores once again. By eleven o'clock, the warm air turned chilly. The sky clouded over and became dark. Within twenty minutes, a hailstorm with stones the size of marbles began. It lasted for fifteen minutes before turning into a torrential downpour of rain.

While Kaela napped, I tried to write in my journal. I gave up and grabbed one of the few books in Sean's library that I hadn't yet read. But my mind kept wandering and wondering about Sean trudging through the rainstorm. I guessed the road would be a sea of mud. Sean was right about Kaela being better off here. I certainly felt grateful that she was warm and dry inside the cabin. The hours dragged by, and I started to worry. I peered out across the meadow. "Where are you?" Perhaps he took cover from the rain, hoping to wait out the storm. But visions of encounters with bears or injuring himself on slimy inclines crowded my mind.

As late afternoon turned to evening, I began pacing the cabin. Where was he? What took him so long?

I sat in the rocking chair with Kaela. "I knew we should have gone with him, sweet pea. If he's hurt, we'd be there."

Dusk turned to darkness and I lit the lantern, placing it on the table by the picture window. The rain stopped, but it didn't make sense that he would travel through the woods at night. Still, if he did, the kerosene lamp would help him find the clearing.

I bathed Kaela, fed her and put her to bed for the night. I found myself slipping out to the porch every few minutes, calling Sean's name.

A couple of hours after dark, I stood on the porch once again. I called for Sean to no avail. This is ridiculous. Call it a night. I decided to try one last time. "Sean … Sean …" I yelled into the darkness.

Turning back towards the open doorway, I heard something faint. I spun around and heard it again. "Sean, is that you?"

There it was again. It sounded like someone calling, but it was far away. "Sean, where are you?"

Deep in the woods across the clearing, I could see a light. It moved slowly towards me, getting brighter and brighter. Then I heard his voice. "Georgia … Georgia!"

I sprinted inside, grabbed the lantern off the table, and ran across the clearing as Sean reached the edge of the woods. I placed the lantern on the ground and ran straight into his arms, laughing and crying at the same time.

"I was so scared. I thought you were hurt or worse," I cried, clinging to him. He was soaking wet, but I didn't care.

"I told you I'd be back," Sean said softly, holding me tight, "Let's get back to the cabin and I'll tell you all about it. You're in for a surprise."

I looked at him expectantly. "What?"

Sean placed his finger on my lips. "Shush … later." He handed me the flashlight and he picked up the lantern.

He changed by the wood stove, shivering from the wet and cold. I waited patiently while he warmed himself by the fire. Finally, he settled on the couch with a hot cup of coffee and filled me in on his day.

"It was an easier hike out than I expected. I reached the truck as the hailstorm started. Wasn't it something?"

I nodded as he swung his long legs up onto the trunk.

"I decided to wait it out in the truck. Then the rain began and I thought maybe I could out wait that as well. You can imagine my dismay as time passed on and I watched the road turn into a sea of mud. Finally, I knew, rainstorm or not, I needed to start back to make it here before dark. As I was leaving, who should arrive? Jack Hill, the grader operator." Sean paused to sip his coffee. "Mmm … that tastes good."

"And?"

"He'd finished for the day and was going to head home early because of the downpour. But Sarah told him I came in early this year, and knowing the road condition, he decided to continue along to make sure I made it in okay."

Sean stopped to get up and refill his cup. My frustration built. He sure took his time to tell a story.

"We sat in my truck for another half an hour making a plan to get you out of here. Because of the weather conditions, Jack wanted me to go out with him and fly back in the chopper for you and Kaela. He knew I couldn't make it back before dark and he was concerned."

"So why didn't you go with him? It made better sense than hiking back in the mud and wet."

"Because he told me Tom Glass, the pilot, was away on mining business until tomorrow, and I knew the rescue helicopter would come from Prince George. That meant you would spend the night alone, and I promised I'd be back. I couldn't do that to you." I reached out and touched his arm. My throat tightened. "You could have been hurt out there in those conditions. Thank you."

Sean shrugged. "I know these woods, been in them my whole life. I finally convinced Jack I'd be all right. He lent me his heavy-duty flashlight and drove me to the path. I expect he's back in Dease Lake by now and the RCMP will be busy making plans to pay us a visit tomorrow."

I stared blankly at him. "Tomorrow … that means this is my last night here," I whispered, with a long look around the cabin, "I can't believe it." Tears welled up in my eyes.

"It must feel a little strange all right. Tomorrow will be a big day for you, Georgia. Maybe you should turn in and get a good night's sleep."

"Are you crazy? I won't sleep a wink. I'm too excited." I grabbed Sean's hand. "Stay up with me, please?"

He laughed. "Okay, but I bet you won't make it through the night, kiddo."

"We'll see. There's some stew on the stove. Come and eat."

A short time later, we were settled back on the couch.

"Tell me more about this cabin. I know it was your Grandfather's."

"Did I tell you this is native land?"

"No." *I know that but I'm not saying a word.*

"My grandfather was a full-blooded Tahltan native. This area was abundant in game and fish, and they traded their goods up and down the Pacific Coast with the Iskut. The Tahltans were quite prosperous. Grandpa married a white school teacher from Alberta, and they settled in Telegraph Creek. As he aged, he tired of the life, and when the gold rush hit in the Yukon, he decided to become a guide."

"But I thought the gold seekers came from Skagway, Alaska into the Yukon."

"Lots did, but not all the stampeders went to Skagway and over the passes. The Stikine River runs through the Alaska Panhandle and enters the sea at Wrangell. They took a secondary route on a steamer from Wrangell up to Telegraph Creek. From there, my grandpa guided them up the Tahltan River and cross-country to Teslin

Lake. They travelled the Teslin River downstream to where it joined the Yukon River at Carmacks."

"Your grandpa was the real deal. Part of the history and the lore."

"He loved the reserve lands around the Tuya River area. After my father went to college to study Engineering and my grandmother passed away, he retired to this land and built this cabin. The Tahltans believe this land to be spiritual."

"I can attest to that."

Sean gave me a puzzled look.

Oops. I pursed my lips and shut up.

"My father met my mother, a Caucasian woman as well, at college. They married and returned to Dease Lake. That's where I was born and raised." He stood up and went to re-fill the wood stove. I studied his profile. That long, straight nose and chiseled cheekbone definitely showed his heritage and added to his dark, brooding, virile looks,

Hmm ... definitely easy on the eyes. "That makes you one quarter Tahltan."

"Right. My father never had the love of the land like his father, but I inherited it from my grandfather. My parents moved back to the city when my Dad was offered a lucrative job, and they remain there to this day. They gave me the cottage in Dease Lake and this cabin.

"One thing I've been curious about all winter is the root cellar. It's only made of wood but nothing freezes. Nor is there ever any frost."

"That's because there are double walls made from wood slats two feet in depth, and they're filled with wood shavings," he rejoined me on the couch.

"Fascinating, a homemade refrigerator without a motor. Tell me the story behind the canned goods. I know why you stocked the cabin, but who did all the canning?"

"Huh … that's a bit sexist. How do you know I didn't can it all myself? I'm a pretty independent guy," Sean challenged, but I saw the glint in his eye.

I gave him a coy look. "Because you spent four years researching, writing, and travelling. Whenever would you find the time?"

"Ooh … safe answer. The truth is, when Laura left me I came here to lick my wounds. My neighbor and her friends in Dease Lake got together and made up care packages for me. They had my friend, Tom, fly the supplies in. It was all way too much for one person for the short stays I made, so it all went into the root cellar."

"Lucky for me you have such supportive friends. That's nice." Knowing I would be leaving, I gave a nostalgic look around the cabin. "I love this cabin. When I first arrived, I was so afraid of everything— the land, the animals and nature. Now that I know I'm leaving, I'm going to miss it."

"You're welcome to come back and visit anytime. I mean that."

"Thank you."

We stared silently at each other, caught in a moment I didn't want to end. Sean ran his fingers down my cheek to my lips. I began kissing them—our eyes still locked. His head came closer to mine. I sighed while he smothered my face with a series of gentle kisses. Finding my mouth, he brushed my lips softly at first, parting them slightly, then his kiss became more urgent until we grabbed each other and his tongue touched mine. I lost myself in a heat of passion I had never felt before. A cry escaped my lips as I felt his hot hand inside my shirt, cupping my breast. His fingers encircled my nipple and my head spun. His hand moved down and rested between my thighs, while mine searched until I found his heat. Our kisses became more frantic as we caressed each other. It wasn't until his hand slipped inside my jeans that my senses returned.

"No, Sean ... please, wait ..." I pulled his hand away.

Instantly, Sean stopped. He held me close to him and we were silent once more.

"I'm sorry," he muttered.

Pushing myself away from him, I placed my fingers on his lips. "Don't apologize. I want this as much as you. It's only that I'm ... well, the childbirth ... I'm not able."

"Oh, Jesus ... Georgia, I'm such a dope. Of course you can't."

I knew I wasn't being entirely honest with him, so I continued. "That's not all of it. I'm beginning to figure out who I am as a person, a woman and a mother. But ... as a lover ... well, I don't want to make the same mistakes I made with Colin. I'm not ready."

"I respect that. Casual sex has never been my style and I don't think it's yours either. You'll know when the time is right, and hopefully, I'll be there when you do."

Sean was right about something else too. I couldn't stay awake all night. About six in the morning, we awoke to the hungry cries of Kaela, still locked in each other's arms on the couch.

Chapter 25

The helicopter circled overhead, inspecting the clearing. It was a Delta six-seater. Sean told me it was Tom's 'baby'. The seats come out for carrying freight. Slowly, the big red bird descended. Hovering momentarily over the open field, it finally came to rest. The noise was deafening. Dirt and debris flew all around from the down draft created by the huge circulating rotor. Sean yelled something to me but it was lost in the din. The door opened and an officer of the Royal Canadian Mounted Police disembarked. He turned to help a middle-aged woman, carrying a doctor's bag, down from the helicopter. The pilot turned off the rotor and it slowly came to a stop. The noise level dropped quickly. Ducking their heads, all three ran across the clearing towards the cabin.

The sudden appearance of these people, combined with the noisy discord of the chopper, upset my balance. The months of being alone, willing myself to be strong for Kaela, came crashing down on me. These were people I could trust. It was their job to be in charge. I let my reserve go and became engulfed in emotional turmoil. Everything around me became surreal. My body shook and I heard myself cry out. "Oh … oh my …" My hands flew to my face. My knees buckled, and I felt Sean's arms support me. He led me to the bench on the porch and sat down with me. He rocked me back and forth in his arms while I sobbed.

"Mrs. Charles, I'm Dr. Lori Phillips."

I pulled myself up and turned to see the doctor kneeling beside me. She spoke softly, her face filled with kindness. She handed me a Kleenex to wipe my face and blow my nose.

"Thank you," I replied. "It was overwhelming to see the helicopter knowing help has finally arrived."

The doctor reached out and squeezed my hand. I looked up to see a huge man with deep-set brown eyes and a handle bar moustache standing behind the doctor.

"It's understandable ma'am, considering what you have been through. I'm Staff-Sergeant Leo Pratt, Dease Lake Detachment," he said, "Are you all right?"

"Yes, I'm fine, thanks."

Sean stood up and shook hands with the officer, "I'm Sean Dixon."

"Glad to meet you, sir," he replied.

Sean walked over to the cabin door where Tom Glass, the pilot, waited. The pilot patted Sean on the back and they exchanged a few words.

Dr. Phillips stood up and held her hand out to me as she addressed the men. "If you gentlemen would give us a few minutes alone, I would like to take Mrs. Charles into the cabin to examine her and her baby. Is that all right with you, Mrs. Charles?"

"Yes, but … I need to ask the Staff Sergeant something first. Please, did anyone contact my parents or my brother?"

"I notified the North Vancouver Detachment, ma'am. Your brother is off the base until tonight and they dispatched a car to your parent's home.

On our way here, my staff contacted us by radio. According to the neighbors, your parents flew to Arizona to spend Easter with your grandparents. If you could give us your grandparents' name and address, I'll call in to the office and have one of my officers contact the local Sheriff. They can dispatch some of their people."

"Their last name is Carr. The phone is listed under the name of John & Betty Carr in Chula, Arizona."

"Thank you. Tom, how about giving me a hand with the radio? The sooner we relay this information the better."

The doctor and I entered the cabin. I picked Kaela up from her cradle and placed her on the bed.

"Oh my Lord," Dr. Phillips said. "What a beautiful child. What's her name?"

"Kaela, her name is Kaela," I said, proudly.

"And she was born when?"

"February 14th, Valentine's Day."

The doctor stripped off Kaela's clothes and started an examination as I stoked up the woodstove. After taking her vitals, she gave her a complete check- up. Finally, she measured her length.

"She looks quite healthy. Everything appears to be normal. Do you know how long she was when she was born?" she asked.

"I didn't have a tape measure, so I cut a piece of fishing line the length of her body." I retrieved it from the dresser. "Here it is."

"Eighteen inches; she has grown two inches in eight weeks," she said, writing it down.

"Is that good?"

"Perfectly normal. Tell me, where did you learn to tie the cord off like that?"

"There's a wilderness survival guide in the bookcase. I studied the section on emergency childbirth. Does it look all right?" The long end of the cord had dried and dropped off. The piece in-between the surgical tape and her stomach was dried and black.

"It certainly does, for an amateur who looked it up in a book. The Obstetrician may need to perform some minor corrective surgery though." She gave me a studying stare. "I don't know how you coped with all of this, Mrs. Charles. Being stranded here alone was bad enough. But to give birth by yourself, it's... you are a brave woman. I am in awe."

"Well, I had some bad moments. In fact, there were plenty of them. But, I did what I had to do for Kaela's sake. Sometimes I wonder if I hadn't been pregnant, if I would have found the strength to survive. She was my salvation, Doctor."

She smiled and nodded her head. "Whatever your motivation was, you did find the strength and you were courageous, my dear. Now, let's get this little one dressed. From the looks of her, I would guess you haven't had any problems breastfeeding.

"No, she took to it right from the start and I had no problems producing."

"Okay, your turn." I lay on the bed beside Kaela while the doctor examined me. When we were done, she sat beside me.

"You will need a little corrective surgery yourself, dear. You have a small tear that hasn't healed properly. But there are no infections. The uterus seems to be back to normal size and your milk is flowing well. Your blood pressure is elevated a little, but under the circumstances, it's understandable. I see you have an injury healing on your ankle. Nasty one that. Although, it looks like all you'll be left with is a nasty scar. Kaela's body weight looks about normal, but we have no way of telling what she may have lost initially, or what her gain has been. But she has good color. Now, you on the other hand, look like you could put on a few pounds. Do you have any questions?"

"Yes, I've been concerned that Kaela isn't getting Vitamin D from my milk. I've been giving her some formula, made from canned milk, with an eyedropper. But I don't think it's sufficient."

"I'm sure some blood tests will be done. But at eight weeks, I don't think you need to worry. Symptoms don't usually occur until at least six months of age, and she will be well-treated by then. If there are any concerns, she can be treated with large doses of Vitamin D and there shouldn't be any lasting effects at all. At this point, I'd say you don't have anything to worry about. Anything else?"

"One other thing—I saved the placenta. I know if something's wrong at birth, it's used for testing, but I'm not sure if it's of any use at this late stage. Should we take it back with us?"

"I can take care of that for you. Shall we let the men in to discuss your evacuation?

"You bet. Evacuation … I love the sound of that word," I mused.

The men filed in and sat around the table with Dr. Phillips. I was busy smoothing the covers on the bed. I picked up Kaela and turned towards the table. All eyes in the room focused on my baby and me. Dr. Phillips was teary eyed, the men quiet. Staff-Sergeant Pratt cleared his throat as I approached the table.

"I must say, ma'am, you two are a wonderful sight to see. I usually send my officers on rescue missions, but this was one I had to do myself. It's not too often we see happy endings in these situations. The sight of you and the little one will stay with me forever."

My throat felt tight. "Please, call me Georgia. That goes for everyone." I sat down at the table and turned my attention to the Staff-Sergeant.

"We would like to evacuate as soon as possible," he began. Nodding towards Sean, he continued. "Sean tells me you're packed and ready to leave. Now we've tried hard to keep all of this under wraps. Once the media hears about this, they'll break down doors to reach you. These things have a way of leaking out regardless of our efforts."

Turning to Dr. Phillips, he asked for her report on our condition and what her recommendations were.

"I'd like to have Georgia and Kaela flown to Lions Gate Hospital in Vancouver. They both are in need of some minor care, some blood work, etc." Then, she addressed me: "Before we flew here, I had no idea what condition I'd find you in. I ordered a Medi-vac plane from Prince George. It arrives tonight in Dease Lake. If you were in immediate need, we'd fly you to the hospital in Prince George. I also talked to a colleague of mine in Obstetrics at Lions Gate. Since there is no immediate danger to either of you, I suggest we fly you to the Vancouver hospital. They'll keep you both there for a couple of days, and you can have the rest you most certainly deserve. How does all this sound?"

"I'll do whatever you say. You can't imagine how good it feels to have someone else make my decisions for me. I'm putting myself in your hands."

Staff-Sergeant Pratt took the floor again.

"The trick will be to keep Georgia under wraps until we can get her to Vancouver. We're going to have a couple of hours wait in Dease Lake before the Medi-vac arrives. During which, I need to talk with you alone, Georgia. I need some information to file my report."

"What if we go to my place?" Sean asked. "Any place that is official will attract attention for sure. You can have my study for privacy."

"All right, I'll go to the office and check in. Then I'll change into my civvies and drive over in my own vehicle. How about you, Doc?"

"I think I'll go back to the clinic and make the final arrangements. Then, I'll come over and bring my scale. I'd like to weigh Kaela," she replied.

"Okay, we're all set." Staff-Sergeant Pratt stood up from the table. "Let's get going."

My body jerked and I stared at him with my mouth open. His sudden abrupt manner shocked me. *I'm going home.* They all stood and turned to me.

"Are you okay?" Sean asked.

I looked from one to the other. With determination, I stood up and shot them all a huge smile. "Damn right I am."

Everyone left the cabin but me and Sean. Dr. Phillips carried Kaela to the helicopter. Sean grabbed the ring of keys and backed out the front doorway. "I'll lock up the front and the window shutters." He finished up and headed for the back door. "I'll meet you out back."

I stood in the middle of the room and slowly turned in a circle. I thought of my native spirit and walked over to the rocking chair. I sat down and reached into my pocket for the crystal Nonnock left me so many months ago. "Can you believe it? I'm going home. I wish I could see you once more to say goodbye. You keep telling me I did it on my own, but you'll never convince me of that."

It all began that night, the night I received the crystal. Staring at it, I knew my life would never be the same. I'd never be the same. *Awareness happened here.* A new growth had started that was in its infancy, and that didn't only mean the birth of my daughter. *She and I are on a path of enlightenment together.*

I stood up, reached out and stopped the rocker from moving. With one last look around the cabin, I walked slowly to the back door. It may belong to Sean, but I'd discovered my true essence here and a small part of that essence would remain behind. I felt bound to this cabin by a spiritual link, and somehow knew I'd return one day. It was a part of my destiny.

As I stepped out of the door, a voice spoke softly behind me. "Goodbye, child. Know that I'll always be with you."

I turned quickly to see the empty rocker moving slowly back and forth. My throat constricted and my eyes watered. "Goodbye," I whispered. Sean and I walked to the front of the cabin and into the meadow. He was about to help me into the helicopter, when I heard a familiar sound.

"Kraa … Kraa …" I spun around to see Feathers sitting on the edge of the cabin roof.

"Goodbye, Feathers." I waved and blew him a kiss. I watched as he flew across the field and disappeared into the trees.

... people are lonely because they build walls instead of bridges

J.F. Newton

Chapter 26

In a matter of minutes we were airborne, zooming across the treetops. Tom circled around the cabin to change our direction, affording me a bird's eye view of what had been my home these past several months. We passed over a rocky crag, and once again Tom circled. Flying a little lower this time, he pointed out a family of wolves. There appeared to be three adults, two males and one female. A couple of cubs were rolling playfully with each other. As we hovered above them, the female chased the cubs into the crevice of a large rock. She stood in front of the den and stared up at us. She had the same torn ear as the wolf I encountered with the caribou.

"Oh, Sean … look. It's my wolf. The one we talked about." The wolf and I stared at each other. I doubt she knew it was me, but I felt like we re-established our connection. "She survived the winter and motherhood like me ... my leaving's complete." As we rose higher and flew on, I twisted in my seat and watched her until she disappeared behind a curtain of trees. "Goodbye, sister. Take care of yourself." Sean squeezed my hand.

Looking out at the vast land beneath me, I realized how remote this area really was. To have survived, I knew a higher power had most surely intervened. Something special had happened to me here and I knew I'd been protected. I vowed to never take life for granted again. From now on I'd give back, pass onto others what had been given to me. At this point, I had no idea how I'd do this, but somehow I'd find my Path.

We landed in Dease Lake. After disembarking, we parted ways to meet later at Sean's. Tom instructed his mechanic to tend to the chopper. Sean and I, carrying Kaela, walked to the parking lot to Tom's truck. We pulled into a gravel driveway in front of an older cottage with a screened porch. There were only two houses on this short street. Sean jumped out of the truck and took Kaela from my arms. With one arm, he helped me down from the cab. We started up the walkway and I noticed a woman peering at us from the other house.

"There's a lady watching us from the house next door."

"That's Sarah. I'll bet she's dying to know who you are and how Tom found us. Wait until the others arrive."

Sean gave her a big smile and a wave. She smiled and waved back. We settled in the living room and Dr. Phillips arrived.

"Sarah came out onto the porch to say hi. She was curious about what's going on over here. I changed the subject and hurried inside."

"When the Staff-Sergeant arrives, she'll be here with some hot cinnamon rolls in no time," Sean replied.

Dr. Phillips set up her scale on the kitchen table and set about weighing Kaela.

"Eight pounds. What do you think she weighed at birth, Georgia?"

"I judged her to be about six pounds. She was definitely small." I replied.

"I talked to my colleague in Vancouver. The hospital is preparing to receive you and Kaela tonight. They're quite full at the moment, but they're going to do some shuffling around to ensure a private room. Hospital security will be informed as well to keep the media away from your room. I have my report in this envelope. You can take it with you and give it to the attending physician. Oh, here …," she paused, while digging in another bag, "I brought you something."

"Disposable diapers! Oh my goodness, they're so tiny … and sleepers. Thank-you."

"I borrowed them off my neighbor."

Sean showed me to his guest room and we put Kaela to bed, with pillows all around to keep her from rolling off, but not before I changed her diaper and put on her new sleeper. I hovered over her beaming. "Look at her, she looks so cute."

Sean laughed. "She does. Okay, proud mama, let's leave her to sleep, I think Staff-Sergeant Pratt is here.

Dr. Phillips approached the officer. "I confirmed the arrival of the Medi-vac. We have to be back at the airport at seven p.m."

"I thought while you interview Georgia, Staff-Sergeant, I'd order in some pizza." Sean looked around. "Tom are you staying?" Everyone nodded in agreement.

He showed Staff-Sergeant Pratt and me to his study. We spent the next thirty minutes discussing my kidnapping, escape, and my time at the cabin. He showed me pictures of Gary and Bobby. Seeing their faces again sent shudders up my spine. My gaze froze on their pictures.

"Georgia?" he prodded.

"That's them."

We were finishing up when the doorbell rang. The officer straightened. "Must be the pizza boy."

The telephone rang. Sean knocked on the study door and poked his head in. "It's for you, Staff- Sergeant. And the doorbell was my neighbor. I invited her in."

The officer laughed. "Ah yes, Sarah Brown. That's fine. Tell her she's under house arrest until we leave." We all laughed.

He answered the telephone more formally.

"Staff-Sergeant Pratt here, how can I help you?" There was a pause, while he listened to the party on the other end. "Yes, Sir. I did leave a message for you. Could you hang on one moment, please?"

He placed his hand over the receiver, looked at me and smiled. "I have your brother, Kris on the line. Let me break the news to him, so he doesn't think it's a prank. Then I'll pass the phone to you, okay?"

I gasped. "Oh my God ... yes, oh yes ..." My stomach flip-flopped and I tried to contain my excitement.

"Sorry to keep you waiting. I've some good news for you, sir. We've found your sister, Georgia. She's alive and well."

I watched his face intently, as he waited for Kris to reply. I leaned forward on the desk, my fingers in my mouth. I chewed my fingernails.

"Yes, sir. You heard me right. Your sister's alive."

Another pause. Squirming in my seat, I couldn't wait another minute to hear his voice.

"Sir, are you there? Mr. Carr ...? Kris ...?" Silence. More agony.

"There you are. I thought I'd lost you. Yes, sir. I can tell you where she is. She's sitting right in front of me, waiting to talk to you."

Whatever Kris was saying in return, I didn't know. Then Staff-Sergeant Pratt smiled.

"No sir, this isn't a prank call. You talked to my office, remember? They referred you to me.

I'm going to pass the phone to her now. I'm sure once you talk to her, you'll be reassured."

Handing me the telephone, he stood up and walked around the desk and gave my shoulder a squeeze. He left me alone in the study.

I stared at the receiver in my hand. Slowly, I lifted it up to my ear. I took a deep breath.

"Kris? It's me ... Georgia."

"Georgia ... is that really you?" he asked, with a raspy, broken voice.

"Yes, Kool Cat," I whispered, using his childhood nickname. "It's me."

Kris half laughed and half cried. "Georgia ... what did Dad use to call you?"

I laughed. "Ginger Cake, of course."

"Dear God. It is you."

We both broke into sobs. For a few minutes there wasn't any conversation, as we listened to each other cry. Kool Cat and Ginger Cake were nicknames made up by our father from our initials. Our Dad considered it a challenge to make up nicknames for all our friends with their initials as well. Marion Greenly from Whitehorse had been Mardi Gras. When Kris and I became adults, my father gave up this practice, save one.

When Colin left me last year for Julie, my Dad took to calling him Crusty the Clown.

"I don't know where to begin with the questions. First, are you okay? Have you talked to Mom and Dad? Does Grandma know? How about …"

"Whoa, one at a time, bro. Yes, I'm okay. No, I haven't talked to Mom and Dad. They're in Arizona, as I'm sure you know. The police down there are trying to reach them. You're the first to know."

"How is this possible? Where have you been, sis?"

I paced around the study, filling him in on the last five months in as few words as possible.

"So where are you now?" he asked.

"We're at the cabin owner's cottage in Dease Lake, waiting for the Medi-vac to arrive from Prince George. We'll be leaving here about seven tonight and flying to Lions Gate Hospital in North Vancouver. Do you think you could get leave and meet us? We'll be there about ten."

"I know they'll give me the time. Hopefully, I'll catch the eight o'clock ferry to Horseshoe Bay. I should be at the hospital by 10:30. You keep saying we?"

I realized he didn't know about the baby yet. He was in for another shocker. "Are you sitting down?" I teased.

"Yes! Why?"

"Well, brother dear, when you come to the hospital there will be two of us waiting for you. Not only your sister but your niece, Uncle Kris."

There was silence at the other end of the line. "Is she yours?"

Convulsed with laughter, I sputtered back a response. "That sounds like a dumb blond joke, Kris. Of course she's mine.

"Oh my God. Marion told us you were pregnant. But that means you had her at the cabin? Who was there with you?"

"No one was with me. I had her by myself."

"You've got to be kidding. Alone? Is she all right? Are you sure you're all right?"

I realized this was something I'd have to get used to. People would always react this way when finding out I experienced childbirth alone and isolated. I was only one of many women over generations who gave birth under dire conditions. But to the general population living in urban and modern times, what I had weathered was unthinkable.

"We're both fine, Kris. I think the pizza is here. This is one treat I'm not going to miss out on. I better say goodbye."

"Me too. I have arrangements to make." There was a pause. "I'm afraid to let you go."

"It's okay ... you'll see me in a few hours. I love you," I said, softly, feeling tears welling up again.

"I love you too. See you later."

I replaced the phone on the stand and noticed a newspaper on Sean's desk. I found myself staring into my own face. It was a picture taken of me last year at a family picnic. There was a worldly innocence in my eyes that I no longer felt. I'd never be that woman again. In a sense, that woman was dead. But she didn't meet with foul play. Instead, she was reborn, and with this birth came wisdom and serenity. I walked to the window. The Cassiar Mountains stood tall, affording the same view as from Sean's cabin. I wrapped my arms around my shoulders in a tight hug, digesting the moments spent on the phone with Kris. After a time, I walked to the study door to join the others for pizza. *How normal.* So began my first step back to civilization.

Sean introduced me to his neighbor, Sarah Brown. She gave me a spontaneous hug. My isolation from civilization left me a little cautious of strangers and I fought the urge to push her away. She insisted I sit by her on the couch. I was touched by her genuine display of concern and took an instant liking to this woman. Her warmth made me feel as though I'd known her for years.

"You poor dear, imagine you bein' so close to us and none of us knowin' it."

The pizza looked tempting, but I could only manage to eat one piece.

"Come on now, you have another," Sarah said. "God only knows what you've been eatin' all these months. You're skin and bones. And you, a nursin' mom."

"Oh no, thank you. It's been quite a day for me. With all the excitement my stomach is a little upset."

Dr. Phillips spoke up. "Once we get you home with your loved ones and you re-adjust to 'normal life', it won't take long for you to get back your appetite. The weight will return quickly."

Tom Glass rose from his chair. "Well, I must get going. I have Curling to attend to. Semi-finals you know; if I'm a no-show the team'll kill me."

Staff-Sergeant Pratt reminded him that he must keep the day's events under wraps until tomorrow. Tom promised he would.

Sean and I walked him to the door. After they said their goodbyes, I gave Tom a hug and a kiss on the cheek.

"Thank you, Tom. I won't ever forget the sight of that helicopter circling overhead."

"Little lady, I won't ever forget the sight of you and the little one at that cabin. It was my pleasure to be a part of helping you. I only wish it had been sooner. Usually I fly over Sean's place a couple of times during the winter while on my mining duties. But this year, I spent the winter back east on family business, and since I got back, I've been too busy to check. I feel mighty bad about that. You take care now." Tom left.

"Strange, isn't it? The way things went, Tom not checking the cabin this year, you coming sooner than usual. Fate can be a scary thing," I said.

When we returned to the living room, Sarah was holding Kaela.

"The wee one was awake. I hope you don't mind my gettin' her. Isn't she a little beauty?" Sarah gushed.

Sitting with these people, I was amazed at the sudden role they all played in my life. There was an instinctual sense of humanity prevailing in the room. It was moving to note how these people came together to aid someone in need, forming an instant trusting bond that surpasses our normal mistrust of strangers. They reached out to me. Each one trying in his or her way to make me feel at home and comforted—and, as I became accustomed to the feeling of being cared for again, so I did.

"Oh my ..." Sarah said wistfully, "It's been years since I held a precious bundle this tiny. She's special you know, like her mama. You've both been spared and protected to do somethin' in this world. Destiny, that's what it is. You mark my words."

With a great sigh, she gently ran her fingers across Kaela's face.

I realized Kaela was giving something in return to this gruff, but gentle woman. Under her rough diamond exterior, I sensed a beauty and wisdom that reminded me of my native spirit. I knew if she remained in my life, she would be another teacher.

The remaining time passed quickly, and suddenly Kaela and I were whisked out to meet the Medi-vac at the airport. They all came to see me off. Sean and Sarah came with Kaela and me in Dr. Phillips car. She insisted on holding Kaela right up to boarding time.

Dr. Phillips gave me a hug and wished us well. Staff-Sergeant Pratt tried to maintain his formal police demeanor, but his eyes gave him away. I threw my arms around him, as I had with Tom, and kissed his cheek. Sarah squeezed me until I couldn't breathe, prattling on about how we were to come back and visit her once my life was back to normal. I promised her I would, and I knew it wasn't idle talk.

Sean helped Kaela and me into the helicopter. He climbed aboard to say goodbye. We sat staring at each other, neither of us quite sure of what to say.

Smiling, I grabbed his hand. "You know, there aren't any words to express my thanks."

"There's nothing to thank. You're an incredible woman. You've touched the lives of so many people in such a short time," he added, and smiled. "Come tomorrow, Dease Lake will be buzzing for days about you. This will put us on the map."

"I guess I better watch the news. You'll all be famous," I teased.

Sean placed his hand over mine. "No, my dear. You're the one who's going to be famous. You better make plans to hide out for a while."

Once again, we stared silently at each other.

"I hope we'll remain friends. I don't want you and Kaela to disappear out of my life," he stammered.

This man who was a savior, stirred my blood. It was all so confusing and my emotions, conflicted. Too much, too soon. "Friends it is."

The two paramedics who'd been talking with Dr. Phillips came back on board. One of them addressed Sean.

"Sir, we're taking off now.

Sean stood up, cupping my face in his hands; he leaned down and brushed his lips lightly against mine. He touched Kaela's cheek with his fingers.

"I'll be in touch. Take care," he said thickly, upon leaving the plane. I gave no words to my feelings but he surely knew ... maybe. All I could muster was one word. "Bye."

As we left the runway, I watched the small group waving on the tarmac until they disappeared from sight. Excluding Sean, it was hard to believe that I'd been oblivious of their existence before this day. After a few short hours, they were etched in my memory forever.

Chapter 27

Since Kaela and I weren't in need of immediate medical care, the paramedics didn't have much to do. But I felt grateful for their company. The next two hours were filled with questions about my experiences at the cabin. I found myself using humor to laugh off some detail that had once traumatized me, and realized it was the only way I could talk about it. Still, they were a nice diversion from the mixed emotions I felt. After months of monotonous sameness, the changes were happening so fast, I wasn't ready to deal with them.

We landed at Vancouver International Airport a few minutes before nine o'clock. Kaela slept throughout the trip and woke up hungry when we transferred to an awaiting helicopter. Twenty minutes later, we landed in the parking lot of the Lion's Gate Hospital in North Vancouver. An RCMP officer and a nurse climbed on board.

Looking out of the window, I was shocked to see two or three television cameras, a dozen news people, and a crowd of curious onlookers, all held back by a rope and police officers. Television lights lit up the parking lot and camera lights flashed as reporters snapped pictures.

I gasped, bewildered. "My God, how did they find out so soon?"

"I'm sorry, Mrs. Charles; these things have a way of leaking out and developing a life of their own."

I looked at the RCMP officer who spoke to me. I wasn't ready for this kind of confrontation, and I knew he could see the fear in my eyes. He was young, but he had a confident look to him.

"I'm Constable Owens, welcome home. We have a wheelchair waiting outside for you. If you'd let the nurse carry your daughter, I'll lead you to the chair and escort you into the hospital.

"I don't need a wheelchair."

"We were told you had a leg injury and it's the easiest and fastest way to get you through the crowds and into the security of the hospital."

I reluctantly let go of Kaela. The nurse gave me a reassuring smile and wrapped her in a blanket.

As I stood, the officer handed me a blanket as well.

"Place it around your shoulders and over your head. It'll afford you some privacy. Cover your face and stare down at the ground. Don't look at the cameras and ignore their questions. We'll have you inside the hospital in no time."

I followed his instructions with the blanket but when we reached the doorway out of the helicopter, I hesitated.

"Don't be afraid," he said, grasping my arm strongly and urging me forward, "Here we go."

The moment I stepped through the doorway and onto the steps, all hell broke loose. Lights flashed, people yelled my name and bombarded me with questions. I stood dumbfounded. Sneaking a quick glance around the parking lot, I felt the officer's grasp tighten, reminding me of his advice. My eyes fell to the ground. He helped me down the stairs and into the wheelchair.

As he pushed me quickly across the parking lot, I pulled the blanket further down over my face, ignoring the barrage of questions. My daughter wailed above the chaos. It filled me with anger towards these strangers frightening my baby. I had a mother's urge to jump up and grab Kaela to my breast to protect her and soothe her confusion. But I remained seated and soon we were well inside the hospital emergency doors. Hospital security stood guard at the entranceway.

The nurse placed my frightened baby, Kaela in my arms and asked me to stay in the wheelchair. We were immediately wheeled into an elevator and up to the maternity ward. I found myself in a private room with the window curtains drawn. Sitting on the edge of the bed, I rocked Kaela. I needed to calm myself if I wanted her to relax and feel safe.

"I'll be right back. I have to call the obstetrician. She's at home waiting for news of your safe arrival at the hospital." The nurse slipped out the door.

Constable Owens lowered himself into the armchair beside the bed.

"Mrs. Charles, I want you to know that you're safe here. No one will bother you."

"Thank you."

"Your brother called our office for a private security company recommendation, which we provided. Arrangements were made for a security officer to be on guard outside your door for as long as you're in the hospital. I assured your brother I'd remain here with you until the guard arrives."

I raised my eyebrows. "Kris thought of that? I guess I never considered myself that important to warrant all this attention."

"This must be overwhelming for you, going from complete seclusion to living in a goldfish bowl in a matter of hours. But believe me, you do warrant the attention. I don't think you realize the impact your story'll have on the world around you. You're a real- life heroine. Society needs to hear stories like yours.

Embarrassed, I paused to think over what he said.

"I guess I can't see myself as a heroine. It's not a role I'm comfortable with."

The nurse returned and asked Constable Owens to wait outside while they settled me in. He excused himself and left.

"I'm glad to see the baby calmed down, poor little thing," she said with a sigh. "I'm Katie, your nurse for the night. I'm going to take Kaela to the nursery and get her ready for Dr. Orn to check over. There's a gown in the lower drawer in the bedside table and a dressing gown in the closet. If you want to shower, there's one here in your bathroom."

"A shower?" I echoed, "I've forgotten what that feels like. I didn't know hospital rooms had their own showers."

"We only have a few private rooms with one. You're lucky to get it. Under the circumstances, we not only felt you deserved one, but it was the best way to secure your presence here with all those news people snooping around."

As she took Kaela from my arms, I felt a sudden panic. There was no bed for her.

"Kaela and I have never been separated before. She'll be staying in my room with me?"

"Of course, dear. Don't you worry. The orderly hasn't brought her crib from the children's ward yet. When the Doctor's done, we'll bring her right back to you. Now, you go enjoy that shower."

I headed into the bathroom, sporting an ear-splitting grin. A year ago, I would have accepted the nurse's authority if she told me Kaela couldn't stay in my room. But had that happened tonight, I would have protested so loudly the reporters outside in the parking lot would've heard me.

Yes, I think I'm going to like the new me.

Stepping into the hot shower, all thoughts left me. I was completely absorbed with the tingling sensation my body experienced from the onslaught of hot steamy water. "Ah ... Oh, man."

I moaned and sighed for I don't know how long, completely lost to my senses. How can one explain such a feeling? With the enjoyment came a feeling of appreciation—appreciation for life, appreciation for living in a part of the world that afforded me such luxury, and appreciation for being able to experience joy.

I returned to my room, towel drying my wet hair, completely oblivious to a figure sitting in the chair. "It's about time you came out of that shower. I thought I'd have to sit here all night."

I pulled the towel back from my face and froze.

My brother sat, grinning from ear to ear. "Oh Kris ..." I cried.

Throwing the towel onto the floor, I raced across the room and flung myself into his arms as he stood up, almost toppling him over backwards. We clung to each other. He pushed me back. "Look at you!" He shook his head. He embraced me again and we laughed.

"I can't believe you're here, sis." Another hug, but this time we cried. Finally, he settled back in the chair and I stretched out on the bed.

"I didn't expect you here so soon."

"I decided to fly over from Nanaimo to Vancouver Harbour rather than chance the ferries on a long weekend. The RCMP sent a squad car to pick me up. I don't think I would've made it into the hospital without them. No one would've believed I was your brother. What a zoo out there, sis. You're a celebrity."

I groaned. "So people keep telling me. Have you talked with Mom and Dad yet?

"Not directly, but on the ride over I was told they'd been reached. They're on their way to Phoenix to catch a red eye to Seattle. They'll connect to Vancouver and be here sometime midmorning. All five of them are coming."

Puzzled, I asked: "Five?"

"Grams is with them. Mom and Dad took her with them to Chula."

"Oh, I'm so glad they're all together. I was about to ask if you'd talked to Grams." I giggled. "Can you imagine the five of them on a plane together? They'll turn it into a big party. However did they get seats on a holiday weekend?"

"I have no idea, sis. But knowing Granddad, he pulled a few strings and called in a few favors."

Our quiet reunion was interrupted with the influx of people into my room. The nurse entered first. Then a woman carrying Kaela. Constable Owens and a security guard followed them.

"I'm Dr. Orn. And here's Kaela, safe and sound," she said. Smiling broadly, she handed me my daughter.

Constable Owens stepped forward and introduced Dennis Campbell, my security guard.

"It's a pleasure to meet you, Mrs. Charles. Don't you worry. No one will get past this door that shouldn't."

Kris stood up and shook hands with the guard and Constable Owens, who said his goodbyes and he walked them both to the doorway. As they attempted to leave the room, the orderly arrived with Kaela's crib.

"Oops, sorry," the orderly said, backing out into the corridor.

Nurse Katie laughed. "Considering visiting hours are over and all the other patients are supposed to be sleeping, it's like grand central station on this floor. You've caused quite a commotion here tonight, my dear."

The orderly set the crib up beside the armchair and left with the nurse. Kris came back into the room and sat down out of the way.

Dr. Orn turned her attention back to Kaela and me. "I've looked over the charts Dr. Phillips sent with you, and after examining Kaela, I concur she appears healthy and stable. Tomorrow, I've scheduled some time to do corrective surgery on the cord. Of which, by the way, was expertly tied off. We took some blood and stool samples and we should have the results tomorrow."

"It's such a relief to have Kaela checked out."

"Don't you worry about her. As for you, we're going to let you have a good night's sleep. The nurse'll be back in a while to take your vitals and give you something to help you sleep. Tomorrow, Dr. Summers will be in to examine you and do some tests. Your family doctor will be in tomorrow as well. We'll let your brother stay a little longer until your medication kicks in."

"Thank you, Doctor," I said.

She turned to Kris. "Mr. Carr, if you would see the nurse on the way out, she'll get you to fill out the admitting paperwork for your sister."

Kris nodded. "Certainly."

She stopped on her way out and turned. "When you're rested and things have calmed down around here, I'd like to sit and have a talk with you about how you managed childbirth all alone in that cabin. Goodnight."

I turned to Kris and found him staring at Kaela. I stood up and moved to where he sat in the armchair.

"Would you like to hold your niece for awhile?" I asked, my voice choked with emotion.

"She's beautiful." He took her carefully and when looked up at me, he had tears in his eyes. "I hope one day you'll tell me all about your experience and the cabin, but not until you're ready, okay?"

"I will and thanks for not pushing me right now." *A lot of people will want to know about my winter at the cabin.* Something was bothering me about telling my story. I felt uneasy about it, but I pushed it from my mind. I wasn't going to examine this feeling, not tonight. *Tonight, I'm at peace. Tonight, I'm safe and happy. Tomorrow, maybe. No... tomorrow my family will arrive and I'll be surrounded by love.*

Maybe the next day!

Katie returned and prepped me for bed. Lifting a sleeping Kaela from Kris, she placed her in the crib.

"She should sleep right through the night. She's a good sleeper and today her schedule was completely turned around," I said.

"Well, let's hope you sleep through the night too," Katie added.

"I don't know about me, I'm too keyed up."

"That's what the meds are for, sweetie. I'll check on you in a while."

Kris and I chatted for half an hour about his life on the base. The next thing I knew, a distant voice reached through my dozy state.

"Goodnight, Georgia. I'll see you tomorrow. I love you."

I opened my eyes briefly, as Kris bent to kiss me on the forehead. "Mmm ... me too."

My eyes were shut tight before he left the room, but not before I heard a "Kraa, Kraa" and saw a shadow of a raven flash across the window.

The next morning, I woke up to a bubbly young voice, chirping my name. It took a few moments for me to figure out where this annoying, high-pitched voice came from. Orienting myself with my new surroundings, I quickly looked to the crib for Kaela. She was still sound asleep.

"What time is it, please?"

"Seven o'clock. From what I understand, you both had a good night's sleep. I'm Patty, your day nurse."

Shoving a thermometer under my tongue, Patty grabbed my arm to take my blood pressure.

"Breakfast will be along in an hour, but the lab technician will be in shortly to get some blood. There's a bottle in the bathroom with instructions for a urine sample—thought I'd catch you before you relieved yourself."

Flashing me a big smile, she took a big breath and started chirping again.

"The whole hospital is buzzing about you this morning. Reporters are stopping staff in the parking lot. They're trying to bribe us into giving up your floor and room number. The other mothers on this floor keep trying to peek through your door whenever we open it. I, for one, am thrilled to be working this floor today. And I must say, I am really happy to meet you, Georgia."

Patty extended her hand to me. Sitting up, I shook her hand and decided she was too cute for words and genuine.

"Thank you, Patty."

For the next two hours, doctors on their morning rounds and day nurses popped in and out to meet me and Kaela. Flowers and cards from well-wishers had already started to arrive. Presents from strangers were left with the security guards at the entrance to the hospital. Dr. Petersen, my family doctor, arrived at the end of his rounds. We chatted for about twenty minutes while he studied my chart and Kaela's.

"Well, my dear, considering the last time I saw you professionally, and all you have endured since then, you appear to be in remarkable condition. A tad thin perhaps. We'll see what the blood

323

tests show. I'm so pleased for you and your family. It hasn't been easy for them these last few months. Have you seen them yet?"

"Only Kris, my parents and grandparents will be arriving from out of town this morning."

"Please give them my regards. Now, Dr. Orn and Dr. Summers will be looking after the two of you for the next while. I'd like to see you both in my office in about a month. When you get home, call my office and set up a time."

"I will, and thank you, Doctor." I must have said "thank you" at least a hundred times in the past twenty-four hours.

At nine-thirty, we were both taken for corrective surgery; by ten-thirty we were back in our room. Neither of us required anaesthesia. Sitting in the chair nursing Kaela, I enjoyed a rare moment of solitude.

Suddenly, the door burst open and there stood Mom and Dad. As we stared at each other in disbelief, the moment seemed frozen in time. My mother let out a soft whimper and rushed towards me. Jumping up, I placed Kaela on the bed. We clung to each other and wept with abandon. The familiar smells of her hair and her perfume piqued my senses. Childhood memories surged from the recesses of my mind, reconnecting me with a lost world of love and security. Strangely, I gained my composure first. I found myself stroking my mother's head and softly uttering soothing words as we rocked back and forth. "It's okay, Mom. Shhh …"

My eyes searched for my father. He had sat down on the bed, his eyes focused on Kaela. To my amazement, his face was wet with tears. I'd never seen my father cry.

I heard a raspy voice, barely audible, speak out, and realized it was mine. "Dad …"

"Ginger Cake," he responded, rising from the bed.

My mother separated herself from me. Taking a moment to blow her nose and wipe her eyes, she made a beeline for her granddaughter. Dad and I hugged in silence. Each of us drew strength and comfort from the other, our motionless stance in sharp contrast to the emotional outburst shared moments earlier with my mother—but no less meaningful.

No sooner had a semblance of peace and order returned to my room, the nurse let my grandparents in. Pandemonium erupted as Kaela and I were passed from one family member to another. Since five visitors at a time definitely broke the rules, we tried to keep the noise level down to a dull roar. As I thought it couldn't get any better, the door opened and a head popped in.

"Can anyone join this party?" a female voice asked.

"Marion!" I screamed.

Locked in an embrace, we jumped and danced in a circle true to our old schoolgirl fashion, tears streaming once again. I stared at her through blurred eyes. "How did you get here? I can't believe you're here."

"Hey, that's my line. I can't believe you're here, girl," Marion croaked. "I saw the late news last night and about died. I called the RCMP and they confirmed the story. So this morning, Barry chartered a plane and here I am."

"But how did you get past security and the nurses?"

"I called Kris at the house and he brought me in." Marion nodded towards the door.

Kris leaned quietly against the wall with a shit- eating grin on his face. "I told them she was my wife." He shrugged.

We all laughed.

"I could be the first celebrity to be kicked out of Lions Gate Hospital. The media will accuse me of being a 'Diva'."

"They wouldn't dare, sis. Could you see the headlines? Hospital throws kidnap victim and baby back from the dead into the street after emotional reunion with family breaks rules," Kris mocked.

Nurse Patty poked her head in. "Hey guys, can you keep it down a little? I could lose my job if Admin finds out I let you all in together," she winked and left us alone.

"Correct that," Kris said. "New heading reads: Hospital fires nurse for allowing family reunion with kidnap victim and baby back from the dead."

Amidst the laughter, I observed my family. Not with my eyes, but from a place within. *Love—that's what it's all about! Why is it we always seem to forget such a simple and elementary truth?*

Chapter 28

"What?" I yelled. "That fucking bastard! How dare he?"

"Oh, Georgia! Such language, dear." Mom exclaimed.

Pacing the living room floor of my parents' home, I looked at my mother's shocked expression. It was my first day home after two days in the hospital, and Grams and Nana were in the kitchen preparing a family brunch. The rest of us were having our morning coffee. My father said nothing, but a slight twitching at the corner of his mouth caught my attention. He looked away instantly, but not before I saw a glint of mirth in his eyes.

Kris saw no need to hold anything back. Laughing, he slapped me on the shoulder. "Good on you, sis. It's about time you showed some anger towards that guy and saw him for the jerk he is. They're only words, Mom."

Mom didn't see the humor. "Foul words, Kris. Maybe they fit okay on base, but they don't belong here in my house. I taught my kids better than that."

"Sorry, Mom," I apologized. "There were days in the cabin when I'd stand at the window staring out into the wilderness. The loneliness would become so unbearable the only thing that helped me was to yell obscenities, as many as I could think of in as many ways I could make up. I can't explain it exactly, except it was so out of character it made me feel alive. A little mad perhaps, but alive nonetheless."

They all stared at me, as though trying to comprehend what I'd gone through. No one ever could. I smiled, "That's one habit I'd better work on breaking."

I dropped onto the couch beside my father. "I can't believe Colin did that. Tell me exactly what he said, Dad. Don't leave out any details."

"He called right away to ask if there was any news about you. After the search was called off, he called again to offer his condolences. We heard nothing from him until March, when he paid us a visit. He wanted to know if there was anything he could do to help. I asked him in what way. He offered his lawyer's help for any legal matters we may need to take care of. I thanked him and informed him that our family lawyer was handling your affairs."

"That's when his real purpose for coming revealed itself," Mom interjected.

My dad gave my hand a squeeze and continued. "He was particularly concerned about the condo. When I told him you'd drawn up a will before you went to the Yukon, leaving it and the contents to your brother, he looked annoyed, but didn't say anything. Then, he asked if our lawyer had applied for a death certificate yet ..."

Mom cut in again: "We were horrified."

Dad continued, "I told him we had to wait seven years for you to be declared dead, since you were only missing, and he told us these were special circumstances. Since foul play was suspected, we could apply to the courts for the certificate now. He suggested it was best for everyone involved."

I couldn't believe what I was hearing. "What did you say to that?"

"I asked him, how so. He said your legal affairs couldn't be settled without the certificate of death, and it would give us peace of mind so we could move forward. Then, he added that he needed to move forward also. He was a new father and he needed the death certificate so he could remarry and give the baby his name."

"The bastard," I spat out.

"That's exactly what I called him to his face," Mom said, defiantly.

"Your mother walked out of the room after tearing a strip off of him, and I walked him to the door, while I told him he was an insensitive asshole.

I laughed. "What did he say to that?"

"He looked like he was about to retort, but stopped. He apologized for upsetting us and scurried out of here red-faced."

"That's not all. Tell her what happened next," Mom said to Dad.

"A few weeks later, I received a legal letter from his lawyer informing us Colin was applying to the courts for a death certificate. It stated that as your legal husband, he was within his rights to make such a request. He also filed a writ against the will, claiming the ownership of the condo should revert back to him.

Granddad scowled. "The coward, skulking around behind everyone's back."

"He gave me that condo as settlement. He has no rights to it. His lawyer drew up the papers. How could he possibly support Colin's decision to fight my will?"

"You're talking morally, sweetheart," Granddad said. "This is about money and Colin's lawyer gets paid whether he wins or not."

"Okay, but what is Colin's reasoning, and is it legal?" I asked.

"It's totally legal, honey," Dad answered. "Under the law, Colin is still your spouse, and at the time you disappeared you were separated less than a year. He filed a Writ of Summons and Statement of Claim under what is called the Wills Variation Act. He based his claim on the fact that he was a large contributor to the mortgage payments, and you signed the ownership papers only weeks before your disappearance. Usually a judge takes into account whether or not the claimant is needy. Colin isn't. But the judge could still rule in his favor."

My anger was building again, and I resumed pacing the room. "Then what the hell is the point in drawing up a legal will? What about my legal rights and wishes?"

"Unfortunately, there was a loophole and Colin found it. Fortunately, with the courts being busy, it wasn't scheduled to be heard until next month."

"Turning up alive just resolved it. Imagine Colin's surprise," I said sarcastically. "Sooner or later I'll be talking to his nibs. He's going to see and hear a side of me he never knew existed."

Dad gave me a wink and a snicker. "Before you disappeared, we all wondered how long it would take you to build a healthy anger towards Crusty the Clown and lay some blame where it belonged. You've only been back a day, but I can see a strength and determination that wasn't there before."

"All that's happened in the past year could either build character and strength, or kill you. I survived, Dad. Sometimes I don't know how or why. But here I am, and for the first time in my life, I know who I am."

Dad chuckled, "Old Crusty is going to finally get the comeuppance he deserves."

We had turned off the telephone ringer the previous night, because it never stopped ringing. Dad cleared the electronic voice mail and screened the calls. Later that morning, Colin left a message expressing his joy and happiness for the family on my safe return. He requested that I call him at his work right away. *What a change from last year when he avoided all of my calls!* I decided to make him wait.

The photographers and reporters stayed outside all that day. I stayed away from the windows and refused to return their calls. As the day wore on, the number of calls increased. They came from all over the world: distant relatives, friends, neighbors, acquaintances, lawyers, agents and publishers, talk show agents, movie producers and well-wishers who we didn't even know. Mom carefully logged each and every one of them. Dad answered the door to flower deliveries and presents for my daughter.

"You know, honey, sooner or later you're going to have to talk to the reporters," Dad said.

"Why?" I demanded, petulantly. "I want to be left alone. I'm going up to check on Kaela."

My parents stared after me as I hurried up the stairs. Alone in my room, I wrestled with that nagging unease I felt whenever I thought about the reporters. I peeked discretely through the window blind to watch the group outside. A light knock sounded on the door. Mom slipped quietly into my room.

"The sooner you give them an interview, the sooner they'll all go away. I know this must be overwhelming for you, but I'm sensing something else. It's a wonderful story with a happy ending, sweetheart. You should share it with the world. What's bothering you?"

The time came for me to face another fear. I gave her a thin smile.

"Standing before the world, accepting accolades of praise, makes me uncomfortable. I feel like a fraud."

"I don't understand, dear. A fraud in what way?"

I breathed in deeply. "Oh boy ... here goes. Let's sit, Mom."

I sat on the bed, twisting my hair in my fingers, as I tried to find a way to start. "Mom, do you believe in multi-dimensions? I mean, do you believe we can travel between dimensions ... not with our physical body, but with our soul?"

"I would have to say I don't disbelieve it. I have an open mind."

"January 2nd, your birthday, was an especially horrid day for me. I needed to see you and Dad—to know you were okay." I paused. "I went into a trance, Mom ... and I was here. I saw you and Dad."

I paused to see how my mother would react to this information. She started to cry softly.

"I know, honey," she said, in a whisper. "I saw you too, standing by the bedroom door."

We embraced and rocked slowly together, silently celebrating a personal and profound experience that was ours alone.

"I thought you came to say goodbye. It was comforting."

"You were wearing the night gown I bought for you for Christmas."

"Yes, for the first time. I put it away until then because I couldn't accept the idea you were gone. After that night, I truly believed you came because I finally wore it. I believed your visit was a way of telling me it was time for me to get on with my life. Is that what's bothering you? You don't have to talk to anyone else about it. The experience belongs to you and me. Let it be our secret."

Here it was—my moment of truth.

"The soul travel only scratches the surface of my experience at the cabin. Mom … I didn't do it on my own. The soul travel, the child birth, the survival, all of it … someone helped me."

"Who helped you?" Mom asked, looking perplexed.

"Kaela … or Nonnock."

"But you told us you were alone at the cabin. Your daughter's name is Kaela, and I'm getting more than a little confused here. So keep talking dear, who is this other Kaela?"

"I was alone in terms of physical beings. The area I was lost in is part of the Tahltan native lands. Kaela's a native Spirit and she guided me. Her white man name is Kaela. When I decided to call my daughter after her, she became Nonnock, her Indian name."

I studied my mother's face to gauge her reaction. Other than a slight raise of her eyebrows, her face was unreadable as she digested this information.

"I see!" she said. It was her turn to study me. Staring at each other in silence for several moments, I spoke first.

"That's all you can say—I see?"

"Uh … yes. My missing daughter has told me she spent five months living with a native spirit in the woods. I need to wrap my brain around this."

"There it is in a nutshell, Mom. If you don't believe me, how can I expect anyone else to? I'm not lying. She's real, at least in the ethereal sense."

"Now hold on. I might be having a little trouble grasping this, but I know you're telling the truth. You know how I know?" Mom smiled, "Whenever you tried to lie to me as a kid with those big innocent eyes, your ears turned red. They were a dead giveaway." We both laughed. "Now seriously, I believe you experienced something, and I want you to tell me about it."

"After I found the root cellar, I knew I had enough food, if rationed properly, to take me to early spring. There was enough firewood and water, so I stopped worrying about my physical needs. The fear of childbirth and the isolation sent me into an emotional depression. I started to doubt my ability to survive again."

I stopped to study her reaction. She didn't say anything, so I continued. "That's when I saw her for the first time. She came to me in a dream, and after that I had visions. She gave me comfort and peace. From our many talks, I grew emotionally and spiritually strong. At first I thought I was imagining her. Then I decided I was going crazy, thinking that my subconscious mind created Nonnock to help me to survive. In time, she gave me a physical sign; it's a crystal I saw her carrying."

Rising from the bed, I went to the dresser and retrieved the crystal. I gave it to my mother and watched as she turned it over in her hand.

"It's beautiful." she said.

I rejoined her on the bed. "The thought occurred to me that my subconscious produced the crystal as proof. But deep down, I don't believe that. That crystal convinced me that her presence was a reality. Without her, I probably wouldn't have survived out there. That's my dilemma. The world sees me as a heroine, and I feel like a fraud."

"You're looking at this all wrong, hon. First of all, let's assume this spirit was a figment of your imagination. Your subconscious mind found a way to cope with a frightening situation. Call it temporary insanity if you like. But you survived, and you seem emotionally and mentally stronger to me than you were five months ago. Now, let's say this spirit is real. Did you ever have any physical contact with her?"

"No, she was in spirit form. I saw her energy. She conjured up a feather once and tickled my nose with it but there was nothing physical about her being other than visual."

"What about when Kaela was born?"

"No, in fact I never saw Nonnock during the birth. She spoke to me in my mind towards the end of hard labor. Why?"

"Because, my dear, you're selling yourself short. Nonnock may be a real native spirit. She may have given you comfort and emotional support. But you're the one who lived in the physical realm with all its harshness and physical demands." Mom stopped to peer at me intently. "It was you that physically gave birth to your daughter and took care of her needs and saw to your own."

She handed me the crystal and I placed it back in the dresser. "I guess that's true."

"Nonnock didn't do anything for you physically. She helped you find strength and the courage to do what you had to do. And honey, you did it, you and only you. I will always be grateful to her for being there, but I'm so proud of you, Georgia. I don't know if I could have done what you did, even if a spirit was there. You're a heroine. Don't you ever think you aren't worthy of praise. Accept it and be proud."

"I never thought of it like that before. She kept telling me the same thing, but I wasn't listening. You know, it means a lot to have your support on this."

"If you can accept the role you played in your own survival, I don't see the need to tell the reporters or anyone else about Nonnock."

"Oh, but I do. My daughter and I were protected out there, Mom. I feel I have to give back. By sharing what I learned from her, someone else may benefit. I conquered a lot of fears this past year, but this is the granddaddy of them all."

Once again we sat in silence, weighed down by our own thoughts.

"You know, when you went missing, people thought you were dead. But, soon they forgot all about you. So, now they may think you're crazy, and soon they'll forget about you again. At least you're alive." Mom shrugged.

We shared a good laugh, and Mom continued. "Honey, think about Shirley MacLaine. Here was a woman who jeopardized her career and opened herself up to ridicule. She spent years building a career, gaining the respect of her peers. Yet, she chanced it all because she believed she had a spiritual destiny to be shared with the world."

I sighed, "And some people think she's one of the enlightened ones, while others think she's a flake and crazier than a hoot owl. I guess I fear the latter."

Mom took my hand in hers and squeezed it. "And in the end, it really doesn't matter which.

She succeeded in getting people to think, to talk, to argue, and that's how change and enlightenment begins. But more importantly, she was true to herself, regardless of what the world thought."

"You're right again, Mom. I've come to a decision. Tell Dad to set up the interview. I'm ready to talk to the reporters, but not about my native spirit yet. I have some more thinking to do on that score."

Chapter 29

The reporters arrived the next day. My parents' living room transformed into a studio with lights, cameras and cables running across the floor. I sat at the dining room table holding Kaela, my father on one side and my grandfather on the other. The rest of my family stood behind us. The table housed numerous microphones representing various news media. I spent an hour talking with the reporters.

They wanted me to tell them in my own words what happened, and how I coped both before and after I found the cabin. When I finished, the questions started, and they all clamored to be heard at the same time. My grandfather's authoritative nature took control. He told them he would point to them one by one, and if that didn't suit, they could all leave. They asked questions of my family as well. One reporter made the mistake of asking Grams how it felt when everyone thought I was dead, compared to how she felt now she knew I was alive."

Grams became so upset at the absurdity of the question that she couldn't hide her sarcasm. "What a stupid question. How do you think I felt? Let's see ... oh ... I was glad when we thought she'd died and upset to find out she was alive." We all laughed while Grams looked indignant.

At the end of the interview, one of the reporters asked me what my plans were for the future, and if I intended on returning to my job at the library. This was a question that I'd been contemplating since my talk with Mom the day before. A couple of hours before the interview, I had talked to my former boss at the Vancouver library. She said they wanted me back and felt morally obligated to offer me my old job as Assistant Librarian. I asked her who'd taken over my job and if they were happy with their choice. I knew the co-worker who had moved into my position, and

I heard myself telling my boss that it was time for me to do something different with my life. I assured her that they had the right person as my replacement, and I wouldn't dream of taking the job away from her. I sensed relief in the voice of my former boss. Secretly, I knew there was a legal obligation on their part to offer me my job back, and that I had released them from a sticky situation. I also knew it was the right decision for all of us.

"I won't be returning to my position at the library. I intend on spending time with my family and my daughter while I write a book about my experience."

This statement invited a whole new set of questions I wasn't prepared to answer. I looked at my father with tears in my eyes. He promptly ended the session.

With the interview showing on the news that evening, things started to return to normal on my parents' street. Most of the reporters moved on to the next story. Only a few remained from the entertainment shows. However, the phone calls didn't decrease in number and the Post Office requested that my parents pick up their mail at the substation because the letters and packages were too numerous for the carrier to haul.

Colin called again the morning after the interview aired. I decided it was time to take him on. After exchanging pleasantries with his secretary, I was put right through, contrary to my experiences last year.

"Georgia, finally. You don't know how hard it's been to reach you. I saw you on the news; you looked great, considering. So, how are you?" Colin's voice came through sweet as maple syrup.

"I'm fine, considering." I tried not to sound sarcastic.

"I thought you might have called sooner, Ginger Cake. But I guess things have been a little off-balance for you and the family these past few days?"

I turned away from the phone and pulled a face. *How dare he call me by an affectionate nickname he didn't deserve to use?* I swallowed my anger and continued the banter.

"The past few days, Colin? Things have been more than off-balance for the past five months."

"Of course, I meant … look, I'm really happy to know you're alive. I mean, these past months I've been so depressed thinking of your surmised death and your family's loss.

"Ah, yes—my family's loss. You were so upset that you planned to sue them for my estate. How could you do that, Colin?"

"Come on. That's only business. It had nothing to do with personal feelings."

"I understand the concept of mixing emotion with business. But kicking someone when they're already down is morally wrong. You can call it business. I call it greed, pure and simple. You hurt my family when they were already hurting. That's hard to forgive."

"I'm sorry. Look. I don't want to fight with you. Anyway, it's redundant now. You're alive and the condo is rightfully yours. I guess you and your baby will move back in?"

My baby? This was the first reference he made to his baby. The fact that he referred to her as 'mine' instead of 'ours' didn't go unnoticed.

"The condo was always rightfully mine. A stinking loophole in the law doesn't change that fact. In answer to your question, I'll probably sell it. I don't intend on raising 'our' baby in a condo."

"Georgia, I'm sorry about the way things turned out. If I'd known you were pregnant, I doubt I'd have left. If I hadn't, none of this would have happened to you."

"Save it, Colin. I didn't want to lose you to Julie at the time, but I wouldn't have accepted your staying because of the baby. We can't change the past, and now that all's said and done, I wouldn't want to."

There was a long pause. I sat at my father's desk doodling with pen and paper, letting Colin make the first move.

"I'd like to see you and the baby. Could I visit you at the house?"

His gall shocked me. *It never occurred to you that my parents might be less than welcoming to you in their home?* But I also knew that they would respect his right to see Kaela. I felt ready to leave the house, but I didn't want to expose Kaela to the public yet. My parents would understand.

"When did you want to come?"

"I'm going out of town tomorrow for a couple of days. How about midweek? I'll call you."

"You do that."

My father wasn't quite as understanding as I hoped, but in the end he accepted it. He realized that Colin and I had unfinished business to discuss, and he wouldn't dream of asking me to take Kaela outside the house at this time. As long as Colin arrived during the day, he would make a point of not being home.

My grandparents returned to their respective homes; Kris went back to his base. Marion returned to Whitehorse, and Dad couldn't get back to work fast enough. Mom and I spent many pleasant hours together. Long showers, phone calls to friends, and helping in the garden became a daily ritual.

We set aside time each day to read the mail. It was an amazing experience to read letters filled with words of encouragement and well-wishes from complete strangers. I vowed to write a few letters in return each day to thank those people who opened up their hearts, and at times, their pocketbooks to buy something for Kaela. Mom played secretary for me and returned all of the recorded business calls. She rejected most of their offers on my behalf. From the rest, she took particulars and said we would get back to them.

It was time to visit my condo. Mom drove us over one evening. Everything looked the same as I'd left it on the morning I flew to Whitehorse. Wandering from room to room, I realized how little it meant to me.

After all the years that Colin and I had spent together here, I felt nothing. Even the negative energy that I had experienced here after Colin left me was gone. My decision was made: I would sell.

Mom shared one of her many wisdoms: "I came here before Christmas, looking for comfort, wanting to feel close to you again. But the condo was only a shell. Your energy, positive or negative, was long gone. I didn't find any peace."

We gathered a few personal effects and some clothes. The next day, I listed the apartment with a realtor. Coupling the proceeds from the sale with a small investment fund that I had left from my maternal grandfather's estate, I could afford to take a year off to write my book. Then there were the offers from publishers and publishing agents. I gave this a lot of thought. Being ignorant in this field, I needed useful advice. I didn't want to be exploited or used because of my naiveté. Thinking of Sean, who'd been on my mind amidst the entire clamor, I decided to ask for his opinion. Perhaps he and his contacts could give me background information on the people who made offers, as well as give me sound advice on contracts.

When the phone rang that evening, it was one of the few times Mom chose to pick it up.

"It's Sean Dixon," she said, handing me the receiver.

My heart skipped a beat at the thought that he'd called me first. "Hey, Sean. How are you?"

"I'm good. I've tried calling a few times but couldn't get through. I'm sure your phone has been ringing off the hook."

The deep resonance of his voice reminded me of the moments we'd shared at the cabin. There hadn't been much time for me to think about him since I'd come home. "We let it go to voice mail or unplugged it. It's been nuts."

"I figured," he said, chuckling. I saw your television interview. Impressive how you handled the reporters. You appeared so poised and self-confident."

"Appeared is the key word," I added, chuckling. "Inside I shook."

"Well, it didn't show. So how're you doing? Are things calming down for you and your family?"

"For the moment, Kaela and I are staying with my parents for a while, and I put the condo up for sale. I'm not sure where we'll go next, but for now we'll stay here. I saw the tail end of a piece on the news the other day on Dease Lake. You were right about all of this putting you on the map. Although, I missed the interviews with some of the townspeople. How's Sarah?"

"She's okay. It's too bad you missed her interview. She had them around her kitchen table eating fresh-baked cinnamon rolls."

We both laughed. "Of course she did. I'm going to contact the station and ask for a copy of the tape. Where are you? Dease Lake?"

"No. I'm in Vancouver."

"Oh …" I mumbled. *So close.* This time my heart flip flopped.

"I had some business to take care of, and the cabin became like Grand Central Station."

"No way ... the cabin?"

"Every day a plane or helicopter circled overhead, snapping pictures or videotaping. A couple of the choppers landed and asked me for an interview. They also wanted inside the cabin to see how you lived, which I wouldn't allow. I decided to lock it up and leave for a while."

"Oh Sean, I'm so sorry. You wanted a peaceful summer and you were driven away."

"It's okay. It helped me make a decision, and that's one of the reasons I'm calling you."

"How strange, I was going to contact you to help me make a decision. What's up?" I asked.

"I hope you won't be upset with me. You left your journal at the cabin and I took the liberty of reading it."

Now, my heart was in my throat. I'd forgotten all about my journal. "You read it?" I stammered.

"Yes and when you told the reporters you planned to write a book about your experience, I felt really excited. It's so well-written ... pure and honest emotion. You're a natural writer."

My thoughts flew in all directions. "I ... I didn't know I'd left it behind."

"I'm glad you did and that I took the liberty of reading it. I showed it to my agent. He was really enthusiastic. We met again today and set up a conference call with my publisher."

My head was spinning. *Sean and a stranger read my journal? They discussed it?* I felt vulnerable and exposed. *And betrayed.*

"You still there?" His voice dropped. "You are upset."

I couldn't help myself. My anger bubbled out of control. "How dare you! I never told you about my native spirit because I thought you'd think I'd gone crazy in that cabin. And now you've shown it to complete strangers?"

Sean started to reply but faltered. "The spirit world comes natural to the Tahltans. If you say you saw her, I accept it as truth. There are dozens of stories of a spiritual nature told and retold in that part of the country. We very much believe in the spirits."

"Maybe so! But the rest of the world will think I'm nuts. You had no right reading it and certainly no right to pass it on to your agent and publisher without my permission."

Once again my trust in someone ... a man ... is shattered.

"I'm sorry. I got enthused and thought I was being helpful. I know you must have every agent and publisher in North America hitting on you and I thought ..."

"That's right, I do, and you were being presumptuous. I don't need another man thinking for me and telling me what I should be doing, thank you very much. If your agent and publisher want to cash in on my story, maybe you should write it ... being their superstar client."

There was dead silence. My temper spent, I filled the void in a quieter voice. "Please return my journal to me at once." With that, I slammed down the phone.

The look on my mother's face filled me with remorse. *A little harsh?* "I'm in the right, Mom. He had no right." I pushed my shoulders back, turned on my heels, and headed to my room.

Chapter 30

The man who came through the open doorway was a stranger to me. Colin had aged in the past year. His hair had thinned, with grey streaks running from his temples through the sides. Even his moustache lacked its thickness. His eyes, etched with lines and dark shadows, searched mine as I came down the hall stairs. I looked deeply into his eyes. This moment was an important one for me. I had no idea how it would feel to see him again. Thoughts of this meeting had prayed on my mind since leaving the cabin. Now I knew. *I feel nothing. Absolutely nothing!* With a new-found sense of freedom, I continued down the stairs. I flashed him a bright smile. "Hello, Colin."

"My God, Georgia, you look great. Television didn't capture that radiance. Motherhood suits you," he said, with a tremor in his voice.

"Thank you."

Looking past him at my mother, we exchanged a knowing look. Only Colin would think my weight loss flattering. Everyone else thought me as thin. However, he had no idea how carefully I had prepared myself for this visit. I needed to look my best. I chose my clothes with care, paying close attention to my toiletries and make-up. As excited as I was about my newfound spirituality, my earthbound ego needed to be stroked as well. I was still a human being with frailties. I wanted to look good to let him know that I had survived not only my kidnapping and my ordeal in the cabin, but I had survived Colin.

My mother remained standing by the front door.

Colin acknowledged her with a quick nod.

"Would you like some coffee?" she asked stiffly, as she walked towards the kitchen.

"Uh … umm … actually, I was wondering if you would like to go out for coffee, Georgia. So we can talk," he said.

Mom stopped and turned to look at me. I shrugged, knowing it would also be easier on Mom. "It's a beautiful day, why not."

I walked over to the hall closet to retrieve my jacket, musing about what I would say next. After Colin helped me with my coat, he opened the front door and stepped aside for me to exit.

"Before we leave … wouldn't you like to see her?"

"Uh … who, Georgia?" he asked.

Are you kidding me? Who? He had to know who I was talking about. Maybe he didn't want to see her.

My mother's eyebrows shot up in disbelief. She shook her head and headed to the kitchen.

"Your daughter, Colin … your daughter."

Colin's face turned red. He rubbed his forehead with his fingers and blinked several times. "Of course I do. Where is she?"

"She's upstairs sleeping. Follow me."

We went upstairs in silence, and Colin stared at his daughter. Surprisingly, I caught a look of sadness in his eyes.

"She's a beauty." When he looked at me, I could see tears in his eyes. "I can't believe you survived after all that time at the cabin, and to think you gave birth all by yourself. I was with Julie when she gave birth and …" Colin stopped,

"Oh God, I'm sorry. That was insensitive. You're truly incredible. I never thought you could do something like that. I thought I knew you, but I guess I didn't."

Colin reached out to touch my face, but I pushed past him and exited the bedroom.

"You certainly don't and I didn't know me, either."

We drove over the Lions Gate Bridge and into Stanley Park. At Second Beach, we bought coffee. Sitting on a log on the beach, I stared out at the ocean, squinting from the glare of the sun on the water. My eyes took it all in, from the blooming flowers in the gardens, the blossoming cherry trees, and the seagulls crying overhead. Springtime in Vancouver! This was my beloved city, my home.

Colin moved closer to me. "What are you smiling about?" he said as I edged away

"I can't help it. Smiling is my favorite pastime these days. A year ago, I took everything for granted in my life. I valued all the wrong things. I can't explain it, but the only thing that truly matters is our love and understanding with nature. A oneness, a sharing; living for the moment one day at a time." I glanced at Colin and started to laugh. "I'm rambling and I can see by your face you haven't a clue what I'm talking about. So tell me, how's your life?"

Colin hesitated. "I'm not sure. I thought I had it all figured out. But then you disappeared and I started to doubt it all. I missed you terribly. Now you're back and I'm looking at you with different eyes. I'm confused."

"When I disappeared, perhaps you were experiencing survivor guilt. I mean, here you were with Julie and the baby coming. And suddenly your wife and a baby you didn't know about are missing and presumed dead. I can understand the confusion. Now we're alive and it lets you off the hook."

"That's a little bitter, isn't it?" He sounded angry.

"No. Just realistic. I think it's normal you might miss me once in a while. We shared ten years of our lives together, and there were some good times in that decade. Because we've moved on doesn't mean the fond memories don't exist, or we aren't allowed to remember them from time to time."

Colin stared at me for a long moment. "Have we moved on? Have you?"

"How can you ask if we moved on? I presumed you did that a year ago. Now you're asking me? I don't think Julie would be too happy to hear this conversation."

"This has nothing to do with Julie. It's about you and me."

My mouth dropped open. "You really are something. There is no you and me. There hasn't been for a long time. And I'll tell you something else too. It's about you and only you," I said, my anger rising.

"How can you say that? I'm trying to communicate with you about how we feel. I want to know what you're thinking."

"Where was the communication when you left me? Where were you when I tried to figure it all out? When I doubted myself as a wife and a woman? I'll tell you where, with Julie, right where you wanted to be. You never gave me an explanation or showed any concern for my feelings then. You shut me out and even refused to talk to me. It's your feelings we're really talking about here, because you're confused." I was wound tight. All my pent-up anger released. I stood up and leaned towards him. "You never even asked to see your baby until I pushed it on you. You haven't even asked me her name. I'll tell you what I'm thinking, Colin. You're a whiffle bird."

"A what-bird?"

"A whiffle bird ... he flies in ever decreasing concentric circles, faster and faster, the circles getting smaller and smaller, until finally–he flies up his own ass."

Colin stared at me, a look of shock on his face, and I stared back defiantly, hands on my hips. After a long silence, he started to smile.

"I guess I deserved that, didn't I? I know I've been a shit to you. I couldn't talk to you because I didn't know how. And then there was Julie, telling me I had to make a clean break. She was so jealous and insecure. I felt like I was being pulled in opposite directions. I'm sorry I hurt you." Colin took my hand in his.

"That's my point. Again, it's about how you felt," I said, shaking my hand from his.

"You've changed. You were never this ... aggressive before."

I gave my shoulders a shake and turned towards the water. "Let's walk."

Colin followed me across the sand to the water's edge. "I guess I grew up," I said.

I knew I could never discuss my native spirit guide with Colin. He'd think I'd gone mad.

"So what do you want now? What's next for you?" he asked.

"I'm writing a book about my time at the cabin. I've had lots of publishing offers and even movie offers. I haven't made any firm decisions as yet. Right now, I'm enjoying my time with my family."

"It must feel great to get away from that hellhole you were in."

I smiled. The thought of returning to the cabin had a certain appeal. I missed the simplicity of daily living. "Actually, it's been hard to adjust to the noise and crowds in the city. The cabin holds a special spot in my heart. I'd love to go back for a visit for the tranquility and beauty there."

"What? I'd think you'd never want to go back to a place where you and our baby almost died. I can't believe you'd even consider it. I certainly forbid you to take … take her with you to that godforsaken country, no mother would." Colin exploded.

My eyebrows shot up. I couldn't believe Colin thought he could tell me what to do.

"Her name is Kaela … not her. First of all, I didn't almost die. I had enough food and shelter to keep us safe. That cabin saved my life in ways you could never understand. Second of all, it's in God's country all right, but it certainly isn't forsaken …"

"Calm down. People are looking at us."

Like I cared. "… finally, you're in no position to forbid me to do anything, especially concerning Kaela. She's your daughter, and if you choose to be in her life, I'd never stand in your way. But, you have no idea what I went through to make sure Kaela and I survived, so don't you ever challenge my ability as a parent. You'd never win."

My body shook with anger. Colin looked chastised. I think he realized that this was one battle he had no argument for. I stared at the waves building up in speed and height as they headed to the shore, and experienced the sound of the crescendo when water and sand met. The waves retreated calmly, and with them, all my anger. Feeling the release of anger as each wave broke and receded, I relaxed, feeling at one with the water.

Colin proceeded cautiously. "I don't understand how you could go back to a place that must have seemed like a prison to you. You were trapped there all alone. If it were me, that place would hold nothing but bad memories."

"In the beginning, yes, it was a prison. But I discovered freedom comes from within. Once my soul was free, it didn't matter what the physical circumstances around me were. When your spirit's free, nothing or no one can imprison you."

Colin stared at me silently for a moment, and then changed the subject.

"What happened with us, Georgia? What went wrong?"

I looked at him as we strolled along the beach and thought carefully about what I'd say.

"Maybe nothing went wrong with us. Perhaps things happened the way they were supposed to.

I believe we come into each other's lives for a reason, either as a teacher or a student. You were a teacher for me. In answer to your earlier question, I guess I'm ready to move on."

"I wish I could be as sure of myself as you seem to be," Colin said, pensively.

"We were kids when we met, young and protected. When we married, I was Cinderella and you were my Prince Charming. I left the care of my parents and placed myself in your care. I allowed you to pamper me as they did. More importantly, I let you protect me. Instead of facing my fears of the world, I turned that responsibility over to you. Somewhere along the way, I became Dorothy, lost in Oz. You became Peter Pan. What did we really know about life and relationships?" I said quietly.

"But lots of kids get married young. Some work it out and stay together," he said.

"That can only happen if they grow together in the same direction, wanting the same things."

"So you're Dorothy and I'm Peter Pan. Are Oz and Never-Never Land that far apart?" he asked, smiling at me.

"I'm not in Oz anymore. And you ... well, you're ... I grew up." I replied with finality.

"I'm what?"

"Nothing. What I'm saying is we have different concepts about life now. We value different things. You're completely earth operative. Material things have a different meaning for me now."

Colin cut into my conversation. "Don't do that, start a sentence about me and not finish it. I hate that. Tell me what you were going to say."

"Oh my God, you aren't even listening. You sure live in your ego." I laughed, shaking my head.

"Don't laugh at me. I'm trying to understand all of this. Tell me what you were going to say."

I let out a sigh. "You've lost touch with yourself, and I can't help you with that. The fact is that the only one who can is you."

"How do I do that? You did it, obviously. You've become so strong."

I gave him a rueful smile. "Part of that was what I experienced up north this past six months. I don't recommend going that route."

Colin looked embarrassed, "I'm sorry."

"Let me put it this way. You have to be willing to go inside and take a good look at yourself. It can be a difficult thing to do, and you may not like what you see. But what you don't like, you can change. It's in your power and yours alone." I paused. "And you have Julie. Don't shut her out like you did with me. I must get home, Kaela will be up soon." I turned and headed towards the parking lot.

"You said I was materialistic. What's wrong with surrounding yourself with nice things, if you can afford them? I worked hard to reach my current financial position. Why shouldn't I enjoy the fruits of my labor?" he asked.

"I didn't mean to sound like I was criticizing you. I'm not judging you either. I wasted a lot of time this past year doing just that. All it brought me was pain and unhappiness."

We reached the car and left the park. Colin headed towards the Lions Gate Bridge. It's so difficult to explain a personal awakening to someone else without sounding as though you're preaching. Words can't do justice to internal vision.

"You also said you want to aspire spiritually. What does that mean? You want to become a nun or a missionary? Are you talking about a religious calling?" he asked.

"No, I'm talking about applying spirituality to my everyday life and work. I believe we have to be healthy and balanced in mind, spirit, and body. But we don't have to become philosophers or nuns to spread love and live in peace."

Colin laughed, "Sounds like the sixties. Maybe you're going through a hippie phase. I'm surprised you're not wearing flowers in your hair."

Idiot. It was the sort of comment I expected from him. If he didn't understand something, he always turned it into a joke. I decided it wasn't worthy of a response, and stared out the window in silence. I remembered Nonnock's words: *When you know who you are, you don't need to define yourself by what other people say about you or how they react to you. So true.* "You know, lack of communication wasn't the problem with our relationship, it was lack of communion." *Let's see what you do with that.*

"What does that mean?"

Exactly. "That we played a role in each other's lives, and that's all. Maybe one day you'll understand what that meant to you."

Colin walked me to the door. "I'm really glad we had this talk and I hope we can still be friends. I'll meet my financial responsibility to Kaela, and I want to be a part of her life. Let me talk to Julie and we'll work it out, okay?"

I shrugged. "Sure."

Colin gave me an awkward hug and said goodbye. Watching him drive down the street, I felt certain sadness for him. I knew he would never be a large part of Kaela's life. Julie would never be mature enough to handle that. And Colin, for the moment, would never stand up to her. I mused about how strange it was that the role in his relationship with Julie had reversed from the roles he and I had played. Julie had a power over him that I never had. *Maybe she was to be his teacher.*

Dear Kaela would be his loss, and I was determined to make sure my daughter wouldn't suffer because of it.

Chapter 31

The doorbell rang. I brushed grass off my pant legs and lifted a laughing Kaela onto my hip. I entered the house from the patio as my mother opened the front door to Alice and Frank Charles, Colin's parents. *What were they doing here?* It had been over a year since I'd seen them. We exchanged pleasantries while Mom led them into the living room. Alice never took her eyes off Kaela. Once seated, she asked if she could hold her.

"Of course." I placed my daughter into her arms. Frank asked me questions about my experience.

He leaned forward, nodding his head now and then, showing genuine interest in my answers. Alice ignored the conversation, her eyes on Kaela. Furtive glances towards Frank, and the rolling of her eyes a couple of times, told me she had no interest in me or my story. As our conversation became more inane and stilted, I sensed a purpose to this visit that had nothing to do with seeing their granddaughter for the first time. Finally, Alice gave an annoyed nod to her husband and glanced at me before returning her attention to Kaela.

Clearing his throat, Frank stared at the floor for a moment.

Here it comes—my warning bell's going off.

"Alice and I would like to discuss a proposition with you. We hope you realize our intent here is for the well-being of Kaela," he said, pausing to gauge my reaction.

"Go ahead," I said quietly; knowing instinctively that whatever I heard wouldn't please me.

"Well, please be assured we're in no way making judgment on your ability as a mother. After what you experienced, we have nothing but respect for the strength of character you displayed to protect yourself and Kaela in the wilderness."

I tilted my head, steeling myself for the blow to come.

"Get to the point, Frank," Alice prodded, looking annoyed.

My mother gave Alice a suspicious glance. She caught my eye and did that raising one eyebrow thingy she does that means, 'Don't bullshit the bullshitters.'

Always the gentleman when it came to 'handling' me over the years, Frank tried to keep me on his good side. True to character, Alice, on the other hand, couldn't care less. *Nothing had changed there.*

"We would like to provide for Kaela. We would take care of her education and cover her every need," Frank said.

"That's generous of you," I said. My brows knitted together. *Come on, I haven't heard it all yet.*

"Of course, she would have to live with us," Alice said.

Mom jumped up from her seat. "What?"

Frank gave Alice an angry look. "Alice, we discussed this ..."

"Don't be a wimp, dear," Alice looked smug.

My heart pounded and I swallowed hard to keep my temper under control. I had to stay cool to handle this situation. I braced myself, determined not to respond emotionally.

"Mom, it's time for Kaela's nap. Would you take her up, please?" I said.

Mom pursed her lips together. She didn't like being dismissed by her own daughter. She reached for Kaela, giving the other woman a glare. Alice hesitated, but had no choice but to let mom take her.

"Have you discussed this arrangement with Colin?" I asked.

"No ..." Frank began.

"Absolutely not, he would have tried to talk us out of it," Alice interjected. Once Frank had brought the subject out in the open, she had no intention of letting him finish the conversation.

I focused my attention on Alice. "Removing myself from the scenario for a moment, he is the father. I think he would expect to have a say in what's best for his daughter," I said, coldly.

"Colin doesn't always know what's best for him, never mind the responsibility of what is best for another daughter," Alice replied.

"Perhaps that's because you've never given him the opportunity to shoulder his responsibilities."

We stared at each other defiantly. As I waited for her to explode, she surprised me by letting out a long sigh and giving me a phony smile. "You see, my dear," she began slowly, her voice high and clear, "Colin and Julie have had a difficult year."

Bitch!

"Colin's divorce couldn't be finalized when you were presumed dead, because they needed a death certificate. It was upsetting enough for Julie when they had to put the wedding off, and then there was the birth. She had a difficult delivery, long and painful. They called in specialists you know. Now there's the added burden of another child. Julie is so fragile, my dear. We've all been so concerned for her."

Double bitch. This was her condescending way of telling me I was out and Julie was in. *Good for Julie; she was welcome to Alice.* Frank stared at his wife in disbelief as though seeing her for the first time. Maybe he was.

Mom came bursting back into the room. "How dare you compare Colin's year to the one my daughter had, or throw Julie's difficult pregnancy in her face. She had every modern convenience and the best medical care. My daughter had none of that, but she survived and so did her daughter."

Alice stood and shouted, "The bottom line is we can provide for Kaela's every need and then some. Georgia, you don't even have a job, for God's sake. And as a single mother, how can you possibly be there for her if you ever get another job?"

Mom yelled back, "She has the emotional and financial support of her family. That's all she needs."

"Please, everyone settle down. Mom, let me end this right now," I cut in. I couldn't stand it any longer. "Alice, although I think your intent has less to do with me, Julie, or the babies, and more to do with protecting your precious son, I'm sure you and Frank could provide for Kaela's wants and then some."

"My point exactly …"

I held up my finger. "But … the one who can provide for her needs is me. My ability to provide for her as a mother is none of your concern, but if you must know, I do have a job. I'll be spending the next year writing a book. I'll be able to work from home and care for Kaela. As for Colin, he'll have to face his financial responsibility to Kaela, like the man he should be. This is one situation you can't control. And if Julie wants to be a part of his life, she'll have to accept the responsibilities that come with him."

"Come along, Alice. I think it's time we left," Frank said, rising.

Alice huffed and bolted for the door. Stopping in the open doorway, she glanced back at me with a haughty smile. "Of course..." she paused, "before we would have taken her in, we would have insisted on a blood test to make sure she really is Colin's baby." With that said she was out the door and gone.

Frank hesitated at the door, his embarrassment obvious. "I apologize for my wife's insensitivity and rudeness. I have no doubt you'll provide a good home for our granddaughter. I'm sorry for the intrusion. Goodbye ladies."

Mom slammed the door after them. "Well, I've had about enough of that whole family, thank you very much. That is the last time any of them will be welcome in this house."

Looking at each other, we burst into laughter.

Mom put a hand on my shoulder. "Honey, I don't know how you stayed so cool. You handled the situation with far more maturity than I did."

"I had more to lose than anyone if I didn't stay in control. It's not often I see you lose your temper, Mom. Good thing you're on my side. And I enjoyed watching you put her in her place."

"As did you, and I'm proud of you," Mom said.

... the more faithfully you listen to the voice within you, the better you will hear what is sounding outside

Dag Hammerskjold

Chapter 32

For the third morning in a row, the doorbell rang. The first day had been Colin, the second, his parents. *Now what?* Since my return home, my life had become so complicated. So many people had come back into my world, most of them wanting something from me. And these were the people I knew. Then, there're the ones I didn't. I understood their interest in my story. *Unique and inspiring. I get it.* But the constant clamoring for my attention overwhelmed me. The peace and simplicity of the cabin called to me and I smiled. Thoughts of running back to the cabin were appealing. *No, I'll stay and fight my way back to normalcy ... whatever that is.*

The sound of muffled voices drifted upstairs and my mother's laughter. I decided to stay in my room and fold my laundry, leaving my parents to their company. Kaela was sleeping after her latest feeding. My time was my own.

About ten minutes later, Mom came into my room.

"Has your company left already?" I asked.

"No. Sean Dixon is downstairs."

The shirt I was folding fell out of my hands. "Sean? Why the heck is he here?"

My mother was smiling which somehow annoyed me.

"He returned your journal."

"He could have mailed it."

"Your words, if I recall correctly were: Please return my journal to me at once. He'd like to talk to you."

I picked the shirt up off the floor and threw it on the bed. "Just another person wanting a piece of me."

My mother started to fold my laundry. "How do you know if you won't even listen to what he has to say?"

I stared at her, puzzled and remembered her laughter ringing out a few minutes earlier. My jaw dropped open. "Oh, Mother ... he's charmed you. You let an attractive man charm the pants off of you."

My mother's eyebrows shot up and her cheeks flushed. "Well, I wouldn't put it quite like that. But, he does seem like a nice man and sincere. I could tell your father's impressed with him and that's saying a lot."

"Just like that. You don't know him any more than I do, and I spent more time with him than either of you," I retorted. *Why was I being so bitchy?*

"And it seems to me, that you had nothing but good things to say about him and the few weeks you spent together at the cabin until the other night."

"That's before he tried to take over my life."

My mother looked exasperated. She moved the laundry out of the way, sat on the bed and patted a spot beside her. "Sit."

I did.

"You and I have had some pretty serious conversations lately about expectations of people. Your father and I have been together thirty-three years. Do you think I've stayed with him because

383

he's perfect or he with me because I'm perfect? We aren't and no one is."

"What does that have to do with Sean betraying me?"

"Because what he did was wrong, yes. He should have talked to you first. But you have to look beyond what he did and think about why he did it."

"And that matters why?"

"Because Colin betrayed a trust and it was a biggie. Not something you let go of easily or quickly. But, Sean was excited for you and in his enthusiasm he did something he thought was right. You can't lump his mistake in with Colin's. Don't paint him with the same brush and mistrust all men."

What she said made a lot of sense. "Is that what you think I'm doing?"

She rose and walked to the window. "Yes I do and I think you should at least listen to what he has to say. Then decide if he deserves a … second chance." My mother stared out the window, obviously distracted.

"What are you staring at?" I asked.

She waved her finger at me. "Come here and look at this."

I joined her at the window. My father was building a screened gazebo in the corner of the front yard. He and Sean were kneeling down examining some pieces of lumber, deeply engrossed in conversation. My heart skipped a beat as I looked at him. He was just as attractive as I remembered.

"Your Dad's been having a problem with the metal fittings or something."

Sean took the blueprints from my father's hands and appeared to be studying them. He pointed to something on the ground and then at the base of the wooden structure my Dad had started to build. He put the paper down and his hands were flying in every direction, while he pointed to this piece of wood and that piece of fitting. My Dad smiled, slapped his forehead and sat on the grass, roaring with laughter. The two men, complete strangers, sat on the grass laughing like little boys, bonding. My Dad high-fived Sean and they stood up and shook hands. There was no doubt my father liked Sean.

My mother sighed and I turned to look at her. She was smiling. Her gaze wasn't on my father, but on Sean. "Mom, I think you're crushing on him, and I don't mean Dad."

She poked me with her elbow. "You have to admit he's a fine looking specimen. Now, go put your face on and I'll join the men. Dad and I have some shopping to do, so we'll leave you two to talk when you come down."

As I headed to the ensuite bathroom, my mother poked her head back in. "Just remember that being sensitive to women doesn't come easy to most men. We have to teach them. Most of the time they're just monkeys with car keys." We both laughed and she was gone.

I looked at myself in the full-length mirror. Sean had only seen me in jeans and a sweatshirt, no make- up, out of control hair, and ragged finger nails. All sanity left me. I stripped off my jeans and t-shirt and ran to my closet. I chose a peach sundress that accentuated my curves, brushed out my now straight hair and applied mauve eye shadow and eye liner, added taupe accents and mascara, blushed up my tanned cheeks and added a peachy bronze lipstick. Another look in the mirror and I was pleased with my appearance. *What would Sean think?* My senses returned and I chastised myself for being so girlie. *Don't forget you're mad at him.*

With my chin thrust forward, I headed barefoot downstairs.

They were waiting for me in the living room. My Dad whistled when I walked in and my mother nodded at me with a smile and a knowing look.

My gaze fell to Sean, who stood staring. "Hello," I said.

"Uh ... hi," he stammered. "Thank you for seeing me on such short notice."

His embarrassment was obvious and he sounded so formal.

My mother broke the awkward silence "Come along, Robert. Let's get that shopping done and let these two chat."

"It was nice meeting you and thanks for the building advice." Dad put his hand out and shook Sean's once again.

"Nice to meet you too. Good luck with the gazebo," Sean said.

My parents left and once again, there was an awkward moment. "Would you like to sit on the deck? There's a nice breeze back there right now."

"Sure." He picked up an envelope on the hall table and handed it to me. "Your journal."

"Thank you," I said, curtly, and led the way to the deck.

As soon as we sat, Sean blurted out: "Georgia, I'm so sorry. I overstepped a boundary."

"Yes, you did," I said, softly.

"I should have talked to you first. I got caught up in my excitement for you and expected you'd be thrilled that I put you in touch with my people. It was wrong of me."

I thought about what he was saying and weighed it, like my mother suggested. "What you did was wrong, but it came from a good place."

Sean shifted uncomfortably. "I understand how it appeared to you. Like I was being controlling and making decisions for you like Colin did. You were right to be upset with me. Forgive me?"

"Forgiven. And I apologize to you. I was a little too … harsh."

He appeared to relax and slumped back in his chair. "Can we start over?"

I smiled. "Let's. When you called that night I was going to ask for your advice on publishing my book. I've had so many offers and I know nothing about the business. But our conversation went a little sideways."

Sean chuckled. "To say the least. You're a free agent. If you don't want to go with my people, I'm willing to help you sort them out."

I knew my story would be controversial because I intended to include Nonnock. An uncomfortable thought that made me nervous and I cringed. "Tell me something. What did your agent and publisher think about my spirit visitations?" I held my breath and waited for his response.

Sean snorted. "They believe in sales figures probably more than they do the spirit world. However, they, also, think it's a great story and will make money. That's the bottom line."

Relief flooded through me, and a great weight lifted off of my shoulders. "Then I would love to meet with them. If your people are willing to work with me, things couldn't get any better. I mean you've done well with them, and if you trust them, so do I."

"There's one more thing I have to tell you. I approached them to offer you a contract. They countered. They'd like us to write it together. They want you to write about the kidnapping and your time alone at the cabin and the birth of your daughter. They want me to write a part about the cabin, the history, my involvement at the cabin and your rescue. Finally, you'd write the last part about your rescue and the after-math. I know they think my reputation and personal experience in this would make it a sure bet for a best seller."

"It certainly flushes out the story."

"If you want to do this on your own, I know I can get them to run with it. Your story is in such demand that you don't need me and they know that. It's a sure bet for a bestseller without shar-ing it with my name."

"I'd be honored if you were to share this book with me. After all, your personal involvement is a part of the story. And how could I turn down the opportunity of working with such a successful writer? I'd be crazy."

"If you're sure, I'll set up a meeting."

"Absolutely and thank you. This is so exciting." My enthusiasm far outweighed any fears I had about the controversy I'd create by sharing my spirit guide with the world. I was ready to tell my story.

Sean had an appointment and reluctantly took his leave. I walked him to the door. Before he walked away, he looked deep into my eyes, sending shivers up and down my spine. "By the way, you look lovely."

I laughed. "I clean up good?"

"More than good, you're beautiful," he said his voice husky and full of undertones.

"Thank you."

I shut the door and danced a little jig up the stairs to check on my daughter.

Two days later, we all sat around the conference table and my confidence was bolstered even more. Sean's agent and publisher were supportive and encouraging. At one point, I brought up the subject of Nonnock.

"I need reassurance from you that I'll have complete literary license to tell my story as I believe it to be. I want the world to know about my spiritual experience with my native spirit. It's part of my story and part of the history of the Tahltan and it all happened on their land. I need to know you won't blue pencil it later, even though it's controversial."

"My dear, controversy sells. We wouldn't think of censoring it," John said. "It won't be only a story of survival, it will have a twist. Readers like that."

Trent, his agent, pushed a copy of the contract across the table to me. We went over the items one by one. It seemed fair to me, but as a novice I was at a disadvantage.

"Take it with you and have your lawyer check it over. We'll meet again next week," Trent said.

Watching the three men interact and demonstrate that their relationship was more than that of business associates, I knew I could trust them. But I took it to my father's lawyer anyway, and the following week I had myself an agent, a publisher and a new focus.

It was agreed that I wouldn't do any more interviews, except the Oprah show in September. Sean would appear with me and we were to push the idea of our pending book. It was decided that we would mention "our twist" to this story of survival, to tease and pique interest. We, also, agreed we wouldn't start the book until September, giving me the summer with my family. Sean would accompany Trent to Los Angeles. They were to meet with a screenwriter to discuss the script involving a movie of his thriller series.

Chapter 33

It seemed to me that my life was gaining some order, with only a few issues left to deal with. One thing, a little harder to deal with, was bringing myself back to life. Even though I hadn't been legally declared dead, some government agencies had recorded that I was. Little things like renewing my expired driver's license proved to be a test of patience and humility.

The telephone stopped ringing and the mailman was back to delivering our mail once again. I was able to take Kaela out in public with only the odd curious stare from strangers. Through the past year's experiences, I found myself as a woman. Now, through the joy of my daughter, I was finding myself as a mother. Motherhood, one of the hardest and thankless jobs a woman could do, was proving to be the most rewarding. Life was good.

The days flew by, and one day at the beginning of August, my realtor called to say he sold the condo. Now, I needed to consider my options. As much as I loved the city, I began to notice its many changes. Raising a child today in the city wouldn't be like it was when I grew up.

The following week, I drove to Horseshoe Bay, north of Vancouver, and took the ferry to Gibsons on the Sunshine Coast to visit Grams for a few days. One warm, sunny morning, we went for a walk. We parked by the marina and headed towards the Landing. We pushed Kaela's buggy past the retail stores, stopping every few minutes to talk with the shop owners. Taking advantage of the lack of early morning shoppers, they stood on the walkway socializing. Grams knew them all. It took us a while to get past the fish store, to the clothing store at the opposite end of the Landing. Everyone knew who Kaela and I were, and gushed over us both.

Finally, we made our way to the gazebo at the end of the long dock, built over the breakwater in the harbor.

"You certainly know enough people, Grams. They're all so friendly."

"Yes, they are. I live a peaceful life here. I'm content."

"Did I tell you the condo sold?"

"You're mom did. Have you given any thoughts as to where you'll live next?"

"Lots of thoughts, but no decision. I don't feel the same way about the city now I'm a mother."

"Perhaps I have a solution for you, at the least a temporary one. You know I'm going to Arizona next month to spend the winter with your paternal grandparents? Why don't you move here and house sit for me?"

"How long will you be gone?

"Seven or eight months. I'll be back in the spring around April or May. You'd be doing me a big favor. I wouldn't have to worry about the house being empty, and I could leave my cats home with you. A friend was to take them in, but I'd feel so much better leaving them with you.

"I think it's wonderful Nana and Granddad invited you down. I know they'll take you travelling all over, and they're always such fun to be around. You'll have a great time."

"Huh … I'll probably spend my time warding off all the widowers they've lined up for me to meet. Your Nan is determined to find me a new companion. I'm not sure that's what I want, but it will be fun finding out," she said, with a twinkle in her eye. "Now, what do you think about staying here?"

I looked out at the fishing boats and live-aboard vessels lining the docks inside the breakwater. To their left, in sharp contrast, the sailboats, pleasure craft and yachts sat moored in front of the yacht club. One side of the breakwater represented the history of a small, hardworking coastal village of fisherman and loggers. The other depicted the values of the nouveau riche and the new breed of city dwellers who were moving back to the country, either as permanent residents to raise their children in a relatively crime free lifestyle, or weekenders who came for fun and relaxation. Glancing up the hillside to upper Gibsons, I could see the subtle changes that were an indication of the growth to come.

"Hmm … you might be on to something here." Moving to the opposite side of the gazebo, I looked north across Howe Sound towards Squamish. The coastal mountains stood tall and proud, their tops peppered with a sprinkling of snow. I knew at that instant that I could live here. Close enough to the city for the amenities and culture I would want and crave, yet, remote enough to offer the nature and natural beauty I found myself longing. And, my family were close enough to visit. "Grams, I'd love to housesit here for the winter."

"Sweetheart, you've made an old woman and a couple of cats happy. Who knows, you might decide to stay here come next spring. It's a great place to raise children."

"Maybe!"

I had a month until I moved into Grams house— a prospect that thrilled me. Instead of fearing the unknown future and new challenges, I felt excited about where it would lead me.

... Now. When I have overcome my fears —of others, of myself, of the underlying darkness at the frontier of the unheard-of. Here ends the known. But, from a source beyond it, something fills my being with its possibilities.

Dag Hammarskjold

Chapter 34

August 15th – Sean's Cabin

The door stood open, with no sign of life. Smoke curled its way slowly up into the bright, summer sky. It was mid-August, and the contrast between my first sighting of the cabin during the blizzard last November and the one I saw today, left me breathless. My eyes took in the colorful array of wild flowers scattered across the meadow. Instead of blinding snow and freezing air that chilled me to the bone, sunlight lit up the cabin and I felt its soothing warmth on my face. Gone were the feelings of fear and despair that shrouded my heart back then; they were all replaced now with a sense of peace and excited anticipation.

I swatted a mosquito buzzing by my ear. *Good thing I sprayed with Deep Woods.* The mosquitoes here were the size of Buicks; the horse flies the size of a Greyhound bus. My stay last winter and early spring had spared me from enduring these forest warriors.

My six month old daughter's stirring in her carryall on my chest broke through my musings. I picked up my knapsack and stepped into the clearing, moving slowly towards the cabin. As I made my way closer, the sounds of a classical piano greeted me. My nose picked up the smell of roast chicken. My grumbling stomach reminded me I hadn't eaten since dawn.

"Mmm ... we're in time for dinner, sweet pea," I whispered.

Why was I whispering? Sudden shyness froze me to the spot and I stood, hesitant, at the bottom of the deck stairs. Had I done the right thing coming back here with Kaela to this isolation? I reminded myself of how sure I felt about my decision when convincing my loved ones back home. I'd been truly excited when Sean invited me to spend a week at the cabin to make plans for our upcoming book collaboration. Smiling, I thought of Jack Hill heading back to the road—too late to catch up with him now. We'd left his truck on the dirt road and hiked the five kilometres to the clearing. He'd hurried back without stopping, anxious to reach home before dark. As I argued with my inner thoughts, a voice from inside the cabin startled me.

"Are you planning to stand there for the rest of the day, or are you coming inside to eat?"

I took a deep breath and entered the cabin to find the table laden with food, wild flowers in the centre, and set for two. My eyes lifted from the table and found those of the man standing by the counter. Silently, we stared at each other, our gaze locked.

"H … Hi," I said meekly.

"Hi," he said, softly. His dark, piercing eyes bore into mine, and my heart skipped a beat. I forced my eyes back to the table.

"You expecting company?"

"Uh-huh. Now you're here, we can eat."

My eyebrows rose. "Me? But I wasn't to arrive until tomorrow."

Sean gave me a bemused smile, "Of course you. I knew you were coming."

"Sure you did. More than likely, you saw me through the window crossing the clearing and quickly set another plate."

"You got me," he said, laughing, "… and just as quickly I ran outside and picked wild flowers for the table without you seeing me. I'm serious. Do you think I cook this much food and put flowers on the table only for me? I knew!"

"Come clean, how?"

He leaned back against the counter, crossed his arms across his chest and nodded towards the woodstove. I followed his gaze to the rocking chair.

What? My native spirit? Now, this made no sense to me. Nonnock was my spirit, not his. Up went my eyebrows. "So … you're trying to tell me that Nonnock took the time and energy to come and tell you I was coming for dinner?"

Sean started to laugh again, accentuating his dimples. That and the twinkle in his eyes made me catch my breath. He was a damn handsome man, and the feelings he evoked stirred me in a way I hadn't felt in a long time. *If you only knew what you do to me.*

He broke through my thoughts. "Actually, it was Sarah."

"Sarah? But I never saw her when I arrived in town this morning. How did she know?"

"She ran into someone who saw you and Jack heading out of town. She figured you were coming here, and called me up to tell me you weren't to leave without visiting her first. Which brings me to the question; why did you hike in? Why not wait for the helicopter?"

I walked over to the couch and put down my knapsack. "Because everyone wanted me to take the easy way here, but I really wanted to take the trail. It's hard to explain. It was important to me to connect the cabin to the outside world."

"I think I understand. So, where's Jack?"

"He left me at the bottom of the incline, on this side of the creek. He asked me to say hello. He wanted to get back to town before dark."

Sean removed my carryall and carried Kaela over to the bed. Removing her outdoor clothes, he picked her up gently and touched her cheek with his fingers.

"She's beautiful, Georgia," he whispered.

Kaela slept as he placed her in the cradle he built for her last spring. We stood together watching her angelic face. I looked up at Sean and my shyness returned.

"It's so strange to be back here. I feel like I've returned home but I'm a little off-balance."

"I can imagine you're running the gauntlet of feelings. You need time to sort them out. Let's eat before dinner gets cold."

Sean took me by the hand and led me to the table. Sudden warmth spread through my body. *Oh, stop it. You're acting like a schoolgirl.*

"… and Georgia?" he said, as we filled up our plates. "I'm really happy you're here."

A big smile broke out on my face. "I am, too."

Later that evening, with Kaela fed and down for the night, we sat on the porch to wait for dusk and the cool night air, but not before Sean lit the bug light.

"I'm happy things have settled down here at the cabin. At least you salvaged some of the summer," I said.

"It wasn't the summer I expected by any means, but I'm not complaining. There are lots of changes to come yet around here."

I curled my feet up under me. "What kind of changes?"

"First of all, I sold the cottage in Dease Lake to Sarah's daughter. She's a recent widow, and her children are grown up and on their own. She's a lot like Sarah and I think they'll be good company for each other."

"How nice for Sarah. I'm really happy for her. So what will you do then?"

"I'm working on plans to build onto the cabin. I'm thinking an addition behind the wood stove with two rooms and a bathroom in-between."

I threw my hands up in the air over my head. "Yay … indoor plumbing."

"I intend to build a loft over the addition, and raise the roof on the existing cabin, so the loft looks down into the old room. The master bedroom and an office will be up there. This whole front wall will be glass, so I can look north to the Cassiars."

"Wow. That's quite an Endeavour for a cabin with such isolation. It'll cost a fortune to bring in the materials."

"That brings me to more news." Sean moved over to the porch railing, hiking one leg up onto the lip, he leaned back against the support beam. "There's an old gold mine northwest of here. It was never fully worked, and it passed down from the original owner to his grandson, who had the mine assessed and found it promising. He sold it to a couple of brothers from the Yukon. They're working a mine up near Carmacks and plan to retire. Carmacks is half-way between Whitehorse and Dawson City. They bought this one for their three sons."

My head went back and an old memory came to mind: "I know Carmacks. Do you know the name of the family?"

"I believe their name is Talbot. Why?"

"I don't believe this. The Talbot brothers are Marion's uncles through marriage; their sons are her husband's cousins."

Sean gave me big smile. "What are you smiling about?"

Sean's smile turned into a mischievous grin. "Nothing."

"It is them. You knew, too." I pulled the pillow off my chair and threw it at him.

"Yes, it's them." Sean ducked and the pillow flew past his head and landed in the dirt in front of the cabin. "Some people have no respect for other people's property." He stood to retrieve the pillow.

I opened my mouth to apologize as the pillow came sailing back and smacked me flat in the face.

Sean was at my side in an instant. "Are you alright? I didn't mean to throw it so hard."

I tried to answer while spitting out the grit and grass that landed in my open mouth. Sean brushed my lips clean with his fingers and pulled grass off my face, while I stared at his concerned face. As our eyes met, we burst out laughing.

Our gaze held and our chuckles hung in the air as Sean's fingers began stroking my cheeks. I let out a sigh and he leaned forward, his lips lightly brushing mine. In an instant, our kiss became hard and passionate. My arms slipped around his neck, and as Sean cupped my face with his hands, his tongue darted against mine. Heat coursed through my veins and my limbs became weak. Our lips parted and we both gasped for air. Still clinging to each other, Sean fumbled for words. "You were saying?"

"No, you were."

Sean picked one more piece of grass off my forehead. "And, what was it I said?" We both giggled and Sean resumed his position at the railing.

"You were telling me about the Talbots."

Sean put his finger up in the air, as if a light bulb went off. "I was. We met in Dease Lake a couple of weeks ago, and they knew me from all the publicity. They've negotiated with the Tahltan Band to develop a road into the mine, and expect the roadway to be open by next summer. As we speak, the road is being built."

"So I take it this ties in with you somehow?"

"She's not only a pretty face." Sean said. I felt my face go hot. "The mining road will pass west of here. At one point, it curves to about half a kilometer west of the tool shed. It eventually merges with the logging road we normally leave the truck on. I plan to build my own road from behind the shed to the mining road. I can use the trees to build the addition. I'll be able to drive straight to the cabin from Dease Lake."

Watching Sean's face as he spoke, I saw the sparkle in his eyes and heard the enthusiasm in his voice. He looked like a little boy who'd received a new toy.

I smiled. "I feel your excitement. But isn't the goldmine on Tahltan lands? How were the Talbots able to open a mine?"

"The Talbots have Tahltan blood; they are brothers. They're working with government environmental groups, the Tahltan Council, the Elders Committee and a number of other agencies. They still have some hoops to jump through before the mine actually opens."

I nodded my head in agreement. "I'm all for development if it creates jobs and helps the people, but culpability and accountability can't be ignored. I, for one, wouldn't want to see this last frontier destroyed for the sake of monetary gain."

"The Tahltan Band is very progressive, and is involved with many developmental projects. But, number one on their list is environmental concerns and preserving the traditional role of the Tahltans as "keepers of the land". Fishing and hunting rights and water and land preservation is foremost."

"So when do you plan to start your renovations?"

"I thought if we spend the winter writing our book in Vancouver, I'll begin after spring break-up. Once the road is finished, I can truck in the materials I need."

"So if you're putting in plumbing, what are you going to do about water?"

"Dig a well."

"I hope you aren't planning to do all this by yourself."

"Good heavens, no. You and I will be busy somewhere in all of this, doing a book tour. I'm going to hire my Tahltan brothers to put in the road first. Then, we'll tackle the building together. I'll hire a well digger from Dease Lake for the water and we'll put in a septic field on the far side of the meadow, away from the stream. I may spend the winter here next year to finish the inside. Jack will plough the road in."

"It sounds like you're planning to take some time off after we finish with the tour."

"I think so. This was to be my year off, but with the book and flying to L.A. to consult on the movie, it didn't happen."

"Speaking of the book, do you think we can finish it by spring?" I asked.

"I think so. If one of us gets stuck, we can collaborate. Two heads are better than one."

"I sold the condo and I'm moving to Gibsons to house sit my Grams home for the winter. That won't be a problem will it?"

"I don't see why. I'll be back in the city in a couple of weeks. Once we work on the outline together, you can work in Gibsons and I'll work in Vancouver. When we need to get together, I'll go over there or you commute to Vancouver. It's all workable."

"Sounds great! Now, I'm going inside to call Marion and gossip about your new neighbors." I stood up and headed for the cabin door.

Sean dove for the door. We reached it at the same time and wrestled to be the first one through, giggling like kids. *Hmm ... this calls for desperate measures.* "Umm ... Sean?"

Sean stopped elbowing me, and we stood wedged in the doorway. "Yes?"

"Remember last spring when I told you I didn't want to make the same mistakes again and I wasn't ready?"

"I do."

"Well ... you said you hoped when I was, you'd be around. Guess what?"

"What?"

I gave him a coquettish look. "I'm ready and you're around."

A slow smile of realization crossed his face and a smoldering look filled his eyes. He stepped back out of the doorway and his voice took on a deep hoarseness when he spoke. "In that case ... ladies first."

I charged into the cabin and headed to the satellite phone. "I won!"

With Sean right on my heels, he picked me up and threw me over his shoulder. He headed to the bed and threw me down, landing on top of me in one full sweep.

"So did I," he said, in a raspy voice.

Chapter 35

Song of Freedom Wheeling with wild abandon,

he thunders forth to race the wind. The pounding drumbeats rolling forth as daily cares are tossed aside ...

In a fiery tangle of glowing mane flowing in his wake,

he sings his song of freedom. Tail held high in proud array, muscles aflame with setting sun;

his liquid form pours through the grass oblivious to worldly cares.

At last his heart, unfettered, thrills, heeding nature's wild embrace!

Freedom is a state of mind. It gallops into consciousness like a stallion, finely tuned, to brush away life's cobwebs 'til the soul bursts free in song.

Anne Carol Marsh

I stood on the dark porch wrapped in a blanket, gazing at the starry sky. A soft breeze cooled the air. Sean came up behind me and placed his arms on my shoulders. Leaning back against his body, his familiar scent reminded me of recent moments shared. A smile broke across my face as I fought to quell the passion rising in me once again. *Later.*

We watched as the northern lights performed a wild dance across the sky; its raw energy and colorful beauty captivating.

"Beautiful, aren't they?" he asked.

"Mmm. I remember the night I decided to stay at the cabin. The lights were like tonight. Only then, they made me feel so small and alone—like a tiny spec that could be swallowed up."

He tightened one arm around me and stroked my hair with the other. "You must have been so scared."

This time around, I felt so safe and lucky to have someone like Sean to share this moment with. "Funny how time and circumstance changes everything."

Mere specs we may be, but our place in this universe is ordained, of equal importance in the large scheme of things. I knew my destiny was bound with Sean's. Our life paths crossed for a reason we have yet to understand. I thought of all I gained from the past year's experiences.

Foremost, solitude is a gift, not a punishment.

I recognized that giving is best when unconditional, and with no expectations. Give only what you can afford to lose and you'll require nothing in return.

Finally, success is not measured by material or financial gain. Being a successful human being is the most important goal worth achieving.

I turned to face Sean. His arms tightened around me and we stared deeply into each other's eyes. This time, I cupped his face in my hands, and slowly kissed every inch of his face, ending with his lips. With his hand cupped in mine, I led him into the cabin and lifting his foot behind him, he kicked the door shut. The cross bar slammed into place behind us.

The fearful child, afraid of the world and all its inconsistencies had disappeared.

Whatever's to come—I'll be ready.

THE END

Dear reader,

We hope you enjoyed reading *Winter's Captive*. Please take a moment to leave a review, even if it's a short one. Your opinion is important to us.

Discover more books by June V. Bourgo at https://www.nextchapter.pub/authors/june-v-bourgo

Want to know when one of our books is free or discounted? Join the newsletter at http://eepurl.com/bqqB3H

Best regards,
June V. Bourgo and the Next Chapter Team

The story continues in:

Chasing Georgia

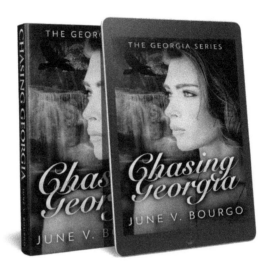

To read the first chapter for free, please head to:
https://www.nextchapter.pub/books/chasing-
georgia

Winter's Captive
ISBN: 978-4-86750-894-7 (Large Print)

Published by
Next Chapter
1-60-20 Minami-Otsuka
170-0005 Toshima-Ku, Tokyo
+818035793528
16th June 2021

Lightning Source UK Ltd.
Milton Keynes UK
UKHW011846010721
386496UK00001B/77